Two Sisters Singing

Published in 2013 by
Liberties Press
7 Rathfarnham Road | Terenure | Dublin 6W
Tel: +353 (1) 405 5701
www.libertiespress.com | info@libertiespress.com

Trade enquiries to Gill & Macmillan Distribution
Hume Avenue | Park West | Dublin 12
T: +353 (1) 500 9534 | F: +353 (1) 500 9595 | E: sales@gillmacmillan.ie

Distributed in the UK by
Turnaround Publisher Services
Unit 3 | Olympia Trading Estate | Coburg Road | London N22 6TZ
T: +44 (0) 20 8829 3000 | E: orders@turnaround-uk.com

Distributed in the United States by
Dufour Editions | PO Box 7 | Chester Springs | Pennsylvania 19425

ISBN: 978-1-907593-81-9
2 4 6 8 10 9 7 5 3 1

A CIP record for this title is available from the British Library.

Cover design by Ros Murphy
Internal design by Liberties Press
Printed by Bell & Bain

The publishers gratefully acknowledge
financial assistance from the Arts Council.

Best wishes & enjoy!

Two Sisters Singing

Carmen Cullen

Carmen Cullen

LIB
ERT
IES

To my mother, Angela Murphy

Chapter One

Bloody war in Europe had brought the Emergency to Ireland. The year was 1942 and I was eighteen. Picking up a pearl-handled mirror, barely glancing at the snub-nosed, grey-eyed girl reflected there, a nervous thrill bubbled up inside of me.

'Lily O'Donoghue, you'll be going to Dublin next month,' I said aloud. 'You'll be heartsore leaving this ramshackle mansion too.'

My hair was a whin-bush of tangles and I tackled the black mop. Outside a swallow darted from the airy eaves of Ballyhale, ready for a sunnier domain than Ballyhaunis. Beyond the stables the friendly bog and hill fields sang a stay-at-home song.

'Stand still, noodle,' my father shouted because Strawberry, his favourite hunter, had clattered into the yard and all the medley and joy of childhood began to play their own seductive tune.

'Edwina and I made sacrifices to get you an education,' Dado's voice echoed in my head. 'You'll be the first Mayo girl to go to a Dublin university in ages.'

I waltzed round the room to see how I really felt, as if the motion would shake things up. A statue of the Virgin Mary on the dressing table whirled with the flowery wallpaper.

You won't be missed because your sister is the only one who counts in this house. After a while you'll be completely forgotten about, I suddenly thought. My dancing stopped. The encouraging eyes of the Virgin looked down at me and I stared into them boldly.

'To hell with Moyra, she deserves a calamity. Even if she is the picture of perfection.'

My words came out as a whisper but that was enough. I'd cursed my sister in front of an image of God's mother and it would stay put forever.

One good reason for getting out of Ballyhale was that I had secretly planned to start a singing career.

'Singers wanted by The Betty Highsmith Singing Agency of Holborn, London. If you have a voice we can place you', an advertisement on a late-night BBC jazz programme on Dado's wartime battery radio had announced. I was going to audition. It prompted another thought. If Moyra came with me it could be an act. She'd play the fiddle and we'd sing together. 'The O'Donoghue Sisters', I could see it on the billboards already.

Leaving Ballyhale meant being cut off from Dinnie, our workman, and the main source for the songs I collected of the people of Ireland, songs rarely heard in respectable parlours. They were as finely strung as shining morning cobwebs. Dinnie said they were strong enough to coax a jig from a corpse.

'Don't bring those come-all-yas into the house, they're too common,' my mother often said with a frown.

'If I were a blackbird, I'd whistle and sing, and I'd follow the ship that my true love sails in,' I'd hum while she talked. It was a new air I'd

learned from Dinnie and I'd decided to sing it for the audition. There were plenty of unfrequented nooks on the farm where I could practise singing. She ought to know them too, if she wasn't so blind to what was going on. My petite sister should be the last person I'd ask to come to Dublin because she never stopped needling me for being useless and singing all the time. Mamma called my looks striking but Moyra was as pretty as a picture, with a waist like Scarlett O'Hara and delicate ways. I found her looking at herself admiringly in the dirty shine of a window in a part of the house we rarely used. We'd slip there to practise new stage routines. Mamma had been particularly cross about my songs that day. A floorboard creaked under the dusty carpet, warning Moyra that I was watching and she swung her chestnut mane, settling it on top with pins and began to walk elegantly as if she was in some wedding scene. I grabbed her hand.

'Come up to Dublin before I get crushed by this place. Tell Auntie Terry you have a religious vocation and we'll plan our stage career together,' I said.

Auntie Terry was a Daughter of the Heart of Mary; an order of nuns who didn't wear habits. She was really Dado's first cousin and it had been arranged that I would stay in her hostel in Parnell Square near O'Connell Street.

'I like it here, but you make sure you go. You're like a bird looking out of a cage when the door is open. Besides, I'll have the choice of the boys in the district when you've gone,' Moyra grinned slyly. 'As a matter of fact I've seen somebody I like. You'll meet him at Ned's twenty-first birthday party next week,' she added. 'His name is Theo.

He's an American and he's come to stay with Ned while he's writing a book.' She had the decency to blush, because news of the visitor had been kept from me.

'Stay if you like. I'll be discovered by some famous singer like John McCormack or Movita and be whisked off to London. It will be too late for Mamma and Dado to do anything because I'll be famous,' I announced grandly.

It was only when I'd flounced out that I realised I should have asked about the American. By rights I should go over to Ned's to meet him. I'd certainly have to get a gawk before Moyra paraded him around at a party.

The Second World War was blazing across Europe. Ireland had remained neutral, but although that was disgraceful in a way in the midst of so much terror, that summer was memorable because of Theo. He had come to stay in Ned's house to write about the first transatlantic flight that landed near Clifden. It turned out he was a friend of Jack's, an older brother of Ned's whom I barely knew because Jack had gone to New York years before. From that family all except Ned had emigrated to America.

My cousin Ned, Auntie Annie and Uncle Tom had a farm off the Claremorris road and I was hardly ever away from it. Ned had hair the colour of dirty corn and his sparkling eyes were like that deep blue in the recently installed Harry Clarke window in Kilasser Church near Swinford. Our parish priest Father Tierney said it was too gaudy to be in a house of God.

On the morning of Ned's birthday I decided to saddle up my pony Nellie, and ride her over to the farmhouse early so I could have a peep at the American. A fog lay on the fields and I could hardly find my way but when I arrived the newcomer had done a disappearing trick. Ned said he'd gone to the post office in Claremorris to make a phone call about enlisting in the American naval base in Belfast.

'Miss Mahon, the post mistress, will make sure to have a good listen to his details so,' I kicked out at a thistle at my feet. 'I'm dying to see this city slicker,' I added. 'Dinnie heard he's a penniless scribbler who never does a tap and Dado calls him a draft dodger.'

'Uncle Michael needs to give Theo a chance. He's suspicious of anyone who can't rattle a few shillings in his pocket. Jack says he's a gentleman and I believe him. There's something else Theo doesn't want people to know. He was born in disgrace and sent to America but recently he found out his mother was a Lloyd from Mayo,' Ned said quietly.

My cousin's house was chock-a-block and the storytelling had started by the fireside when Theo and I were finally introduced. Ned and I were horsing around. I was sitting on the flour-bin trying to hold back laughter, because I'd tricked him. He thought his shoes had shrunk because I'd stuck lumps of bog cotton into the toes and he was cursing like a madman trying to get his feet in when Moyra descended from the hall with her nose in the air. A raven-haired dazzler lounged in the doorway wearing a white shirt and a dickey bow like a *habitué* in some smoky nightclub joint.

'Lily, I'd like you to meet Theo of New York.'

'Welcome to Mayo, Theo. I hope you enjoy your stay,' I said.

He was grinning at me in a charming way which my sister clearly didn't like. He had a slight limp which lent him a daredevil air when he walked to shake my hand and I flinched from Moyra's hawk-like gaze. Even better, he held on to my fingers.

Ned's house was divided in two by a short corridor. It meant that when card-playing started in one half, the younger set filtered into the other part to get up to high jinks. As soon as Moyra left to help with the party food, the Yank blew me a kiss. During the first set dance he swung close.

'Here's a war dollar for the prettiest colleen in the room. Take it with you when you go to Dublin to remember me.'

Before I could get a word in about loyalty he slipped a bright coin into the lace pocket of my blouse. To make it harder to give back, his bog coloured eyes were for me only.

'You have lips sweeter than jewels of Arabia,' he whispered. Now was the time to stop his *plamás* before Moyra really blew up but there and then she high stepped it into the middle of the room. Only a desperate act would banish him.

'I'll meet you at the stables at midnight,' I lied.

He thinks he can come over here and flash an inviting grin at any Irish girl he likes and she'll fall at his feet, I thought. But a smile stayed on my face as the dancing continued.

When the cuckoo clock in the back parlour chimed midnight, singing out 'Lá Breithe dhuit', or 'Happy Birthday', we dancers spilled outside. Moonlight was the draw and the night sky was sequined, high as the blackest silken canopy and strewn with an embroidery of stars. A group of us laughed and chatted, and gave quick chasing runs at one another. Moyra had moved off and was standing under a chestnut tree on the front lawn. She'd wandered there in a daydream, probably to make up a romance about Theo. Ned's friends began kicking at the pebbles on the path and he went back to get his hurley so he could hit a few pucs.

The moon outlined Currach Hill nearby and honeysuckle night scents drifted by. I could see that our Yank from New York was enjoying it all, because he took a deep appreciative breath as if he'd stuck his nose into a glass of peaty whiskey and blew it roundly in my direction. In the middle of everything, I had to walk round to Nellie whinnying in the backyard as a creature completely forgotten. The newcomer and I turned at the same time.

'Damn, what's the loveliest girl in the world doing in this godforsaken place? I want to snatch you out of here and show you Dixie bands and ballrooms and a nightlife you could only dream of,' the Yank said.

A warm hand grasped mine and before I knew it, his face loomed near, pearly pale as a button. Rain clouds were beginning to mass, some drops fell but it was grit crunched by feet that made us both turn. Moyra was watching, like the Currach Hill witch, ready to cast a spell.

'Stealing the cream again Lily? You only want him because you can't get a boy of your own,' her tone was icy.

'Theo can make up his own mind who he likes,' I perked up. I had to because the *amadán* was squeezing my waist and I pressed the silver dollar in my pocket. He'd given it to me and she couldn't take that away. Shortly after that Mamma came down and marched us both off.

'Come along, Uncle Tom has started the storytelling. You'll meet far more suitable boys at university Lily,' she said loudly enough for anyone to hear. Maybe she was right, because a love song in her heart was ringing out like a promise of the future.

Chapter Two

Noisy birds flocked over the drooping corn in the farm fields. The days had been seemingly endless and then suddenly August was over. It had been a long summer and, despite Moyra, Theo and I had begun to hold hands and cuddle. Heavy showers - thrashing Dado's crops grown especially for Ireland's wartime Emergency, as it was described by Mr De Valera - had kept us indoors on the morning we'd chosen to go on one last walk away from prying eyes. But by mid-afternoon the stone walls and grass glimmered in the sunshine. As we set out at last we took a trail through a grove of oaks which screened off Ballyhale, hiding us from onlookers. The sweet meadow sent up heady spurts of scent.

'I love you Lily,' Theo said, thrillingly, and I bent to pick a buttercup.

'Butter-lover,' I tilted the flower under his chin. Bristles grated against my hand and I grumbled.

'How do you expect a girl to kiss that stubble?'

'It's as soft as a new-born babe,' he laughed and pushed his face against mine. Even more exotic was his cologne. There was more banter and I was about to trip him up for fun when he dropped onto the grass and pulled me after him. A bush waved above, alarmingly.

'Moyra will find us,' I struggled away. We rolled into a hollow. The back of his ear was intoxicatingly close and I placed a quick kiss there. Before I knew it strong arms had pinned me down and lips pressed against the love spot on my neck that always sent me into a tizzy and I gave him a thump to go away. He pounced on my open mouth.

'I want to be with you always Lily,' he said.

Theo began to unbutton my cardigan and summer blouse. It was either squeal out loud or let him continue. Oak trees shielded us on one side and brambles thrust in towards us. Before I knew it he'd spread out his coat and thrown his shirt onto the bramble bushes as if it was a tinkers' camp. I was no travelling woman, but queen of the wild looking for homage, I could have told him. Hazel eyes bright as a stream came close.

That was when I heard a branch cracking. The sound was followed by a hiss of air as if somebody had been caught in briars. It was Moyra, or an animal from the field. I leapt up. My fingers fumbled and flew about to button my blouse. It was too late because a lumbering creature was breaking through like something that hadn't a bite for a week. There was a clap of noise and two mad eyes blinked. That devil of a sister of mine had driven a cow on top of us.

It became certain we'd had our last walk when I stepped into an outhouse to see Theo later that evening. He was sitting on a round of timber where a space had been cleared and his face broke into a smile.

'I had to meet you Lily. Your mother bumped into me after we'd parted and suggested I ought to stay away because you need every minute to prepare for Dublin.'

Then he picked up a sod of turf and threw it at the back wall moodily.

'I'll write to you when I get to the hostel.'

There was a scraping sound outside. Somebody was approaching, but a warm forehead was pressed onto mine to stop me rising. For some reason my attention had been taken up by a daddy longlegs scampering across a willow creel. It had paused, anticipating danger, and lifted a leg.

Be nice to Theo, your time together is precious, I thought. Close as two birds on the branch of a tree, our breathing came and went. A thought of all the name labels still to be sewn on my clothes intruded and I started. It let me see a face peering through the window. Before I knew it Moyra was in and had grabbed my hair with fingers like claws and pulled me up.

'Kiss me Theo,' I said breathlessly and held him tight.

'Mamma is looking for you, but I put her off. If you go now she won't know where you were. I'll stay in case she comes in,' Moyra offered. To make sure, she pushed me out of the shed with the strength of a mule.

She'd only come in because Mamma put her up to it. My mother, Edwina Lloyd, a southern Protestant, belonged to the old school where connections and money mattered more than anything. She was a hypocrite if she wanted to break the connection between Theo and me because she herself married my father Michael O'Donoghue, a handsome Catholic and owner of a failed butcher's stall, converted to his religion and let him step into her farm. The one thing she wouldn't want to admit was that we were alike and I could be just as stubborn.

Later on, at teatime, Theo's name came up in the conversation and Moyra called me deceitful. She said that for my own sake it was just as well I was leaving.

'Maybe I won't go to university. I want to be a singer,' I said hotly.

'What kind of singer?' my mother paused with the teapot in her hand. 'Speak some sense to her, Dado.' Her pinkie finger swam out as she poured.

'Put it out of your head. Edwina and I have already discussed this. After all the money going into you we'll expect you to be a teacher at least,' my father said as he banged the table. Shortly after he stormed out and Mamma rubbed my hand soothingly.

'Make enquiries about getting singing lessons in Dublin,' she murmured.

'Moyra can take classes. You're always saying she has a sweeter voice,' I said abruptly. 'Unless you want a statue stuck by a piano sounding like a wind-up doll,' I glowered.

'Your sister's not a prima donna, ready to jump up at the drop of a hat to sing street ballads. Make sure you behave once you are away from here. Father Tierney disapproved of your looseness with Theo. He has a Dublin friend called Father Lonergan who has agreed to keep an eye on matters,' Mamma hit back.

I couldn't wait to leave. This was the limit. I'd keep up with my studies and use them as a cover to do what I wanted.

Chapter Three

Dado's face had a squeezed look, making wrinkles appear mysteriously when he laughed and better-humoured than it was right to be. He broke into a broad grin on the morning I was leaving for Dublin.

'I'm feeling low at the thought of going,' I said and looked grave.

'A trip in the car to the station is just the solution to cheer you up. Dinnie managed to get some petrol rations from the Local Defence Force supplies in Knock. Nobody says Michael O'Donoghue can't do it in style.' He flung his head back and laughed. Later on, as if he couldn't wait to get me away, he hoisted my trunk, as if it were a sheep's carcass, into the back of our new Ford that he'd taken out of storage.

Driving away from the house, Dado began to whistle. Mamma and Moyra appeared at the hall door of Ballyhale with long faces. Perched on the low curved wall of the front steps leading up to stone lions, Mamma took off her apron and, misty-eyed, blew a kiss. It made an ache start inside me. Rising from a hollow in the road where the car had dipped, the roof of the big house appeared for the last time, floating on a river of air. Dado beeped and I blinked back tears, taking a deep whiff of that lovely smell of leather seats, trying not to think too far ahead.

'Aren't we great swanks in our new car?' he nodded happily and I knew once more he didn't care about my homesickness.

Turning off the main road and nosing down a boreen, a figure peered out of the ditch. Sea-blue eyes and a brown face told me it was Dinnie. It was a late opportunity to delay my departure and I stuck a hand from the window.

'Slow down Dado, I want to have a last word.'

'Where are you going with that shoveleen on your back Dinnie? Are you waiting to say goodbye?' my voice sounded squeaky in the wind.

'Act the young lady. You'll get a poke in the eye from a branch,' my father pressed his foot to the floor, his eyebrows came together dangerously and we jerked forward.

'It's far from bog and dirt you'll be up in that college, you're not to be worrying your head about me. Make sure you bring me home a new air,' Dinnie's voice lilted and ended as quickly as the last notes of a dawn chorus, as the car moved forward.

A sombre mood flowed into me when I thought of complaining, Moyra-loving, Auntie Terry. Her hostel for young ladies will be more like a prison, I thought glumly. The only good thing was the nuns didn't wear a habit and if I planned to stay out in the evening I could pretend I was one of them. I was jolted out of trying to imagine how I would paint a disparaging picture of my sister to my aunt when the car swerved and got stuck. I clambered out. Heaving it out of a rut with Dado, my thoughts drifted away once more. Dismal streets and a string of garish gas-lights swung into view. Just letting my back be viewed leaving, I'd dress up like Auntie Terry to get out of the hostel after bedtime. Anyone looking would think I was on my way to minister to the poor but really I was setting out for a university party.

'I hope we don't hear any bad reports from Sister Terry,' Dado shot a warning glance at my dreamy face as we clambered back in.

'There won't be a more successful student than your obedient daughter,' I panted, and flopped noisily onto the seat. A bow-shaped solid gold brooch that had belonged to my grandmother glinted on my Connemara tweed suit and I put my hand over it like a promise. Keeping it on would be a reminder to be on my best behaviour.

There was a hurried kiss from my father at Ballyhaunis Station and his face drooped with sudden regret. It was too late to miss me but I caught a last glimpse of the Ford in a cloud of dust, driving more slowly than usual. A porter lifted my trunk onto the shabby platform with paint peeling off the station doors, another mark of wartime shortages. Water dribbled from a broken gutter. Star-shaped leaves fluttered on the red-tinged sycamores and, lowering my trunk, the porter stared up the line to spy a puffing steam engine. Voices came from beyond the arched entrance. I heard the name Andrew and the words 'draft investigation' and another passenger strolled in. He tipped a hat back on his head like Roy Rodgers beside his horse and placed a valise on the ground with a copy of the *Mayo News* on top. 'Battle of Stalingrad Rages', a headline flapped. It hit me that I was on my way to God knows what. Daring deeds and death and destruction had a bitter hold on the rest of Europe.

The stranger was probably a reporter investigating a recent German plane crash near the town, I decided. Mamma said the injured pilot was kept in Counihan's Hotel under lock and key in case the IRA decided to spring him. It was impossible to read beyond the headline because the man folded the newspaper and placed it in his briefcase, taking out an envelope addressed to 'The Recruitment Officer'.

'*Dia is Muire dhuit*. Good day to you,' I saluted, curious about the information on his bag but he didn't answer and looked away.

'Direction of Dublin', a sign swayed on the platform and my thoughts turned to Moyra. Instead of letting her crow about how she could do no wrong, I'd have to get her to Dublin for our singing career. She was at home with Mamma right now, going about the boring jobs of the house. That should convince her to leave. Swinging my handbag up, the latest in fashion in Ballyhaunis, a giant bee rose from a clump of weeds, droning like a war aircraft and I was sorry for my frivolous thought.

'I *belong to Boston city boys, a place you all know well*,' I sang the lyric to myself as I moved away. 'The Boston Burglar' was one of my favourite songs, passed on by Dinnie and impossible to resist. He said he got it from the tinkers at the end of Feathery Lane beside Ballyhale. The tinkers roamed the length and breadth of Ireland and kept an ear out for new ballads; many of them were never written down. The song was one of the low-brow airs my mother forbade me to sing in the house. 'Believe me, if all those endearing young charms', was her idea of something respectable and I could see her now at one of her soirées for ladies of the neighbourhood, lilting sweetly, poised beside Father Tierney on the piano. Our parish priest was Mamma's favourite accompanist since she'd converted. She should realise how much singing means to me too, I thought. Her voice was haunting my brain like a bad omen.

The chugging of the train into the station erased it from my mind. Even finding that the only empty carriage smelt of hen-dirt didn't dampen my spirits. The train moved off, stone-walled fields rolled by and I closed my eyes, determined not to think of the shining fields of home. Beyond Castlerea the passengers went onto the line. I decided this must be the usual wartime crisis of a train running out of fuel and settled down for a wait. Passing the time meant sticking my head out a window, trying to count the number of sheep in sight or singing a bar of a song for a friendly ear. Fuchsia in ditches glowed red, like painted fairy bells. I seemed to hear our own church peals of St Patrick's in Ballyhaunis and see the rapt face of Father Tierney, guardian to the gates of paradise for all the well-behaved parishioners and ready to bar from entry the flightier ones like me. A pimply-faced ticket-checker slid in the door and shuffled.

'Do you have your ticket Miss?'

'Divil a bit. I forgot to get one.'

The dainty clasp on my new bag sparkled to nearly blind him as I grinned, drawing the ticket out instead. Isn't it strange, I thought, as I watched him scoot away, that he may well be working on this train for the next twenty years while I was heading for a life of God knows what? I sighed again contentedly. Your new life is beginning, I told myself. The wheels hummed and only at the last minute I remembered about Theo and how it wasn't too late to go back.

There was bedlam in Westland Row Station in Dublin when we whistled in, making me draw away from the carriage window with fright. People rushed about. It was impossible to see Auntie Terry and as I leapt off a high step onto the platform the steam hissed. Spots of soot fell on my cherished costume and then the crowd split in two, revealing her. She'd poked her face in the air and was staring intently. A flowing cream coat gave her a fashionable look and I ducked behind another passenger who was alighting.

'Auntie Terry, look over here,' I called out weakly.

'Stop making a show of yourself,' she mouthed back. Moving forward she pulled down the stiff netting attached to her hat and more grime landed, making the stains on my suit worse.

'Damn it, I don't believe this,' I grimaced.

'That's no language for a well-brought up girl, Miss. It doesn't bode well for someone wishing to excel in university. How is darling Moyra?'

Not bothering to hug me, Auntie Terry's hands twitched, as if itching to give a slap.

'As happy as the day is long. Why wouldn't she be surrounded by everything she likes?' I declared. Not bothering to wait for more news, taking my arm like a child, she commanded a passageway through the crowd as if it was a forced march.

Outside the station we were assailed by the noise of horse-drawn carts and more motors than I'd ever seen before. My aunt must have arranged transport to the hostel because an imperious hand flagged down a van with 'Findlater's Provisions' in cheerful red lettering on the side.

A young man with dark good looks and the figure of Cuchullain himself veered in.

'Sorry I'm late Sister,' he nodded meekly. Now was the time to show Auntie Terry she wasn't completely in charge and I stepped forward.

'Hello there. I'm Lily, I'm coming to stay in Dublin,' I lifted a hand.

'Don't be bothering Matt, a capable man doesn't want to be hindered by clumsiness,' my aunt pulled me back. 'Matt Corrigan's family comes from Mayo; decent people I knew well,' Auntie Terry nodded at me frostily. A smiling Matt lifted a fiddle and placed it behind his seat. An arm was outstretched to pull me on. Not only did the fiddle give a sense of Moyra but it meant I didn't see the ticket checker. He was hoisting my trunk up but pressed a letter into my hand. His birdlike eyes darted. An American eagle imprint on a corner of the envelope leaped out at me. Theo had left a letter with the Dublin mail at Ballyhaunis station.

'Straight to the hostel, Mattie,' Auntie Terry sidestepped the trunk and beamed at her hero. The letter burned in my hand.

'I believe you like to sing, Lily. You might try the Irish Club. They hold good sessions,' Matt caught my anxious glance but Auntie Terry had spotted the messenger at his task and snapped her fingers. When she took off her hat to fix it back more firmly, ready to attack, I saw something else strange. A mole had been revealed at the back of her ear in exactly the same place as mine.

It would be an excuse to take her mind off my letter if I pointed it out but before I got a chance to say anything I was surprised to see her blush when she noticed my gaze.

Chapter Four

Dublin was even noisier outside the station. A car horn blared to get Matt's van to move. There was no doubt Auntie Terry had been confused by my look because she pulled the netting on her hat down so hard the whole thing nearly came off. It didn't matter now though because Matt used the excuse to finally hoist me into the seat beside him. My inquisitive aunt squeezed into the narrow space behind and at the same time Matt saw an opening in the traffic and pulled out. We were off and trundling along, I kept up a flow of chatter until the envelope seemed to be forgotten about and the wide thoroughfare of O'Connell Street stretched before us. Trams shunted in both directions and Matt veered his van around the statue of Daniel O'Connell. You could see there was even less petrol here than in Mayo because all sorts of horse-drawn carts jostled for space. As soon as possible I'd drink in Theo's love pledges and write back, or else I'd never hear from him again, I decided.

This was the first time I'd seen gas bags for fuel on top of car bonnets. Wartime Emergency rule had turned Dublin into a circus and a fit of giggles made me lean out the window but Auntie Terry grabbed my arm. She was already treating me like a prisoner. Glancing around hopefully, I pointed and said loudly: 'There's Clerys Stores.' It was an excuse to get out and there was bound to be a ladies washroom where I could read my letter in peace. 'I couldn't find anything decent for Moyra's twentieth birthday in Claremorris. She'd be thrilled to get a parcel in the post.' I nudged Matt to stop the van.

'We mustn't be late for Sister Angelica. She's looking forward to meeting you again,' Auntie Terry smiled sweetly, yanking me back. Once she had brought Sister Angelica on holidays with her to Ballyhale. It was the year I had a bad fall when I was riding Nellie and our new guest told me to offer up the pain for the Holy Souls.

'You're the one who needs to do penance. You must have committed some awful sins to have to be a nun,' I said and everyone had laughed. Now my aunt tapped Matt to go faster and the van put-putted past McDowell's Happy Ring House and Nelson's Pillar. She wouldn't stop me poring over my lover's sweet-nothings in the hostel, even if I had to lock myself in my own room.

Cool air with a hint of rain blew down the street. The kicking antics of a donkey drawing a cart kept together by bits of wood and wire, forced us onto a footpath and rounding the ornate front of the Rotunda hospital, preparing to turn up the edge of Parnell Square, a terrace of high houses with steps and railings stretched ahead. Some had brass plates, others were shabby. Poorly dressed children gathered on the steps of a crumbling tenement. 'The Irish Club. Singing Session Every Weekend', a sign announced as we passed and I dug my fingers into Matt.

'Bless yourself Lily. It's the Dominican Oratory,' Auntie Terry pointed at the building beside it.

We swung wide round the next corner. Peering from the top step of what had to be the hostel, with her thick hair standing up like a badger's, we could see Sister Angelica waving a welcome. From a window above her a girl with golden curls shoved her head out. Drawing into the footpath a brass knocker on the front door gleamed and a statue of the Sacred Heart in the fanlight held outstretched hands to the street. Matt leaped down and before I could say, 'Let's have a dander round the city', he pulled the trunk down.

'The room is tiny I know, but look how high-up it is,' Auntie Terry said. 'You'll be like a bird perched to look out over the city.'

Shortly afterwards the trunk had been hoisted up, and Auntie Terry's tall figure bowed to get into an attic at the front of the house and she waved a hand across cluttered beds. We were in a dormitory with a sloping roof and the beds in pairs with pulled-back curtains to section them off. Framed pictures of Our Lady of Lourdes and the Infant of Prague hung on the end wall over a row of enamel sinks.

'There'll be no fear of being lonely in this cubbyhole,' I stared around in dismay at the cramped space. There and then I thought, as soon as Moyra comes up to Dublin we could rent a room together. It would be that or be packed tight with girls I wasn't getting on with.

'You can sleep under the window and Rita Kelly is in the bed beside you to keep an eye out for you,' said Auntie Terry, smiling grimly because really her words meant 'keep watch on me', and with that she backed out. While I watched her leave, I could hear faint sounds coming from the street below. Shiny as a black beetle, a car crawled past. Now was the time to read the letter. I bent down to check the daylight. The ticket-checker's envelope was squashed from my sitting on it.

> *Dear Lily,*
> *I have only a few minutes to write before the train leaves. I tried to meet you this morning but it was impossible. Moyra will have to tell me how you got on. You are on my mind every minute.*
> *Write back as soon as you can,*
> *Theo*

I still had his silver dollar in my pocket. I took it out. It gleamed in the dull light. Moyra could be trying to get him for herself now but he loved me too much and she'd never have her way. The hard feel of the coin made my spirits rise. Theo and I would run away together. The thought took hold of me and I imagined us sailing on a liner. The shores of America beckoned. A voice penetrated my dreams.

'Lily, can you bring your trunk downstairs and we'll pack it away,' Auntie Terry was calling up. When I came back up to the room later, the letter I'd waited so long to read was missing.

Chapter Five

The first thing I had to do was reply to Theo in case whoever stole the letter was trying to make mischief but at that moment a blonde girl burst into the room and threw an armful of bed-linen onto a mattress. There were shrieks of laughter from the other girls downstairs and Auntie Terry's voice rose above them, complaining. I wouldn't put it past her if she'd come in and sneaked the letter away. Right at this moment she could be writing to Moyra.

My visitor was the Goldilocks who'd stuck her head out of the window as Matt drove up to the hostel. Her curls framed an impish face and this funny cannonball began to hurl about, tossing sheets on beds. Reaching me she stuck a hand out and grinned.

'I'm Rita Daly, the fool who got to do all the work because I was the first in this room. You must be Lily, Sister Terry's relation. She told me all about you. She said you were a lovely person and that we would get on together,' the smile widened.

'I think you must know a different Auntie Terry to me,' I said but she began to bounce on her bed to check it for hardness and before I knew it I'd joined in the fun.

'I'm missing a letter from my boyfriend. It was here a few

minutes ago,' I said. Rita had started to arrange her clothes on her bed shortly before and I knew she thought she was being accused. Theo should have sent the letter in the normal way and this wouldn't have happened. A deep silence lengthened. She delved into a plain wood press, making banging noises.

'I'm not blaming you. It was only a summer affair.'

'Don't worry about boyfriends. You won't have much time for that from now on,' her red face stuck out from the cupboard. A mouse scampering across the floor provided another distraction. It made Rita shriek and jump on a bed but I stared, mesmerised. Tail twitching and sides beating in and out, it had stopped at my bedside locker. That defenceless look was reminding me of a spider I had seen in a turf-shed not so long ago. I should write to Theo straightaway. He might be tempted to join up for the war because I was no longer around. That night before the lights went out I began writing and as soon as I did my feelings for Theo arose inside me again.

Dear Theo,

Thank you for your letter. Sorry about the short reply. All is going well. I can't wait to see you again.

Lily

The following morning Auntie Terry made an exception for Rita and me, arranging for us to dine in the nuns' parlour. Brightness flooded the room from the sun pouring through high windows and Sister Angelica's voice had a soothing quality, murmuring grace before meals.

'This is Sadie, Matt's sister. She organised the lift from the station for you yesterday,' Auntie Terry announced and I smiled at a buxom girl bringing in toast. If I wanted distraction to forget my Ballyhale romance this girl probably knew as much as Matt about the music world in Dublin. There was no time to signal to her because Auntie Terry stood up abruptly, suggesting we should meditate on God and eat without talking. The presence of a crucifix on the sideboard added weight to her message.

Prominently placed on the mantelpiece as an altar of adoration, a candle flickered in front of a statue of St Joseph and, after a few nods towards it, Auntie Terry and Sister Angelica ate in silence. I stared at myself in the shine of the teapot. Across the table Rita refused to meet my eyes.

'I'd like to go to a good ceilí. Where can I find one, Sadie?' Matt's sister was leaving the room, and I was unable to stop myself as the words had boomed out. I hummed under my breath, ready to run.

'Don't forget your grace after meals,' Sister Angelica's head jerked up. She wiped her mouth vigorously with a napkin. 'In the name of the father and of the son and of the Holy Ghost'. There was nothing wrong with paying your respects to God but I was eighteen and had my own way of communing with him. One week, not a year, was about all I'd manage to stick it out in this place. The tram from Nelson's Pillar on O'Connell Street which would take me to the university on Earlsfort Terrace would leave at noon. There might be some information about student accommodation when we got there. As soon as I found out, I'd write to Moyra to come up to Dublin immediately to start our stage career. Before I could ask Sadie about the ceilí, she saw Sister Angelica's cross puss and was gone.

Chapter Six

Rita and I stepped out of the hostel eagerly an hour later, so that we would make it in time for college registration, and a grey dispirited-looking city greeted us. The grimy streets were a shock. Kids climbed over an abandoned cart pulled up on a footpath to get at a few discarded turnips. Rain hit the pavements in a steady rhythm and we pulled our coats round us and ran to the tall column with the statue of Admiral Nelson on top, disappearing into the mist. An advertisement for Fruitfield Sweets brightened up the side of our tram. Passengers already on board had a woebegone air, but we stared in wonder at the passing parade outside. Somebody had polished up the carriage windows and soon they caught a hint of sun and sparkled. Racing alongside, a sooty-faced *gorsún* grabbed at the tram railing for a free ride. It would be hard to see these children day in, day out and not give every penny I had to the starving mites. A stale whiff caught our throats as more passengers clambered on and Rita held her nose and kicked my shin trying to make me laugh and the tram bell tinkled in tune with our merriment. A pillar-box on Westmoreland Street reminded me of the letter to Theo, and I pulled it out slowly, letting Rita's glance hold mine.

'You remember I told you about my boyfriend yesterday. Well you were right. He's charming and too cocky for his own good,' I said. As soon as the words were out I let his darling face come into my mind.

'I'm sorry I gave out. I'd love to see him myself,' she nodded and Theo's face grew clearer. Passing the green verges of Trinity College there was an instant memory of the sweep of Currach Hill and my mother, carrying a bucket of still-warm milk up from the cow-house to make butter.

The memory strengthened when a small woman waltzed towards us, peering about her like my mother on a mission. I should behave myself in the hostel for Mamma's sake and forget the foolish idea of renting a flat. The bored voice of the conductor interrupted my thoughts and Rita got in the way of my legs, leaping up.

'Next stop Stephen's Green,' the conductor called out and the tram jerked to a stop. A puddle rose up as we sailed off and staggered upright. Before us a flower-seller laughed, arranging bunches of chrysanthemums and dog-daisies, creating bright splashes of colour against a handsome archway. A gust of wind blew leaves over the railings of the park and our skirts lifted, making us forget that ignominious landing.

'We're like people standing on the deck of a boat, sailing to the new world and sad to leave the ones we love behind,' Rita said.

'*Goodbye Tom, and goodbye Jack, and goodbye Kate and Mary*', I began to hum. There was trepidation about what lay ahead and a surge of excitement too at the thought of meeting different people. Uncertainty gripped me, about how I would make myself known in this great new world. Whatever we might be thinking, the flower-seller was marching towards us. Hands on hips, gathering a crowd, her voice rasped.

'Get yezzer own patch to beg on before I call the police!'

'Take your bag and run,' Rita grabbed it up. The letter to Theo lay inside. Although I saw a letter box at the crossroads before the college, it was better to keep going and we raced on towards a group of young people milling outside black railings.

Our university was a long Victorian building with wide steps and a row of pillars. Students were standing around either on their own or in groups. Lily of Ballyhale, you're as good as anyone else, I told myself, in an effort to combat sudden shyness, and I dangled my jacket over a shoulder displaying Dado's bow-shaped brooch. It was enough to reassure me until the group we joined surged forward, sweeping us into a large central hall.

'You're wet as far up as your knees from the fall,' Rita announced to take my bounce away.

The entrance lobby was high and spacious and filled with more lads than you'd find at a hurling match along with just a handful of girls. Uncertain where to go, I twisted and turned. A cleric brushed against me, knocking my jacket off. Another stepped on my brooch. There was a row of seats against the back wall and an older student was sitting there with a violin case on his knee. Slim and sandy-haired, he must have seen my jacket fall because he strolled over and picked it up, handing it to me.

'Come this way Lily. Miss Hourigan, the Dean of Women Students, wants to meet all us girls in her office,' Rita pulled me away. Looking back at my helper he raised a finger gracefully. He was broad-shouldered with wide-awake eyes like a deer, even if he was a bit on the short side, and I strained to keep him in sight.

Miss Hourigan's door closed with a soft click. She was plump and bedecked with rings and immediately launched into a pep talk about young ladies behaving respectably to represent their college. Trying to keep the picture of the sandy-haired man in my mind I barely watched her motherly face. Soon she was gazing in my direction with such a kind expression that I suddenly remembered the idea of renting a flat.

'Are there any questions?'

'I'm Lily O'Donoghue. I'm looking for somewhere to stay in Dublin,' the words were out before I could stop myself.

'You're Sister Terry's niece, isn't that right? I'll have a word with her and see what she says.' Now Miss Hourigan was frowning disapprovingly. Ahead of me a girl sniggered. Auntie Terry would hear everything.

'It won't be for a few weeks,' I said but her steady gaze was memorizing my face carefully.

Later that evening Rita pushed the beds together to have a dance to help us girls in the room get to know each other. Keeping the noise down for fear of the nuns, we sang songs and Rita made speeches about good behaviour and we clowned around. A few girls from the house had a great fondness for our old Irish tunes. Shadows played merrily on the walls as shoes were kicked off. The only pity was we had to take the lead as men. The Kerry Slide is a poor sight with four young women bobbing and passing and no one in trousers to lift the spirits. It brought back to me so strongly the presence of Theo and memories of our summer of fun and I remembered the letter I hadn't posted. I had a flash too of that mysterious student with the violin coming to my rescue in the Main Hall of the university.

Swinging my new friend too fast we bent over laughing at the giddy feeling. Being crafty was the only way to deal with God's holy sisters, I decided. If one of the nuns came up and complained I'd lie and tell them we were getting rid of high spirits before we entered the convent. I'd get that flat for Moyra and myself too.

'By the way, I found out Rory Masterson is the name of the student who picked up your jacket at registration. He's in third year and a leading light in the College Music Society. You should join,' Rita said later.

The *ruala buala* was over and moonlight glimmered in our low window. Staring into a square of night, sighing for something new, my tired mind only came up with Theo.

Chapter Seven

The practice of making a 'Rambling House' out of our room went on for the next few weeks and then a proper university routine got underway. Another letter arrived from Theo about a month after my arrival in Dublin. I was rushing out to college and put it aside. Life was already hectic and even though I meant to, it seemed impossible to find time to answer his letter. Not long after that he sent a terse note. It was more of a scrawl and stated he wasn't going to let himself be snubbed by somebody who didn't have the common courtesy to reply to him. As far as he was concerned I could say that I loved him as much as I liked but he wanted nothing more to do with me. I felt a rush of blood to my head, I can tell you, when I read that. There and then I wanted him to be beside me more than anything. All that day and the next night I pined for him. It must have been why I didn't see the debonair Rory Masterson until we collided at the university, rushing in the opposite direction from each other on an upstairs corridor. Rita was with me and she called out too late.

'I'm very sorry,' I coloured and glanced away. The music sheets he was holding slid about at our feet and bending to pick them up, he looked over my head with a faraway gaze. Next he tapped his fingers on the floor moving his lips and I tossed my head back. Not even the best-connected musician in Dublin was going to keep me from my classes, I decided. Rita had told me he was a third year student and surprisingly, as if he wanted to make friends rather than tease me for being so clumsy, he followed us into the lecture.

I want to sing, to be in the swing of the university music scene or I might as well not exist, I thought. It was a few days later when Rita and I had caught sight of a notice stuck onto a side wall inside the university announcing auditions for *The Merry Widow*. 'Music Society Members only', the print declared and I thought of Rory Masterson. We'd only glimpsed the notice as we were running inside to escape a downpour and, with drops still dribbling down her face, Rita jabbed at it excitedly.

'You should give it a try. Rory Masterson might remember you from knocking into him and sending his music sheets flying,' she grinned and stamped her wet feet.

'It's not my style. Unless I say I want to sing one of my own songs,' I frowned, ignoring her amused expression. According to the poster the auditions were to take place in the Aula Maxima, an austere building with a prim-looking front on Stephen's Green. Even if I did slip in I wasn't going to beg for anybody's favour.

The best thing would be if he could get a chance to hear me sing when the auditions were over, then we could talk casually about other opportunities. Nobody else should know though, especially Auntie Terry. A thrill of fear bubbled up. She'd have Mamma up for me in a second and I clasped my hands, wondering how she could be deceived for this first time.

When the day of the audition finally arrived Rita had to go and visit a sick aunt in Clontarf. It didn't matter because she managed to goad me into going on my own. That evening we were on the first landing waiting for Auntie Terry to leave for late devotions in the Pro-Cathedral in Marlborough Street and I pointed to my watch to say she should be gone already.

'I can't wait any longer, it's eight o'clock,' Rita shook her head but, as if on cue to catch us, Auntie Terry glided out of the reception area in front of the nuns' parlour. My name was called and catching sight of my style her long nose quivered.

'You're dressed up beautifully Lily. You must be off to church. We can both go to devotions together.'

'Say you're going to meet Father D'Arcy the college chaplain, I'll do the rest,' Rita murmured from behind and before I knew it she'd abandoned me, sailing out the front door. My foot began to tap.

'Holy God look at the time. I have to go,' I said. Swinging a coat over my dance dress I fumbled with the buttons. 'Sorry Auntie Terry, I've an appointment with Father D'Arcy, the new chaplain for the university, to discuss some spiritual matters. He's calling here and the two of us are going to walk down to the Gresham Hotel and have a chat.' The banister was cold but my hand was warm, ready to sprint.

'I don't think I know Father D'Arcy,' Auntie Terry looked doubtful. 'Is he the handsome fellow with red hair I saw the last time I went to the college with you?'

'No. He's the small fair-haired man with a squint,' I smiled blandly and ran past her.

In a long black coat of Sister Angelica's that she must have filched somehow to pretend to be a priest and hair tucked into a beret, a barely recognisable Rita had been true to her word. She waved from the other side of the street. Behind me, Auntie Terry stared across. Any second now she'd march over. Luckily, I could see out of the corner of my eye that my aunt's friend, Father Lonergan, somebody Father Tierney was in touch with, had stepped from the darkened recess of The National Ballroom nearby. He was coming closer just as Auntie Terry was about to uncover Rita and she paused and her head dipped in my direction.

'I forgot Father Lonergan was calling,' she said sharply. 'Arrange a meeting with Father D'Arcy, Lily. Tell him I'm looking forward to getting acquainted.' The collar of her blouse was smoothed down. 'Run along dear. Make sure you knock on my door when you get home to let me know you're back.'

Her face brightened as if Father Lonergan was Archbishop McQuaid of Dublin himself and I tottered with relief across the road.

As I walked in for the auditions the Aula Maxima was buzzing with noise and I positioned myself behind a bunch of girls close to the back wall. Some people already had librettos in their hands. Others hummed and walked up and down. Piano playing could now be heard from the stage area. A striking, dark-eyed girl was putting out cups for tea on a table close by and I smiled over. I thought she might claim me as a new member. On a low platform at the top of the hall Rory Masterson became invisible when a group of musicians strolled up. The sound of smashing crockery distracted me and I swung around. The girl with the teacups had caused an accident and a saucer slid in my direction. She smiled apologetically when I picked it up.

'Oh thank you so much. I'll get into terrible trouble if there are breakages. My name is Connie and I work in the library.'

'Pleased to meet you,' I replied warmly. 'I was passing by and heard the music and looked in. I see there's a microphone. I love singing.'

My ears grew pink. I'd be in confession for a week with all these fibs and I began to arrange the cups on the table hastily.

Up on the low stage a series of notes flew from the piano and a voice tested the microphone.

'*Hello Patsy Fagin you can hear the girls all cry, Hello Patsy Fagin, you're the apple of me eye.*' Even if this was the time to leave before I really was found out, my foot tapped. It was a tune I loved. Rory Masterson had a light-timbered voice and I started to sing under my breath. Safely covered up by the stage performance, my voice got louder and closing my eyes, blackbirds were flying overhead. I was beside the monkey-puzzle tree on the lawn at home and a seesaw on a tar barrel dipped crookedly.

It was the reason a line of song ran on in sudden silence. Rory Masterson stopped playing. It was impossible to end now and I faltered. Opening my eyes I could see my accompanist had left the piano and was halfway across the floor. I'd upstaged him and worse than that, I was a girl who should know her place. All he had to do was run and tell Miss Hourigan. He brushed by, blocking the exit and swinging a leg. When I tried to get by he looked at me pleasantly and held out a hand. 'I'm Rory. Welcome to the music society.'

'How wonderful it would be to stay but I'm afraid study calls. Toora-loo,' I raised two fingers in the air, barely glancing back at my new friend, and I bolted while there was still time.

Chapter Eight

No lights shone in the hostel when I arrived back but the door had been left ajar and I pushed it in and crept up the stairs.

'Everything was left unlocked for you,' Rita raised her sleepy head in the dormitory. I'd have to thank her properly tomorrow, I told myself, and just as my head was hitting the pillow my eyes closed.

There was no opportunity to say how grateful I was the following morning either. Rita was up before me and Auntie Terry stood like a policeman at the bottom of the stairs. A burst of laughter came from the passageway down to the basement kitchen.

'There was a telephone call from Moyra yesterday evening,' Auntie Terry said, not giving out instantly and her face softened at the mention of my sister. It was a reprieve from having to explain myself and I floundered.

'What did she want, is she coming up to see me?'

'Moyra has good manners,' my aunt drew herself up. 'She doesn't need a reason to ring up and say hello to her aunt. By the way, you never called in to say goodnight. Yourself and Father D'Arcy seemed to have plenty to talk about. Perhaps you should start going to seven o'clock mass with me every morning, or I could put your name down for a retreat for those who feel themselves attracted to the religious life,' she smiled smugly. I just shrugged and muttered. The arrival of Rita, appearing from behind in the nick of time, allowed me to kiss the doubting woman on the cheek and back out.

Auntie Terry was so innocent she'd think Moyra really was ringing to enquire about her. Instead this was her ploy to come to Dublin for some devious purpose. I would have to find out. Heading for the university, feeling drops of rain, my feet flew along.

The following morning I changed my mind. I thought that perhaps Moyra was writing to tell me how much she missed me, a letter had arrived for me too and I shoved it into my bag. I have a sister to sing with and I don't need the musical society. That's what I would tell Rory Masterson the next time we met and I leaned dreamily against a wall.

Chapter Nine

Dear Lily,

I have something I find it very difficult to tell you but I must write it even so. Theo called to see me last night and he leaned towards me and kissed me when I went into the hall to say goodbye. I never thought this would happen. Please forgive me . . .

I'd been wrong about Moyra writing to tell me how much she longed for us to meet. She'd taken over Theo. A dull ache started inside. I'd opened her letter shortly after I arrived at the university and was in the ladies reading room. Girls lounged on seats or read at a long table. Miss Hourigan had been in the room, hidden in a corner, when I entered. My new friend Connie had arrived too and, not seeing me at first, brought a book to the Dean and peered over her shoulder. This couldn't be happening in such a normal world, I thought and, as if to confirm it, chatter began at the fireplace. The letter grew large on my lap.

Moyra didn't mean that she was sorry. She'd been praying all along that I'd leave for university so that she could get her hands on Theo. Just because I'm younger she thinks she can have her way, I raged inside, the letter slipped out of my hand and I slumped into the soft chair.

I must have groaned without thinking because the girl beside me frowned. She had a cute blonde bob and wore a Rita Hayworth-style dress as if there was no such thing as a clothes coupon. I had seen her sometimes on Rory Masterson's arm. She'd have a canary if I began to sniffle.

Leaning on the seat to get up, a photograph enclosed in the envelope slid out. Three of us, Moyra, Theo and myself, were posing beside Ned's ivy-covered farmhouse. Moyra's lips were partly open and her expression soft, like somebody too vulnerable for life. Theo had been snapped in a speech-making pose. He had one hand on his chest as if he was declaring undying love but it was obvious now he was staring at my sister. Luminous and green, Currach Hill lifted behind us all and I flung the picture down.

Come single belle and beau, unto me pay attention, Don't ever fall in love, 'tis the devil's own invention. The words of one of Dinnie's ballads began to drum. Now I saw the front lawn of Ned's house with that swing from a chestnut branch. I had tried to touch the sky from it as a child. I even smelled yellow furze and earthly muck and heard the gurgling of a stream and the drip, drip of water into a rain barrel; soft water my Aunt May insisted was best for washing your hair. Finally there was a valley of little fields and clumpy bog spreading at my feet, but still the ache remained.

'Excuse me,' the girl beside me said and stood up to leave. Leaning towards me, Connie was by my side. She'd left Miss Hourigan to gather books. A warm cheek touched mine.

'Hello Lily. I saw you when I came in. I have a break until this evening and was thinking of going for a walk and a cup of coffee, if you have the time. I want to thank you for cheering me up at the Musical Society auditions,' Connie chirped.

'I couldn't care less if I never took another breath of air,' I said and tried not to notice the merriment in her gaze. My world was destroyed forever. Although Miss Hourigan's eyes were boring into my back, I stood up and tore the letter into small pieces at the fire and then watched the greedy flames consume them.

On the university steps, streams of girls pouring from Alexandra College opposite were too much like the bright thing I once was. Flower-beds in Stephen's Green were a reminder of all the beautiful names Theo had called me and young men strolling were nothing but callow lovers. Steely grey skies behind the shops at the outer rim of the park promised a downpour. Harsh light outlined the edges of buildings, just like the roof-top of Ballyhale when rain clouds gathered. Some drops fell and, as if to hammer home my misery, the thunder-filled sky reminded me of a storm of last summer. I remembered racing as fast as a hare up the front avenue of Ballyhale. There were the lichen spotted stone lions on the steps, coming closer and then laughing, Moyra flinging the front door open, dragging me in from a continuous cloudburst. Her coat landed on my shoulders. Finally my sister patted and wiped my face, leading me towards the sitting-room fire.

Whatever about now, she loved me then, I decided. Kicking a stone at my feet I lifted it and threw it towards the park pond with force. Forgive and forget, the words repeated silently with the rhythm of the rain and I growled.

'The curse of God on Moyra,' the words were a mutter, as Connie and I put our heads down and ran.

There was a flash of lightning and pelting rain and because it was closer than Bewley's I pointed to The Shelbourne Hotel looking at Connie, and we splashed on. At least we'd have quiet and a chance to talk. My hair was plastered down, our clothes stuck to us and not looking in time, Connie fell over a pavement grating, tearing her stockings. We'd be reported as university girls acting like tramps and I handed her my hankie for her bleeding knee and helped the limping figure.

Life-size statues of Egyptian goddesses holding gas-lamps flanked the entrance to the hotel. A guffaw of laughter travelled from the bar and chandeliers twinkled in the lobby. In the large drawing-room another surprise awaited. A few heads were raised and people expecting Chopin or Bach were glancing towards a grand piano. Leaning on the lid, the elusive Rory Masterson, larger than life, was leafing through some sheet music. He probably hadn't forgiven me for stealing the limelight at the auditions. I soon realised it wasn't true because a smile lit up his face and I managed a cheeky bow. Here was a chance to forget about Theo. The tinkling notes of Patsy Fagin trembled in the air. It was the tune I'd sung at the musical society auditions but I pretended not to notice.

'Did you ever hear of "The Rose of Mooncoin"?' I said because suspending thought, I'd drifted over to the piano. A new statuesque me began to hum, with a smouldering glance like Mary Pickford in *My Best Girl*, a film I saw when a travelling cinema brought a silent movie to Claremorris, and not the drenched defeated girl who'd wandered into the Shelbourne. Outside the window, the trees of St Stephen's Green seemed to dance in harmony.

On your green banks I'll wander where first I did join, with you lovely Molly, the Rose of Mooncoin.

The fluid notes poured out. Tea cups tinkled. English voices spoke nearby and a soldier's jacket lay draped on a chair.

'A song for you Connie,' I mouthed towards her, leaning into my new accomplice, sailing on a river of song. Rory put on a moony face. At the last minute I saw him raise a warning hand.

'That sort of singing is not permitted in here Miss. We have strict rules. It doesn't suit our clientele.'

The head waiter was moving purposefully towards us.

'Devil a bit of harm a bit of singing does and as far as I can see you could do with something to liven up this place,' I said.

'Well look who we have here. If it isn't Lily O'Donoghue and Miss Bradshaw from the library,' a crisp voice rang out from the back of the room. Miss Hourigan was beside Connie and glaring in my direction. She must have been following us since we left the reading room and stood back to take in our bedraggled state. She sniffed like a bloodhound on the trail.

'I have a cold. I came in for a tot of whiskey,' I said.

'Don't you know it's the flu. Your eyes are watering. You need to go to a chemist to get something for it,' Connie announced quickly. Before I knew it she had run and grabbed me and propelled me past Miss Hourigan. Behind us music played on, words about romance and a pining lover. I saw Rory throw a regretful glance but it was nothing to the triumphant look of Miss Hourigan, raising the sails of her coat for pursuit.

At the reception door I signalled smartly to the piano man. 'We'll meet again', it said, until he smiled at the stern Dean, like two conspirators about to close in on their prey.

Chapter Ten

I need a key to the hostel. The thought began to take hold as Connie and I ran on. I was going back to a house to be locked away and I needed to speak to Moyra to thrash things out. A key would allow me to meet Connie or anyone else I liked. Reaching a sheltered corner of Stephen's Green we hid for a while. Connie told me all about her flat on George's Street and then mentioned a concert in the Mansion House with the soprano from Mayo, Margaret Burke-Sheridan, which she thought she could get me into and we parted firm friends. A solution to the problem of the letter rose up. The only other way of stopping Moyra's romance was to tell Auntie Terry about it.

Pausing outside the Gaiety Theatre, a confusion of ideas going around in my head, a poster of the actor Micheál MacLiammóir stared back at me from a billboard. I could play the actor too, putting on a woebegone air until Auntie Terry asked me what the matter was. The feel of the roughness of a beechnut in my pocket reminded me of Connie's absorbed figure admiring trees in St Stephen's Green. At least we had become good friends and I took it out and rubbed it hard to give me courage.

Continuing up the hill past the trees of the Rotunda Gardens and rounding the last corner of the square I could see my aunt was waiting for me in the bay window of the hostel. The image of a head nun stewarding her charges made me halt.

There was worse to come because, beside her, Father Lonergan stepped back and I gazed down at my dishevelled state. A passing coal horse and dray gave enough cover to speed to the other side of the road. Bending low before the railings of the Abbey Church I started to creep. It wouldn't get me into the hostel unseen though because a dog raced to chase a cat from the steps of the National Ballroom, nearly tripping me up and my aunt tapped at the window. The first thing she'd ask when I walked in was had I arranged a meeting with Father D'Arcy.

As soon as I stepped in the door there was no cool reception but instead Auntie Terry bestowed a hug on me. A workman was banging a hammer in the room above and a burst of laughter from beside us broke the rhythm. The candle flame before the statue of St Joseph on the hall table flared up and unexpectedly Auntie Terry placed a motherly hand on my shoulder. I had a sudden thought that maybe Moyra had blurted something out to Mamma and she'd been in touch. Auntie Terry must have had love affairs in her life too in the dim past. The idea strengthened.

'Are you content here dear?' my aunt asked gently.

'As happy as the day is long,' I said. *On your green banks I'll wander where first I did join.* The words of the song from the Shelbourne registered inside me and I thought of Rory. The divilment Theo was up to had affected me less than I imagined. If I didn't concentrate I'd be forgetting about Moyra and rambling on to Auntie Terry about my latest singing achievement.

'You seem out of sorts. I've been neglecting you too much. I should go out of my way more to look after you. I'm freer in the afternoons than the mornings. We could start off a pattern of having tea together. There are so many family things I have to catch up on. God knows your father is no great correspondent.'

Auntie Terry raised a hand in a tender way to smooth back strands of hair from my face and plucked a stray one off my jumper. 'It's understandable you might miss home, though I must say the Dublin air is agreeing with you. You have a sparkle about you I hadn't noticed before. You seem to be making the most of your new life.'

This is too good to be true, maybe I shouldn't speak out, I thought. So I hesitated. Beside us a chink of light came through the door of the reception. It had slid open and to prove it a draught blew towards the candle before the statue, making it waver and go out.

'You wouldn't want to hear about how I'm behaving, going to political meetings and cavorting with boys. It's scandalous stuff,' I joked.

'There's no need to make a fool of yourself. That's the kind of silly talk that made your parents beg me to reserve a place for you here. Of course they also had to keep that Yankee cousin of Ned's and you apart. You had the parish scandalised,' Auntie Terry began to look grim.

My hands grappled for a newspaper by the coat-stand. 'Axis Forces depleted in Battle of Alamein', I gripped the page for dear life. This was the end of complaining about Moyra. The next thing she'd be asking me about my summer affair.

'Theo is the Yank's name and what I do with my life is my choice.' I looked over the rim of the paper. There was a sharp puff of wind as the reception door opened wider. If Sister Angelica wasn't a nun I'd think she was eavesdropping.

'As well as that we were just good friends,' I added loudly. 'You shouldn't believe everything everyone else says. As a matter of fact I couldn't care less about him now.' Putting the paper down let me swing around. 'See, I'm the healthiest, happiest creature on earth at this moment and please God, long may it continue.' My hand touched the statue of St Joseph behind for good luck.

'God bless you my child, you're incorrigible,' a smile tugged at Auntie Terry's mouth. 'I don't think I have to worry about you at all. It seems to me it's the rest of the world will have to watch out when you're around.'

'You can be sure of that,' I nodded. 'But I'll have to leave you now Auntie Terry. I have some study to do and a few clothes to wash.'

My feet edged out and I thought of Connie's description of her secluded flat. A longing grew for the sense of independence it offered. My friend was able to come and go whenever she wanted. A splash of sunshine caused a bunch of keys beside the statue to shine dully as if on purpose and I saw Auntie Terry lift them. A clock ticked in the hall as I paused.

'I'm going to have to write an essay for a tutorial this evening and I need to use some books in the college library for reference. It will be half-nine or a quarter to ten at least by the time I arrive home. If I borrowed a key no one would have to stay up to let me in. You'll get it back tomorrow I promise.'

My eyes stuck to the cluttered keys bunch like a limpid.

'Heaven help me; you'll have me a grey old lady from worry by the time your three years here are finished. Take mine for tonight,' Auntie Terry nodded. She extracted a big hall-door key from the bunch and tossed it over. The key spun.

'Thank you St Joseph,' my fingers grasped the heavy metal. Unless it was too big to copy, he'd saved my life.

'I love you Theo,' I said into the empty bedroom later to practise getting my own back on Moyra. It echoed in a forlorn sort of way. Feeling parched and wanting a glass of water got me up.

'Good evening Father, I don't think we've met,' I rehearsed next, clutching the key and skipping down the stairs. That was when I spotted Auntie Terry. She was putting a photograph to her heart before placing it face-up on the hallstand. It was a replica of a framed picture of me as a baby beside our drawing-room mantelpiece. I wasn't the only one watching Auntie Terry. Sister Angelica was spying from the hostel reception area.

Remembering a locksmith on Dorset Street, I recalled music coming from his sunken shop. He might let me hear a new song while cutting the key. It would be another string to my bow, to put Rory Masterson in his place. Freedom here I come, I thought.

Chapter Eleven

It hadn't taken too long to have the key copied. The musical locksmith's key lay snug in my coat pocket when I spoke to my aunt the following morning. Sunshine lit the hall like a sign from heaven and as if the new key were visible, shining in its woollen hidey-hole, I smiled too widely.

Flurries of activity ran through the house. There was a smell of lavender polish from the reception desk and calls shouted out between people upstairs. Girls who had finished breakfast appeared from the basement. Most of us were students. You'd know the working girls by their smart clothes. The smell of Ponds talcum powder floated. The brooch of Dado's which I had loaned to Annie now twinkled on her coat. She worked in Brown Thomas and was our best source for silk stockings. Auntie Terry stood back to let a girl fly past and tapped the air with her restored key.

'Thank you for being so prompt with this, Lily. I expect your essay went well.'

'It was a paper on 'Paradise Lost'. Hopefully I made a good start. The rest has to depend on divine intervention. Offer up a prayer for me Auntie Terry. It's the only chance I have,' I said with a grin.

'Of Man's first disobedience, and the fruit of that forbidden tree . . .' She had begun to quote from the poem as I grabbed my coat. Sometimes my aunt was a surprise. I shouldn't forget how much she knew, or might still learn about Theo for instance, and use it against me.

'Keep up the study. It should be no problem for such a smart girl,' her voice trailed after Rita and me, as we made our getaway into heady weather.

The streets of Dublin had a washed look from rain and we skipped around puddles. Rita was the one I should tell about Moyra. I'd already let her know about the key earlier on and now I clutched it in my pocket. She'd probably say not to worry about my sister and that the kiss wasn't serious. On the other hand all she needed to do was come to Ballyhale and judge for herself. A sudden wind blew her beret off sending her curls sky high and she had to race after it down the street. She must have been infected by my good mood because she clung to a railing, breathless and laughing.

'We won't be doing this next week when we have our days off college. I can't even go home,' she grimaced. 'Not that I should be feeling too sorry for myself. My mother has insisted I stay because there's an epidemic of TB near our hotel in Tullamore. Whole families are dying, poor things. At least I can get some study done when everyone is gone.' Sighing she picked up her bag and swung it onto her shoulder as if she was going to start on her resolution straightaway. She was presenting me with a perfect opportunity to get her to observe Moyra. Rita had a habit of being blunt about the truth though. She might say it was all my own fault that my sister took Theo away from me.

'I know a better place to study. We could do it together. You could come home with me. The only problem is I have a pony, Nellie and a first cousin Ned, that you won't be able to resist. Yourself and Moyra would get on like a house on fire. I nearly forgot about Dinnie. He'll have new tunes bursting out of him,' I plunged on. Instead of grabbing me in a hug, Rita frowned.

'If you're absolutely sure, I'll go. That is if your mother doesn't want to spend her time dinning some sense into a madcap daughter,' her grin broke out. Moyra would be in trouble because soon I was being chased down the street by another determined demon, brandishing her bag and yelling with delight.

A few minutes later we passed a horse-drawn cart and with a sign for 'Findlater's' on the side which stood out. Some crates were strapped on behind. Blue eyes flashed merrily.

'Do you want a lift Lily? A penny to bring the pair of yiz to Stephen's Green.'

Here was more escape because Matt, Auntie Terry's driver, had stopped beside us. His voice lilted beguilingly and straightaway I hitched my skirt up.

'Rita, you know Matt, Sadie's brother. Come on girl, you can get to college faster. He's a musician. We might learn some tunes,' I pulled at her.

'It's not ladylike to travel through the streets on a horse drawn delivery cart. Miss Hourigan or one of the chaplains is bound to see us,' she said drawing back.

A pair of priests had paused beside us to cross the road. They seemed to think they knew us and one raised a hand in greeting.

'God Bless.'

'I told you we'd get into trouble. You're as giddy as a wild goat,' Rita the killjoy dragged me away.

'Is Sadie sick? She hasn't been at work for a while,' I called to Matt, but he hardly heard as he turned into a stream of traffic.

Old leaves danced in the wind and I had to skip around. Now Rita was standing at a Clerys window beckoning and hopping. I would have walked past her with my nose in the air but right in front of us was a mannequin sporting an evening dress so striking even I had to gaze, entranced. Despite the war, a beauty had found its way to here. I'd wipe Moyra's eye with it, if Mamma had one of her soirées during the college break. She'd never get this in Mrs Ryan's in Ballyhaunis.

The dress was pure white. A scalloped front rose in a heart shape. There was a jaunty hat on top and the outfit was complimented by a fitted, sky-blue jacket. Fifty pounds, a sales tag broke the news on the sleeve. Someone would swap me a few clothes coupons and, despite myself, the five pounds my father had given me for books began to burn a hole in my pocket. I pushed the thought away.

'Isn't it beautiful? It would be ideal for a dress-dance, or appearing on stage. It will only take a few minutes to have a closer look. They could reduce the price if we asked. Let's go and see.'

All her strictness about study forgotten, Rita was pulling me into the shop. On a convenient shelf inside the store entrance, costume jewellery dazzled enticingly. Even if it wasn't bought, it would be a delight to see such a dress close-up and we pushed in further. A counter assistant raised an eyebrow and smiled politely.

'My friend would like to see the evening dress in the window and you might as well get the blue jacket you put with it and the yellow beads and shoes too,' Rita exclaimed.

Digging an elbow into her barely shut her up. I'd try it on for size, getting my own back on her for making fun of me, when she saw me decked out.

'Certainly Miss.'

Over our heads receipts in brown canisters flew along ceiling wires. There were calls across the shop floor and the rustle of paper as parcels were wrapped. Following the assistant to a dressing-room a few minutes later, Rita swung the dress round to look at it. She was right about a stage show. It would turn Rory Masterson's head if I could wear it to college. I'd stroll through the Main Hall like a beauty queen.

'It would be better if the skirt was shortened and a few seams let out,' Rita looked at me doubtfully in the dressing-room mirror as I shimmied around. She was right that it barely fitted but the material lapped out and I clasped my hands. Bending down to search in the bottom of my bag for some stage make-up Annie had found in Switzers, there was a ripping sound. Tugging and squirming to get the dress off, the sound repeated.

'You've done it now. You've torn it and we'll never be able to give it back,' Rita hissed and I grabbed up my bag.

'I'll leave the five pounds on a shelf, that's all I have,' I clutched my other clothes in the small space. Peering out between the curtains, still in the dress, when the assistant had turned her back I sidled with Rita outside.

I've stolen a dress, I said to myself and the thought made me shiver. I bundled my own clothes tightly and ran.

There was no policeman's whistle or an angry shout from Clerys as we fled down O'Connell Street. Staring onlookers made us walk sedately. Soon the dress was having the opposite effect because we strolled through the streets as if I was a film star, Rita's arm linking mine as if we were making our way towards my adoring public at the university.

Reality set in, it was more like suffering pain from a kick in the stomach, when we walked in the gates of the college a short while later. I should have hitched up the dress or taken it off because puzzled faces gazed in our direction. Up ahead, Rory, my so-called friend, was lounging at the entrance pretending to ignore me. He was in the company of some other third-years, Rita and I could see them fall silent and stare. There was a loud guffaw. I had to get past.

'Lovely day gentlemen,' I called out gaily.

It was all Rita's fault. She should have insisted I take the stupid dress off and now I had to answer to my father as well for spending my book money on something I didn't want and we scurried along with our heads down not daring to raise them.

She'll pay for this afterwards, I vowed.

Rita and I met in the students' canteen in the basement of the university an hour later, after our first lecture. The room was overheated and throwing caution to the wind, ready to be accosted for stealing at any minute, I draped the dress on the back of the chair and glared at my friend.

Beyond us a queue of people inched past a white counter, pushing their trays as they went. In one corner a tea-urn hissed, sending up puffs of steam. My cup of coffee had turned tepid and I pushed the bitter-tasting thing away.

'I hate Rory Masterson. He didn't have the decency to say hello because he has no backbone,' I tapped the table with a spoon. Rita shook her head as if the blame was mine. Then as though he had heard us talking, Rory appeared. He had his violin case in his hand and was peering in from the door. I dropped the spoon onto the floor and bent down to pick it up, tapping Rita on the shin to hide me. Rory could find another target to sneer at but the distraction prevented me from noticing something else, until I sat up.

'Guess who?' Cool hands covered my eyes and there was a familiar scent of Damask perfume and the press of a body that had to be my sister. It was a struggle to break free.

'Moyra, is that you? What are you doing here? I suppose you sneaked up to Dublin with Theo?' The words were out despite myself and as I turned to face her she grew pink.

'You must be reading my mind Lily. Theo has a letter from the American Embassy about enlisting for the war. He is here hoping to get a temporary Irish passport so that he can get his writing finished.'

The long white dress gave her an excuse not to say more and she picked it up. Glancing through the crowded canteen in case the stolen item was noticed, she'd be the one caught, because a college porter was walking purposefully over.

'Perfect for a secret wedding,' the devious girl murmured and tucked the dress away in my bag before he reached us.

Chapter Twelve

'Moyra, this is Rita,' my trickster sister was trying to smile as if there was no question of her being in Dublin illicitly with Theo, keeping her eyes glued to my face. The noise of the canteen filtered back and the porter, forgetting his errand, stopped yards away from us and began to chat. An older student from a few tables away stood up to recite and there was a round of applause.

'He bade me take life easy, as the leaves grow on the trees', he declaimed and I used the cover of clapping to glare at my suddenly calm sister.

'I have to do some study. I'll leave you two together,' Rita gathered up her belongings waving to us both and I watched Moyra's gaze follow her and then stare into the distance. Brightness had returned to her cheeks and she stuck her head in the air and continued the poetry under her breath as if she was a student.

'How is everything at home?' I held back, savouring my moment to let fly.

'You know the way it is. The weather isn't great. There was an unexpected fall of snow and a sheep got lost. Dado has fenced off part of the back field to grow more corn for the Fianna Fáil fifteen-acre tillage scheme and Mamma says she's going to join the local amateur dramatic society. She thinks she's missed her vocation,' Moyra drawled away as if the conversation was of no consequence. Then restless fingers began to sweep the table before her. Voices were raised close to the poet and there was a rush of people to get to the next lecture. I examined my unfinished coffee carelessly.

'Mamma is a natural. She'd steal the show. Maybe it's you and not our mother who's itchy to do something different.' Despite my best efforts I was glowering now.

'Lily, I only came to Dublin to help Theo in a strange city and you're trying to read more into it. If you want to know, I'm really here to explain about that letter I wrote. Whatever happened at home between Theo and me was accidental. He didn't know what to do with himself after you left. He's not really interested in me. I'm in second place compared to you.' She pushed her hair behind her ear and tossed a defiant head back as if she didn't care whether I believed her or not.

'Boyfriend thief,' I fired back. This was so like her to twist things round. In a minute she'd turn on the tears. She shook her head and pursed her lips as if to hold them back.

'I'm sorry, Lily,' she whimpered, 'I'm not going to let it happen again. What matters to you is too important and I don't want to hurt you.' This was typical of Moyra. She believed it was just a matter of talking things over and everything would be all right, forgetting she was dealing with her sister. She was the biggest crackpot ever.

'He's a sneak. Have the *amadán* if you want,' I shrugged.

'I don't want him,' she grinned.

'Take him. There are plenty of other nice boys around.'

'He can go and get another I hope he will enjoy, 'cause I'm going to marry a far nicer boy,' I leaned across the table, singing into her face, thinking of her deceit to keep me angry and the surprising tenderness of my own hurt heart.

'It's got cold in here,' she shuddered.

'You don't say.'

She was right about one thing. Theo was as much to blame. If he hadn't kissed her she'd still be daydreaming about romance instead of being a thorn in my side. I had a picture in my head of the brave Theo running away from me as if I'd thumped him as hard as I could.

'Don't worry, Theo might have strayed but he's mine really,' I testified.

Sunshine came through the canteen windows and the sound of conversation and the clattering noise of cups spread around and a mottled colour crept up Moyra's neck as if she didn't agree. Staring moodily outside I was sure I saw Matt, driving through a side gate with his dray and provisions. I raised a hand to wave. A fat tear rolled down my sister's cheek. There was a crashing noise of somebody dropping a tray and I stood up and drew my arms together to stay stern, not to be broken down.

'This place is like a hell-hole. I don't know about you, but I need some fresh air.' Before she could answer I'd snatched the bag containing the dress and marched outside.

Skies were grey and a cold wind sent a newspaper page scurrying along a narrow verge behind iron railings. Arriving at the back of the university, glancing round to see if Moyra had followed, the Iveagh

Gardens appeared through a gate in the boundary wall allowing a glimpse of glowing autumn trees.

'Don't bother coming with me. I need a walk in the college grounds to clear my head,' I said coldly. But she didn't listen because she began smiling at me fondly.

A tentative hand was dropped on my arm and I pushed it away. Sunlight was chasing the clouds across the sky and a wild wind blew her hair, scattering it this way and that like corn in a breeze. Trying to manage her bag and keep the strands down at the same time was creating a difficulty for her. It didn't stop a calculating look, taking me in. She patted her hair, twisting a loose plait into shape.

'This is a nuisance. Do you remember the time your straggly mop got caught in the bushes when we went out picking blackberries?' she bubbled.

'I wanted to get the fattest berries at the back but as soon as I tried to worm my way in, my clothes and everything else got trapped by thorns. You'd think I was nailed down. Mamma was madder than I'd ever seen her when I came home in torn clothes and you took the blame,' I couldn't help replying. It wasn't the first time that Moyra had saved me. She always put me first when we were young.

In the end we went walking in the gardens, resting in the shelter of a wall, and gradually the breeze abated. There was a hush in this green backwater, removed from the noise of the street. A gardener settled his wheelbarrow by a bed of jaded roses to sweep up leaves. Reaching a fountain, in the centre of a grassy space, rubbing the parapet, the rough feel of the stone walls of Ballyhale came back and I cupped some water and aimed at Moyra.

'This is to get my own back, witch.'

'Stop Lily, you'll have me drenched,' she ducked. Leaping from danger, she began to race round the flower beds trying to get away. 'Catch me if you can,' her voice floated.

Water from the fountain splashed in a gay flow and I saw small drops hit the edge. The bright look of her was impossible to resist, like a snapshot, a perfect picture of a carefree girl with her hair flying in the wind. A young nun passed us, her eyes flickered shyly making contact and then slid away. Moyra pulled a bag of sweets from a pocket and proffered me one. There was a Claddagh ring on her wedding finger I'd never seen before. Trying to keep my eyes away, it hovered like something alive.

'Don't mind that. It's only a bauble from a lucky bag,' Moyra glanced down.

The bag of sweets fell to the ground and she thrust her fingers in her pocket. The wind had loosened the plait and her face was shrouded by a veil of hair. Everything was coming out now.

'I have a favour to ask you Lily. You know the way I believe in your hope to be a singer and always take your side against Mamma. I'd like you to do the same about my being in Dublin with Theo. I already told them at home I came to attend an interview for a nursing course.'

My sister was blushing furiously. I had a desire to yawn, to get away, mixed with a need to hear but she started to fix a scarf and buttoned up her coat.

'I'm sure I'm not the only one who saw you. Where am I to say you slept last night?

'It doesn't matter does it? I was in the Clarence Hotel, where

Dado usually stays when we come to Dublin.' She turned sideways, with a secret look. Sweets lay scattered on the ground from the fallen bag. Watching Moyra bend down, her brass ring had been edged off, leaving a black circle.

'Theo has something private he won't disclose too. I only found out yesterday.' Her free hand grasped the sweets bag. 'Writing a book is a cover he's using for being here. He said he can't do much about what he planned, though, because he wouldn't want to hurt either of the O'Donoghue sisters.'

Chapter Thirteen

From the minute Moyra started explaining herself in the canteen I didn't believe it and now she was going home and things still weren't resolved. We were walking to Westland Row Station for the afternoon train and she swung along beside me.

'You'll be home next week and you'll see Theo hasn't changed,' she had a faraway look in her eyes as if I wasn't there and at one stage skipped across the road until I spotted her disappearing into a newsagents. She's meeting Theo at the station, I thought suddenly. Let her try and be friendly if she wanted, from now on I'd be on my guard against her treachery. As for Theo, Mamma would hear about him soon and then he'd be banned from the house the same way he was when he was with me. There and then I imagined Ballyhale as a beacon of light, shining like a refuge always there to welcome me home.

Walking down Nassau Street, fog had settled on the buildings and on the cricket pitch of Trinity College. Maybe in Mayo the same mist was wreathing across Croagh Patrick and obscuring the small hills around Ballyhale and, with that, I began to soften at the thoughts of the happy days we two sisters had spent together. Too soon I remembered Moyra's secretive smile and my heart was a stone again. A pair of war planes droned overhead then revved up as if a chase was going on. They could be Messerschmitts using the railway line to guide them to Belfast. There was a picture in Auntie Terry's *London Times* this morning of fighter planes over Holland like black hawks in the sky and I imagined the pilots overhead peering down intently as if they could see us.

Disregarding any potential danger, Moyra strolled on. When we were children no two girls could be closer, diving through sunshine-warmed, green-tinged days. Now she loitered at the back gate into Trinity as if she wanted me to catch up and I heard her brief familiar whistle. 'The Whistling Gypsy' had been our first tune I mastered on the violin when Mamma bought us one each to banish us from under her feet. After that I spent hours in some comfortable nook, figuring out melodies, sometimes getting so engrossed that the outside world of nature dissolved and I fancied lime splashed stone walls or narrow mountain streams knitting themselves into my tunes like notes from a fairy rath. At that moment I could have told her that it was too late to make up, but instead I nodded coldly and walked past.

The greatest sport for Moyra, I recalled, was to be singled out for praise by Mamma and I kept that favouritism in mind, not looking back. It was why I liked it when Granny Lloyd, who lived in the lodge at the bottom of the back lane, asked me to sing for her alone. She would keep her fist over a lump of sugar in the bottom of her pocket and close her eyes and declare the ghosts of the house were getting a great treat for the ear. Once she took a drawing out of her pocket instead of the usual gift.

'Your parents mustn't know this boy's mother in America sent his likeness. I can see my brother in him already,' she said mysteriously and dabbed her eyes with the corner of her apron and put it away.

The piercing whistle of a train leaving the station brought me back to the present. We had now rounded a corner onto Westland Row and a train was trundling across the overhead bridge. But when I looked back for Moyra she'd sneaked into the side entrance.

'I'm telling Mamma all about you, show off!' I shouted. It was too late for the warmth of forgiveness anyway, because a crowd surged out, nearly knocking me down.

Chapter Fourteen

Leaving the station the Liffey Quays beckoned. Moyra would do whatever she liked now that my back was turned. Halting at the loud call of a girl's voice to a departing Isle of Man boat, that leaden feeling returned. A Findlater's delivery cart had pulled into the kerb and it became impossible not to smile. Matt, the favoured Mayo boy, was peering down. He didn't seem to understand my moving away because he slackened the reins and the horse shifted into a resting position. My sister must have been on board the train by this stage because another train whistle sounded. Matt raised a cap with a twinkle in his eye.

There was a flurry of wind lifting the horse's tail. Twisting around, it nodded like Strawberry. My new friend reached out a hand to pull me up.

'Roll up, roll up! Rides to anywhere in Dublin for sixpence, do you want a ride for sixpence, Lily Queen of The West? Matt Fitzgerald, at your service.'

Leaning in closely, smelling the horse and harness, I realised that Moyra's memory was beginning to fade, because with this sharp scent, I could be in Ballyhale.

'If it starts to rain, you can put that on,' Matt pointed to his horse's cover, thrown over a few crates. The Liffey stank but for all the difference it made, it might as well be honeysuckle or wild roses from a country lane.

'If you're inviting me for a ride you should be ashamed of yourself, what would Auntie Terry say?' All thoughts of study forgotten, I leaped onto the cart and we were away.

'We'll go to the university by a roundabout path. I've an order to drop off some bags of yellow maize and oatmeal at the Magdalene Home for poor unfortunates in Sean McDermott Street,' said Matt. The horse looked back at me with soft brown eyes as if he understood. Not even a badly-behaved sister could take this away from me. I grinned back and grabbed the reins and clicked them lightly.

The cart bowled merrily past a Guinness barge being unloaded. I watched for new fashions and caught sight of shopkeepers covering their wares in case of a downpour.

'*Bless 'em all, bless 'em all. The long and the short and the tall. Bless all the sergeants and W.O. Ones. Bless all the corp'rals and their blinking sons.*'

It was a rallying tune I'd heard in The Palace Theatre and I belted it out to see if Matt knew and he hummed along.

As though our happiness flaunted sorrow, more warplanes sounded, higher up and further away. Across from us the tricolour waved above the Custom House. A train snorted over the Liffey's Butt Bridge and before I knew it we had passed the quays and were heading up Gardiner Street, far away from the university. In this part of the city the women had to be very proud of their washing skills because clothes hung over the railings of buildings or on ropes, strung from one window to another.

Somebody who knew Matt called out his name. 'Shaw's Sausages', an advertisement proclaimed on a passing bus. The houses became shabbier. Going towards Mountjoy Square I barely noticed the road climbing. It was then I saw a skinny whippet like a dog at a tinker's campsite run out from a side road. A careering piebald pony was next with a cart tipping behind. I clutched Matt's coat but something told me it was too late. Matt and the deliveries cart had crashed into it. Now I was slipping over the side of the van onto the road. There was a crunching sound as my head banged and after what seemed like an age I was sitting up dazed, on an unfamiliar street and surrounded by pots and pans.

'Give her air. The poor thing, she's as pale as a ghost,' a grimy face peered into mine and fiery liquid was forced down my throat. I spluttered and my head reeled. The street was topsy turvy and I felt around blindly. A longing for coolness was overwhelming and I must have asked for water because Matt was beside me in an instant. It seemed he was saying he would bring me to his home to fetch me a drink since it was nearby and I nodded dumbly. As I staggered to my feet he said something about the place being poor because he was putting money away to go to London to do some special study to get on in life. Then he made a comment about Sadie being more sick than Auntie Terry knew. The next thing I remember was being hoisted onto his cart and the sound of wheels grating on an uneven road.

The cart moved swiftly into unfamiliar streets, grimy and poor.

Glancing at Matt to tell him not to worry, a hard expression had replaced his smiling looks. Something seemed to be goading him as we careered along. Pulling up at his address, worse poverty assailed me. The houses were low with sagging roofs. A black-shawled biddy watched from one doorway and a gaunt-looking girl came from behind her and threw a bucket of slops into the road.

If Sadie was at home she might make a hot cup. It would help to keep my eyes open, so I could tell Rita of this extraordinary event. We had halted outside a tenement with a broken window and water dripping from a pipe making a green pool and I began to make notes to myself for my friend's benefit. Inside Matt's rundown building damp wallpaper curled on the stairwell walls. A bad smell surged out from a room used for a toilet.

'Can you open up Sadie? We have a visitor,' Matt called gruffly. Rita would never believe anybody could live in a place as bad as this and putting a smile on my face I stared at the peeling door. There was no going back because Sadie answered in that singsong voice she used at work and Matt pushed the door open and ushered us inside. In the cool interior I could have told him that the pain from the fall was beginning to ease but instead I stared around dismayed. This dismal room had the bare appearance of a prison cell. Sadie and Matt were as poor as church mice. Rita would barely recognise the healthy girl who served us breakfast in the nuns' parlour. Her eyes were huge and feverish. Bones protruded everywhere and lank mousy hair was plastered to her head. There was only a plank for a table and some butter-boxes served as chairs. Out of keeping with the poverty, tattered books were piled beside the fireplace. Glistening damp had spread along most of the back wall, a mattress was rolled against it and a bed, half shaded by a skimpy curtain, was pushed into a corner. The only right looking thing was Matt's fiddle, polished to a shine and propped beside the fireplace. Trying not to groan because a dart of pain went through my knee, I swung my leg stiffly. The girl before me braced herself to get off the bed.

'Don't stir yourself Sadie. I'm very sorry to intrude *a stór*. Matt insisted on coming here.' There was a movement from behind as my friend rushed to help her.

'Say hello to Lily. I brought her here to get a cup of water. She took a tumble from my cart,' he nodded back at me briskly. The swirling in my head got worse but I tried to hold the girl's gaze. Red began to patch Sadie's cheeks as if my being in the room was all her fault. Pushing Matt away gently she swung her legs from the bed and stood shakily.

'How did you manage to let her fall, Matt? Sit down Lily and I'll get you a drink.'

There's something about this illness they don't want to talk about. Maybe it's TB, I thought. My own head got worse when I stood back to let her pass and I reached for a butter-box. She was scrawny as a sick cat. I'd say all this to Rita. What was worse, with all the rationing, there wasn't a decent bit to eat.

'We'll have to go up there when we come back from Ballyhale and bring her some country butter and bacon,' I'd declare. The thought cheered me up.

'Don't be worrying your head about me. I'll be better in no time,' Sadie grimaced. 'You're the one with a cut on your forehead.'

Outside in the hallway children could be heard calling in loud voices and she put a finger to her lips and bared her gums in a smile.

'The childer are coming home from school. Aren't they lovely to listen to?' Beside me I heard the sweet sound of a cup banging against a bucket as it was dipped in.

'They're probably all gossiping out there about the girl I brought home on me cart, but let them,' Matt started to frown. He gripped the cup he was handing to me until his knuckles grew white. At the same time Sadie convulsed and clutched at her front, bending in two. Water splashed on the floor as Matt jumped.

'Don't upset yourself about me Lily. I have a sister married in England. She'll come over for a few weeks to take care of me. Matt should never have brought you here,' Sadie groaned, feeling back for her bed. However bad this was, Auntie Terry would know a good doctor to get in touch with. I could feel my head spinning. They were muttering amongst themselves. It was nearly impossible for me to hear I was so close to fainting, but I drummed the memory into my head to tell Rita and pinched myself to stay awake.

'The curse of God on that baby-snatcher Nora Kennedy,' Matt had said in a low voice.

'Nurse Kennedy took care of things. I wouldn't be able to work again, if it wasn't for the same woman,' Sadie muttered back and I saw her glance at me fearfully.

'You darling girl, this shouldn't have happened to you. That bastard of a soldier!' Matt spoke too loudly this time. Still pretending not to hear I put on a display of dizziness anyone would be proud of. It also helped that his voice was drowned out by the shouting coming through the thin partition of the tenement room. A door slammed at the other side. It gave Sadie the chance to drag herself to the bed shivering and she pulled a thin blanket over her wretched body.

That was when I did wish Rita was beside me because the bunched-up blanket had revealed red rags, bloated looking and swimming in a basin of blood. The baby's cries next door turned to piercing screams and Sadie's lips quivered. I'd have to make a huge effort to fake that I'd noticed nothing this time and blew out bubbles like someone in a lunatic asylum.

'My poor dead child,' Sadie said before I could utter a word.

'He's where he'll have peace and quiet, away from this wicked world,' Matt murmured and I pretended to sway. Maybe I should be a nun, ministering to the poor. I could come here as one of Auntie Terry's order, like I'd always promised myself. If I wasn't careful I'd start to giggle from nerves. This is the real world and I can't handle it, I thought sadly.

'Your aunt mentioned you'd be going home to your sister Moyra next week. She's asked me to bring you to the station for the train. You're lucky to have her. No matter what happens you'll look after one another,' Matt said suddenly and began to help me to my feet.

'I'll tell her to watch out, that virtue can be snatched away before she knows it.'

The joke was out despite myself and I turned bright red. I wouldn't tell Rita about that mistake. It would be hard enough to get her to believe about Nurse Kennedy and the baby.

Arriving at the hostel some time afterwards there was a letter from Theo, completely typed this time to prevent a mistake.

I hear you'll be home on Saturday. I've joined the Local Defence Force and will be patrolling in Knock all day Sunday. Meet me at midnight beside the shrine. I'll explain everything,

Your own true love, Theo.

Rita looked starry-eyed when we studied the note at bedtime.

'You can't let him down Lily, even if we both have to take a risk for the rendezvous. We can go incognito,' she said dreamily as if it was she who was being plied for a date.

'Have a look at this. You might like to take it down to the country to show off.' Annie from Switzers poked her head through our curtain. It was a stylish pair of slacks only worn in Hollywood films.

'You could go out as a man,' Rita said breathlessly.

I'd have to tell her about Sadie later and the image of blood came back, as haunting and evil-looking as an abattoir's drain.

Chapter Fifteen

Theo's letter was foremost in my mind as Dado drove Rita and me home from Ballyhaunis station the following weekend. He must have been with Moyra in Dublin and he still thought all he had to do was step out of his hiding place and I'd float into his arms. Instead of his willowy figure appearing out of the bushes, children were the first to acknowledge us, running to the wall of Colmchille National School as we passed, staring with eyes like saucers at the car.

'*I'll take you home again Kathleen*,' Dado started to sing. It was only a mile or so to Ballyhale. I should prepare myself for Moyra's sweet-talking too. At least I had a best friend to keep annoyance at bay and I hugged Rita and swayed to Dado's tune all the way home.

Driving up the avenue, lines of elms stood out like tongues of flame. Bran, Dado's nuisance of a gun-dog, raced along by the side of the car, making me want to fly like the wind up the track. Then we were swinging onto the front gravel and there was rundown Ballyhale, each window lit like a jewel by a low-lying sun. Another car sat by the front steps and I stared curiously. It was a visitor for Dado and, pulling up, my father's voice roared above the engine.

'There's no time to talk, we can have a chat at the fair in Castlebar tomorrow, Andrew,' Dado said. Churning up gravel, the visitor backed out. It was the man I'd met on the station platform the day I'd set out for Dublin.

Mamma wasn't waiting for us. Nobody rushed out and I had to walk through the house to find a preoccupied-looking woman standing in the backyard with a pig-feeding bucket in her hand. It was as if we'd only made a journey from the next parish. She looks older, the new thought was instantaneous until she glanced up and smiled. The horrible smell from the bucket would make you hold your nose and she swished a stick through it to loosen food from the sides, I barely managed a smile as Bran hurtled around from the side path.

'This is a nice kind of welcome Mamma. Are you not going to say hello to Rita?' I frowned.

'The train is hours late. I thought you'd never get here.' She banged the stick at the edge of the bucket and my face grew red.

'Typical of Lily, is all I can say, getting out of feeding the pigs.' It was Moyra, stepping out of an outhouse to save the day. She'd make the actress, not Mamma because, despite all I knew, she only blushed slightly as if she'd never had a Dublin liaison and leaned in and whispered.

'Remember we have our secrets. Don't let me down, Lily, or you'll suffer. Hello Rita, welcome to Ballyhale,' she stuck a hand out and took the bucket from Mamma at the same time, swinging the swill away when the stench spread. As a blackbird carolled, Bran pricked up his ears for a chase and stupidly swerved round the bucket making it rock. Moyra was just about to hoist it onto a wide ledge beside the horse trough by the stables to get it away from him and now she yanked it away and set it down. The lull was the perfect chance to expose her carry on but she surprised me, taking Mamma's arm.

'I got Ned and Uncle Tom to speak for Theo to become part of the Local Defence Force. It's one way of keeping him out of the American Army,' she announced and I stared open-mouthed. My two-faced sister kissed Mamma on the cheek. The blackguard had been working on our mother all along to accept Theo. I scrambled around for something to say and pretending not to hear, Rita bent down to talk to the dog.

'Your sister has sense, we can trust her to behave,' Mamma said calmly, and without waiting to see if we were ready to follow, waved Rita and me into the house. Let me back to Dublin, I wailed inside. I might not know what to do about Theo, but it would serve Moyra right if he appeared, cocking his hat and smiling at me alone. It would be a good way to get my own back on my sister. I walked away proudly.

Thoughts of revenge kept me going all day until they had to be put aside quickly when Mamma prowled into the bedroom that evening. Rita was hanging clothes up. It was too late when I saw she'd revealed the new white dress. I'd shoved it under my other clothes at the bottom of a bag in case it might come in useful. Mamma stared accusingly.

'I don't remember buying this for you.'

'It's Rita's, she lent it to me,' I lied and knew Mamma took in our glances.

'Well don't let me see you wear it in Ballyhale. It's too revealing,' she said smiling calmly.

'*Bless 'em all, bless 'em all . . .*' I had to hum my war song to distract her too. Rita was now sitting on the case with the slacks, hiding them inside.

'Sleep tight girls, you have a busy day tomorrow.' Mamma's thin voice came from beyond the door after she left. There was the sound of a key turning outside. A burst of sunset came into the room and I was distracted by the way it lit up Rita's hair. So I was too late to stop us being locked in. I grabbed the handle and shook it. The only sound was the faint echo of my mother's own bedroom door banging. It looked as if I'd have to fight against her as well and I hit our own door with a clenched fist, not caring if she'd hear.

Rooting through the case, it was time to take the trousers out. They swung through the air provocatively. I said to Rita quietly, 'We'll take a cycle to Knock first thing. It's Saturday, all the stalls will be open and you can buy a souvenir. The Shrine is at our side of the town and we might catch a glimpse of the emergency soldier, Theo.'

If Mamma wanted a battle she would have it. The thought lingered. Already I had a heady sense of Annie's exotic trousers, as if we were speeding off between cascading hedges.

It was noon the next day when Rita and I set out and I pulled one of Dinnie's caps down over her ears, not to give away her sun-burst curls. My trousers fitted like a glove and making sure no one would follow, we tip-toed through the dairy and out the back. Not even a dog barked. My bicycle was stored in a shed beside the apple trees where Dinnie kept his gardening tools and as though we'd never been parted, fitted snugly into my hands. Rita jumped on an old rattler that used to be Mamma's. Wind rushed past in a river of air. I rose off the saddle for better speed.

'Wait for me, I can't keep up with you,' Rita's voice called from behind.

The bicycles shot through the back gate. Rocking over a bad road surface, flat tyres bumped and fields and hedges came together in a heady sensation. Veering round a sharp bend, a familiar dark grove of pine trees blocked out the sun. On the other side, a sea of bog rippled. A donkey drawing home a creel full of turf ambled towards us.

'*Dia is Mhuire dhuit*, God be with you.' I waved to the driver forgetting about my trousers until Rita choked back a laugh and I pedalled faster. Rounding the final bend where the Protestant church reared against a grey sky, we swung off.

'We're going to have to walk in the rest of the way. These trousers are sticking to me,' I panted.

'I told you not to wear them,' she giggled back. It was walking our bikes to the shrine that saved us next. Some instinct had caused me to look behind and there was Dado driving a herd of cattle along the road we'd just travelled. At breakfast he'd said he was on his way to the fair in Castlebar. Our escapade was over. It was stay ahead and take a back road home, or be caught and despite Rita's protest I began to push and run. To the right a procession of Sunday pilgrims was blocking our way. Tethered donkeys and carts surrounded a water pump. Beyond the pump and close to the bus park, the usual corner-boys lounged. If anybody knew us as we passed we'd be shown up in front of the town and we'd never get home. Despite Rita's protests to take it easy we ploughed on. Reaching Murphy's Hotel I kept my eyes down. It was the first real test of my rig-out and every one of those layabouts was staring. Somebody was bound to call my father.

'*Na bac linn a bhuachailí*,' I said jauntily and Rita waved.

'*Dia is Muire dhuit a leanbh*.' It was Dinnie, escaping from work at home, stepping out from the shop door of my father's butcher stall and about to go into Murphy's Bar next door. He was supposed to be helping count sheep on Currach Hill and Dado would spot him too.

'Is that all the go in Dublin? Because if it is, maybe a fellow wouldn't know if 'twas a man or a woman they were meeting. But sure, please yourself girl and why wouldn't you?' Dinnie tipped his forehead.

'You know me Dinnie. I have to feel fine and easy,' my gaze shifted. I was going to have to let him get caught by Dado to give me time to get away. Signalling to Rita airily we pedalled off.

'We might meet in Murphy's tonight,' I cried back to remain calm, not daring to look in case my song-gatherer had been spotted. I could go to the pub, dressed the way I was and apologise to him. It was a tricky solution but there was no time to delay and we pedalled off, heading towards a boreen which I seemed to remember met another path leading back to Ballyhale.

A coach load of pilgrims trundled past and the sound of singing came through the opened windows. '*Sweet Heart of Jesus, font of love and mercy, today we come, thy blessings to implore*.' Up ahead Pat Gibbon, a boy from my year in school, had heard the singing and gazed open-mouthed at a girl in pants. Tonight I would go into Murphy's Hotel wearing my trousers and an old coat and cap of Dado's and not be known from Adam, I daydreamed.

Thorny bushes reached out to scratch us as we shoved the bikes through the rutted boreen. Rita complained of nettle stings and I thought about the possibility of a night-time jaunt. Brambles were making the lane impassable until finally the haggard of Ballyhale came in sight and we barged through with shouts of success.

'*I am a roving journeyman, I go from town to town.*' Dashing up the back lane Mamma was singing while she was hanging out a load of washing in the yard.

The tune was one of my own 'come-all-yas' she said she never wanted to hear and I leaned over the yard wall to hide my trousers.

'I have the key of your door. It's the only one that locks the store upstairs as well, it's packed to the gills with provisions for a Christmas party I want to keep secret from your father.'

She began to slap out the clothes to her tune. The only thing now was to stay behind the wall and shiver with the cold. Tonight it would be pillow shapes in our beds. That would show her. But the washing lifted lightly and Bran barked at our feet to get us out, as if everything was on her side.

'Knock church is a wonderful sight in the moonlight,' I murmured to my friend, reclining on the bed beside me later that evening. Then I shoved Theo's note into her hand as I'd been reading it once again, sighing on purpose so that she'd say something. Her face grew dreamy.

'You'll be telling me next walking in the middle of the night is no fun on your own, mad-cap,' she said calmly.

Down below us, Dado's voice was calling roughly to the sheepdog and he shattered the air with a piercing whistle. He had barely said hello since I got home. It occurred to me that if he was preoccupied then maybe it had something to do with Andrew, the visitor.

'We'll go tonight and have a laugh together. You must be dying to see the boy of my dreams,' I clapped my hands as though I couldn't wait for the moment.

Chapter Sixteen

A photograph fluttered onto the ground from Dado's coat pocket that night. I was borrowing it for my disguise and had stepped in behind the curtain of my parents' bedroom because Mamma and Moyra were talking outside. The picture would be the first thing Mamma would see if she came into the room and then she'd look for the coat to put it back in the pocket. It was a photo of a baby I'd never seen. Something made me notice a resemblance to that drawing Granny Lloyd had once given me when I was younger. I had a sensation of my grandmother's presence there and then, stooped, with thin grey hair piled up with pins and powdery soft cheeks to kiss. It was the time Granny told me how the picture came to her from America and how like her brother the drawing looked. Mamma had things hidden too. As if to prove it, in the fading light from outside, I now saw *To my darling baby boy with lots of love, Eliza Lloyd*, inscribed in slanted writing across the back. The voices got louder and I looked out the window wondering if I could jump down.

From the very minute I'd stepped into Mamma's room that evening to borrow Dado's big coat I had been questioning my motives. Theo had made a decision to go for Moyra and that had to be accepted. As if in agreement now her soft voice penetrated from the corridor to put me in my place. Whatever she wanted, Rita was out on the lawn waiting for me behind the monkey-puzzle tree determined I should do the opposite and there was no choice but to go on. Putting my face to the glass to see if she was visible, Ballyhale was bathed in moonlight. If she stepped forward she'd be caught too and my knees began to tremble.

'Lily is under her father's authority here,' Mamma was talking now and I twisted and turned. I peered out the window through the ivy-cluttered glass again, imagining the long jump, leaves tapped against the pane warning of danger. A lone robin sang and I breathed in deeply. I could stay here until the corridor was empty. Rita was safe. She would blend in with deepening dark until she decided I wasn't coming. It was jump or be discovered because the door knob began to turn and in desperation I grasped the brass fittings on the window to pull it up. A sash creaked and I cowered, instinctively pushing the coat up against the glass to quieten the noise.

'Lily, what are you doing here? Mamma is coming in. Get out fast and I'll cover for you.' Moyra was inside and had noticed my feet. She must have realised I was up to no good as well because she pushed the door closed and pointed at the window.

'Hurry on or you're caught,' she ordered curtly. A flower bed below was miles down but with no time to think I was out. As I hit the ground pain shot through my foot and I hobbled forward. My body bounced up and barely glancing at my sister's face in the window, wondering what she had guessed, I was staggering away.

In what seemed like an age later I saw Rita, dressed in a coat of

Dinnie's, peering from behind a line of pampas grass behind the monkey-puzzle tree. Grabbing her arm to shove her on, a yellow light from Mamma's window shone like a search-lamp behind us. We ducked past her prize rhododendrons. Moyra must cover up for us. It was too late to go back and I crossed my fingers in prayer. Up ahead, Rita crashed through laurels and undergrowth. My trousers tore as I chased after her but, breathing heavily, we were out on the moonlit avenue. This business of having to hide to get what I wanted was another reason to give up Theo. But the thought drifted away.

'We'll be in Knock in no time if we start to run.' Moving quickly to get to the gates, Rita and I had to flap our arms to keep warm. It must have been the quiet all around that made her whistle the old dance tune 'Nora Creina'; I did a quick jig and then we were out on the road. We were just two girls out to enjoy ourselves on a night adventure, I convinced myself, and we snuggled up to one another. If the moon went in, singing would keep us going for our rendezvous with danger. Human shapes were being made by bushes. Rita drew Dinnie's jacket tighter across her chest, the one she'd plucked from the scullery and a fox yelped nearby making us cling together more.

'Look at you. You'd think you were a dandy down from Dublin trying to snare a poor innocent country girl.' I twisted her cap to a jaunty angle.

'You're hardly a perfect picture of manliness yourself. As soon as we get to that town, I'm turning back.' She shoved me away and grinned.

Past the high stone wall that marked the boundary of Ballyhale House, a bat swooped down before us from a line of trees and straight ahead a dipping hawthorn swelled out. Despite an urge to chat, the ghostly air was creating silence. The photograph came back. There was something unexplained about it, I decided; a mystery from the past. A cat whimpered in the field beside us like a demanding baby and I stared straight ahead. A skeleton in the cupboard, the words came into my head with the same stealth as the fluttering of an ash tree overhead. In an effort to dispel the image I imagined Rita and myself skulking in the shadows of Murphy's Hotel. Something tickled my neck and I shivered.

'I have a strange photograph here that Mamma doesn't want me to see.' Rita had paused for a minute to listen to the sound of a distant car and I waved it in front of her. Chubby features paled in the moonlight as she bent close to look.

'It's not just any baby. I could have a cousin somewhere that I know nothing about,' I shrugged and laughed. The noise of the car was getting closer. Beside us a rank smell of rotting straw blew through a five-bar gate and we scrambled over, scratching hands on briars and drenching the ends of our trousers.

'Mother of God, not even a story of finding a missing baby will get us out of this,' Rita swore. The car roared past and we cowered lower. A few minutes later we were trembling as we jumped back onto the road and watched the red tail lights disappear. She was right. The picture of a baby would have to wait. We had nearly been caught because of it and I tucked it away carefully.

When the lights of Knock appeared glimmering like pinpricks in the dark, we lengthened our stride. Here and there an oil lamp flared in a terrace of houses, closed up for the night. A bicycle whizzed by and the rider saluted. Before we knew it we were on the slope of the Main Street. Figures strolled purposefully in the gloom and we passed a donkey and cart parked on one side. Inspecting Rita from the rear, Dinnie's old working jacket was too short and I pulled it down. A man in a doorway who must have thought he knew us waved. Venturing alongside the hotel the dark shape of the church blotted the skyline. There was a figure inside the gate, and we pulled up. If it was Theo he was too early. It was a long way to go to twelve o'clock and I rehearsed what I would say about giving him up. A gurgling stream welling onto the road suddenly reminded me of the sheen of his black hair and how I'd like to see it again. At least we could have a peep at the handsome look of him in the moonlight. Now the figure by the gate was emerging from the shadows. A trilby sat back on his head. Even from here he was bulkier and too small for Theo.

'It's us Theo,' I croaked. The voice that answered had an American twang. The man turned in our direction, his hat tipped forward. This was Dado's friend who'd parked in our driveway and that I'd first seen at the station.

'We'll have to get out of here. It's not Theo. He'll tell them in Ballyhale,' I ran with Rita into Murphy's doorway. Pushing further in, we reached the hotel bar. A murmur of men's voices and the light-hearted sound of a fiddle travelled out. Smoke from the fire was thick in the snug and we slid through. The photograph peeped out of my pocket like somebody watching.

Chapter Seventeen

Once inside there was a thicker pall of turf-smoke and a smell of sweat. We'd moved deeper into the bar but nobody shouted from behind and the doorway was empty. It was important to get home as quickly as possible but heads turned in our direction and murmuring voices paused. Over the counter a pendulum clock blended with a stained wall and rough oak beams. I stumbled and pulled upright and Rita started a fit of coughing. Hardly daring to look around it seemed luck was on our side because one familiar face leaped out. Dinnie was tucked into a corner by a glowing turf fire with a fiddle by his side and he looked across calmly. The hearth area was wreathed with more wisps of smoke and he gestured us over. If there were to be trouble at least we'd be hidden in a dense haze.

Our disguise was working because a friendly nod was made in our direction from one of the box-players and two *sugán* seats were cleared. Daring to glance towards the door again all seemed normal and talk surged back. Blown from the open fireplace some ash swirled in eddies making Rita turn green. At least here was where I really longed to be. I signalled to Dinnie and he lifted the fiddle and plucked at a chord. He had brought us into a charmed circle of sound.

Seated on the hob, cap on knee, a *bodhrán* player tapped a rhythm. There was a lull and a song note entered the air. Up to the rafters went seductive words, as if the hills themselves had found a voice and I sank back in delight. Scrambling behind the wall on the journey had left muck on our faces and it began to flake but I closed my eyes and started to tap, all thoughts of pursuit forgotten, until Rita poked me.

'Don't look now. There's no hope for us,' her pushing became more insistent and I opened my eyes. A sickly smell rose up. Two glasses brimming with porter had landed on a stool before us. That would have been all right but a trickster beside us slid a bottle of *poitín* from his pocket. I could nearly hear the glug of it all going into the glasses. A log thrown on the fire made it flare red.

'This will warm ye up lads. There's more where it came from,' the *poitín* dispenser raised his empty bottle briefly. It caused a circle of faces to watch expectantly. Rita lifted her glass and sipped. If the impostor at the shrine came in now, I thought, he'd find us slumped forward and I gulped the fiery liquid down.

'Swallow it or we'll never get out,' I gasped. The horrible mix was like medicine, exploding inside.

One of us was bound to laugh. Dinnie's voice boomed about as he sat up straight. Rita's hand, hard as a brick, was under my arm and I jerked up shakily.

'You'll be tipsy in a minute, let's go.' A fiery glow took over and her words came from a distance. The stool in front wobbled.

'That's Lily O'Donoghue,' a call came from the crowd but now Dinnie was before us, clearing a way. Fear turned the lobby into a blur. Voices retreated though and at last we were outside.

This is what happens when I try to stand up to Moyra, I groaned, gulping in some air in the dark street. Across the road, starkly large, the cross on the church seemed to bear down on us. I banged against a telegraph pole trying to grope forward. Pulled by Rita we rushed into the middle of the road then reversed into the shadow of the high gateway that acted as a cattle entrance to Dado's butcher's stall. A dog barked.

'You have to get us home,' Rita hissed. The wall of our hideaway was damp and we steadied ourselves against it. Knock was a dead place. Sleeping houses and the narrow empty main street were palely white. A few shouts came from beyond Murphy's Hotel but we were distracted by another noise. Moyra was coming for me because a car was nosing round from a side road. Lights played along our wall. I ducked and a hypnotised Rita nearly stepped into the glare. It had to be Moyra because I knew our car engine. Peering out, Theo was driving it. He must have cancelled the patrol when my sister got word to him that I was out in the dark. Two drunks emerging from the entrance of the hotel stumbled in the path of the car, getting in the way. The clunk of the engine halted and a door opened.

It was nobody's fault that Rita sneezed. We were in the cold after a warm pub and an icy wind was blowing through this tunnel of a gateway. Theo's voice reached us. I took a deep breath and stepped out to take my punishment. Lit by the glow from Murphy's Hotel and perfectly outlined, he swayed languidly before us and in case I hadn't been seen, Rita pushed me further. He was in uniform, giving him a toy soldier look and he removed his cap, letting it dangle. A different thought surfaced in my mind – perhaps he was hoping to tempt me into his arms.

'You should have come when I was alone, Lily,' that voice with its American lilt murmured and despite myself my heart leaped.

'You're someone to complain. It's lucky I'm here at all,' I shrugged. 'Don't be teasing.'

His gaze developed a puzzled look, like a boy's, as if he was displaying the depths of his soul and I should reveal mine too. Neither of us took any heed of Moyra emerging from the passenger seat of the car. Her legs shone in the hotel light. She propped herself against the car bonnet, smiling primly and snapped her fingers. She had come to my aid, the gesture said, but she was running the show. Walking across the car's beam to take Theo's arm, her face grew grave. Rita must have seen the calf look she gave him as well because she muttered, 'Holy God' and her hand pressed mine. It was that which provided me with the opportunity to notice Dado's friend. He had been there all the time we were in Murphy's. The person he really wants is Theo, a thought came suddenly. He was stock still behind the car, like Bran marking a bird on one of Dado's shoots. Theo, the dumb soldier continued to smile at me, longingly.

'This is for you Theo,' I raised a hand in the air with the photograph in it to alert him, pointing behind. He paid no attention and then I thrust the picture at him to get closer, shutting his fingers over it, like a playing card trick.

'Look behind. Somebody knows who you really are.'

He looked at the picture in the dim light and frowned.

'Don't mind her, Lily is a tease. She really wants to say she likes you,' Rita said smoothly trying to grab the photograph back. That was when we all jumped. The IRA had saved us because a shot had sounded too close for comfort and Dado's friend melted away.

Chapter Eighteen

Before we knew it, our holiday was over and Rita and I were back in Dublin. My sister had never really explained why she and Theo were out together that night and now Dublin's shabby streets met my gaze. Our cab had swung wildly from Westland Row Station into a heavy flow of traffic. Stepping from the train a large poster for the Madam Butterfly-Margaret Burke-Sheridan Concert had been pasted high up on a wall. Today's date was printed across it and the singer looked down alluringly. This diva was another Mayo girl but she'd made a success of herself. It was a reminder of the invitation Connie had given me to this concert before I left for Ballyhale, when she said she could sneak me in. Leaning back to see, delight bubbled up. It was something to look forward to. I decided that Rita and I would go together.

'I'd give anything to have Margaret Burke-Kennedy's autograph. I dare you to go to her house and get it,' Moyra had said to me once and, in the middle of the busy street, annoyance at my sister returned.

My fears that she would tell Mamma about our escapade had stopped me from just ignoring her altogether and in fact the days after the midnight walk had been idyllic. Dinnie sang in the cart on journeys to draw turf from the bog, peaty air filled our lungs and bog cotton spread around like flecks of foam. Once, the three of us laughed and linked hands to edge around bottomless holes. The following day Rita borrowed a pony from Ned and we galloped like the wind through the fields. Moyra kept away from Theo all the time but I knew it was only a pretence because one afternoon I saw her slide into Granny Lloyd's shuttered up house. My cheeks burned red when she didn't come out for hours.

She didn't even come to the door to say goodbye, I remembered now. Rather than playing about with Theo she should be visiting me in Dublin. It would be like the old days. Connie would get her into the concert and we'd stroll arm in arm down O'Connell Street, laughing. Later on in the week, after my study, we could go to a dance in the National Ballroom or the Crystal, or maybe to the cinema.

My sister didn't deserve all this thought and I concentrated on the back of the cab-driver's head. His large ears stuck out like handles.

'*Oh Danny Boy, the pipes the pipes are calling,*' a clear tenor voice travelled back to my mind, delivering one of Dado's party pieces. Jerked to a halt on O'Connell Bridge, a sickening smell swept up from the river and Rita pulled a tartan seat rug across her nose, choking dramatically. She gave the impression of acting again when she sat bolt upright in the seat.

Suddenly I saw Sadie, Matt's sister, being escorted along the footpath beside us by a policeman.

'Don't pay any attention to that old codger, come with us, you're not well enough to be put away,' Rita said loudly and poked at me to make me look.

Sadie was in her overall. A police barracks was the last place she'd want to go. We should visit the girl in her bare room later on, to see what had happened and bring her food instead of escaping to an opera, I thought as they marched past.

Sweeping past the pair the cab had rounded the top corner of the square. Beyond us Auntie Terry must have sensed we were coming because she appeared on the top step of the hostel. Here was another actress because as soon as we halted she stared hard through the windows as if we were hiding someone. Then she waved repeatedly to urge us to get out. As soon as we alighted she grabbed my bags and heaved them up the steps.

'Try not to dawdle, girls. There's been a burglary.' Her lower lip trembled. 'Don't just stand there, unless you want it broadcast to the whole nation,' she wailed.

It would be impossible to get to the concert now because inside the hall a sideboard had been pulled out, straddling the floor, ready to barricade the entrance.

'Welcome back to chaos, girls. The whole place is in an uproar,' Annie had come into the passageway. She must be going out, though, because she'd restyled a dress so it looked like a Japanese kimono. Madam Butterfly, I thought despite myself and disappointment twisted inside like a knife. I should be worrying about the hostel instead of thinking about the concert and, as if to reprove me more, Auntie Terry leaned on the sideboard to catch her breath. To stop violin chords swelling in my head, I nodded caringly.

'This is terrible, was anything taken?' The memory of the music got louder.

'Just some letters of mine, I'm sure the burglar thought the box they were in had some cash or bonds,' my aunt pulled herself up. 'Sadie saw it happen and has gone to the police station to give more details.' Auntie Terry took my arm and a fluttering Annie got in our way with her kimono.

'You remember you said you'd love a walk. Maybe we could go and see Sadie?' I nodded at Rita cautiously. It wasn't fair to Connie. If she was going to the trouble of getting me in to a concert we should go. A way out would be to go and visit Sadie first. My thoughts began to crowd each other out.

'It's been a long journey,' Rita said enigmatically. Her eyes narrowed questioningly but I could tell she had guessed. At least Rita was on my side and I pressed into her gratefully. That overture from Madam Butterfly could be playing in an orchestra pit opening out before us right now because it was rising and falling as clearly in my head as cherry blossom dipping in the wind. If we rushed to the Mansion House after seeing Sadie we'd make the first aria. Annie bowed Japanese style in front of Rita. Before Auntie Terry could put two and two together and guess we were up to no good, I murmured kind words and brought her down to the basement for a cup of tea, better than any daughter who has come home after a long absence.

'How did I ever land up sharing a room with such a crazy person? We should be staying at home.'

Rita gave me a puck, nearly knocking me down as soon as we got up to the bedroom. The room was empty and the noise of girls milling about on the first landing, still talking about what had happened came up.

'We're only going to pay a quick visit to the Mansion House after seeing Sadie. Connie told me we could get a private conversation with the singer. It's too good to miss. You could get her to sign a programme for your mother. Please come with me Rita,' I pleaded with her but she still complained, swinging her legs onto the bed. Ten minutes later she left with me, but only on the promise that I write to Theo and tell him all about it afterwards.

Slipping through Mountjoy Square we jumped from one pavement flag to another. It had been raining and pools of gaslight shimmered like guiding marks. The bell of Gardiner Street church rang out for evening mass and an old woman pulled a shawl over her head. A haggard-looking girl started to cover her sewing machine in a shop window and we talked about how we might go to her and ask her to make something for us, to help her earn a few bob.

'No surrender. Keep our ports. Up the IRA'. The words fluttered in the breeze from a torn poster and a crouched figure in a recess, like an irregular on the run, darted out. A lump of bacon from home, which I was bringing for Sadie, swung against my side.

'Any few pennies for a poor man,' a beggar appeared, causing me to step back into a shop doorway. Inside an oil lamp glowed on a makeshift counter. Over the head of the shopkeeper, a few tins of condensed milk lined a single shelf and the added sight of a tin box of Marietta biscuits, probably there since before the war, made me instantly hungry.

'Nurse Nora Kennedy arrested for the death of Rosy Ryan, theatre dancer'. A sandwich board heading just behind the shop door leaped out in large capitals and I froze. Without even having to think I remembered the name. It was the same person Sadie and Matt had argued about in their room.

'Not Nurse Kennedy,' I said with a yelp and a sense of menace rushed in to surround us. The shopkeeper cast a sharp glance towards me. She began to wipe the counter vigorously then removed the mantle from the oil lamp, ready to close up.

'Is something the matter Miss? If you're reading about Rosy there was no badness in her. Even if she was expecting a babby she never deserved that,' she said crisply. I felt greyness now all around me, as if I was about to faint. It was the murky world Sadie inhabited, ready to latch on to innocent girls like Rita and I.

'Come on, Lily, or we'll never get to where we're going.' The sound of Rita's voice was welcome as the dawn but my purse fell from nerveless fingers. A gas lamp outside, the glimmer man had set too low, flickered off. Moving to the step, the forgotten war-dollar Theo had given me rolled and glinted. It must have got stuck in the purse lining. It was a bad omen. Here was another one trying to hide his real self. Any day now he'd be sending a new letter telling me he was going to marry Moyra.

'You're right, this is not the place for us,' I said and I clung to my friend.

'You must think it's clever to walk around an area where there's a murderer. Put your bag in front and button your coat over it and pretend you are expecting a babby and Nora Kennedy will jump from behind railings,' she joked. She'd heard the shopkeeper. The next thing she'd turn on her heels and leave me.

'Like you say, there's probably nothing to worry about. We're not the low kind of girls who'd let ourselves down like Rosie Ryan,' I said taking her by the arm and inching her forward. Lighting the way, the glimmer man's gas light flared. There was no going back.

Chapter Nineteen

Our trip was taking us into a shadowy world. The sooner we get out of here and see the lights of The Mansion House the better, I thought, as we walked on.

'If we do go back without seeing Sadie, Auntie Terry won't stop complaining,' I said to Rita to goad myself on and then clung to her closely. We passed mean-looking alleyways. Walking in our chosen direction meant going by the Magdalene Convent in Seán McDermott Street, that home for fallen girls where Matt was to make his delivery the day I fell off his cart. A single light shone high up on the plain red-brick front.

'Auntie Bridie in Clontarf told me the nuns take in unmarried girls if they get in the family way and then they're stuck there for the rest of their lives,' Rita shivered.

'In my parish, if a girl gets herself in trouble she ends up in the county home with dim-wits and half-dead people who hardly know their name. I'd kill myself if it happened to me,' I laughed to break the tension and we tiptoed past.

The hands of my watch told me it was seven o'clock and I swung along quickly. At this rate we'd soon reach Sadie's. At the Mansion House all it needed was Rita to hear one song from Madam Butterfly and she'd be hooked.

'*Céid míle fáilte romhat, Eilín Aroon*,' I began to whistle, in case there was a chance Margaret Burke-Sheridan might like to hear a bar from an Irish song.

On the deserted street a lone car passed and beeped to get our attention. Washing hung out of the windows of gaunt houses and a few faces peered down. Broken panes of glass let scraps of coloured curtains escape. Despite the dark, children raced up and down singing out each other's names. Rounding the corner onto Sadie's street, a scrawny young lad halted his dilapidated fruit seller's pram. 'Are you looking for someone, Miss?'

'We're friends of Matt Corrigan and decided to call to say hello,' I fibbed in case he got more curious. He'd be telling me next a policeman had brought Sadie home and was waiting to nab anybody else looking suspicious. Pram wheels creaked as he watched us move on. That urine smell was worse than before when we stepped into the tenement and a mouse darted past our feet making Rita jump. If our luck was in, Sadie wouldn't be home yet and we could leave our gift and go. Rapping on the familiar rough door, silence descended.

'Trust you, Lily, to bring us into a rat-hole,' Rita cast a fearful glance back and I drifted to block her exit. Unexpectedly a command from the first floor landing distracted us both.

'Get back here this minute or youse will get a right scelpin,' the voice shrilled. The words were barely out when a pair of waifs appeared on the steps above us. They viewed us solemnly. Moyra and Lily, I thought instinctively. It was because they looked so inseparable, despite their difference in height, just the way my sister and I used to go around. In the gloom you could hardly see the dirt etched on their faces but as they clattered down the stairs blotched skin and thin frames showed up their pitiful condition.

'If you're looking for Matt or Sadie they're not there. They've gone to live in Inchicore for a while. I'm Eileen and this is my sister Fidelma,' the bigger of the two piped up. 'The gardaí came looking for them on account of Rosie Ryan dyin'.' She blessed herself with the sign of the cross and her bird-like fingers quivered with excitement. 'Rosy was a dancer at a theatre. Me ma was at her funeral but she didn't tell the auld fella. She said he'd have a fit. Granny says it doesn't matter because where she's gone we're all the same, good or bad.'

It was a long speech for a small girl and there was a gasp of pity from Rita and she reached out to hug the pair tenderly. This was like when Mamma grabbed her two daughters together in her warm embrace. Moyra had Mamma on her side now and all that was over. More importantly at the moment, Rita was only waiting for the chance to sweep the children away for a treat and I tapped her on the shoulder.

'We can see Sadie some other time. Give this to your ma, Eileen.' I pushed the bacon forward. Bony hands reached out. Eileen's thin ribs stuck through her tattered cardigan and now I wanted to take the children away as well. Sewage smells came in like a wave. The girl's eyes lit up as she snapped the meat from my hands.

'When I grow up I'm not going to be a dancer like Rosy. I'm going to be a singer,' she rocked up and down.

'Of course you will and I'll help you. We can be famous together. *Céid míle fáilte romhat, Eilín Aroon*,' I crooned lightly. Her thin voice began to soar. Soon the wren of Summerhill was sending her notes upwards on the wings of hope and I took her hand. Beside her Fidelma harmonised.

'The Summerhill Sisters,' I clapped my hands. 'We'll have to get a contract for you to. You'll make it to the top in no time.' But it was all make-believe and there had to be something else. My fingers felt the silver dollar, gleaming when I fished it out.

'Keep that as a souvenir to make sure I'll come back.'

'We should put half of the posh girls of UCD here and let them see what life is really like,' Rita interrupted hotly.

'Thanks for the presents Miss, but we can't stay. Ma is going to kill us. We're supposed to be minding the new wee scrap Nurse Kennedy brought.' Eileen bit the money as if it couldn't be real. Following her glance she was staring up the stairs. A thin woman with a careworn appearance and a baby resting in the crook of her arm glared down.

'Let's go home and forget about the concert,' said Rita.

Chapter Twenty

Finally I persuaded my friend to change her mind about the concert and as we crossed the Liffey the calm river rested in moonlight. Down on the waters you could see a dead animal that looked like a drowned cat being set upon by an army of rats.

'Imagine if that was a baby that had fallen in there.' Rita shivered, upset once more, stuck to the spot. We'd never get to the Mansion for our date and I had to pull her away.

'Hello there, girls. Would you like a good time?' a low voice called. It was the car that had prowled past us on our way to Sadie's. Here was a chance to release some tension and soon we were exploding into snorts of laughter, holding onto each other and gasping at the man's funny-looking, leering face. Picking up speed, we began to run. The old pervert in the car was having a different effect than he intended, getting Rita and me to our concert in record time.

'We weren't supposed to be coming here,' Rita snuggled into my side in a dark broom cupboard. As soon as we arrived at the Mansion House Connie had given us a hurried signal to hide and I pushed aside a forgotten fur coat to try and breathe and then I hugged Rita gratefully. The sound of Connie's voice came in faintly. Our cubbyhole was behind the reception desk. When we arrived at our fairy tale venue we saw well-dressed ladies glittering on wide steps. Inside champagne corks popped at a bar and a blaze of candles flickered on marble fireplaces, as if there was no such thing as war or blackouts.

I thought longingly about the concert that was about to start, wishing I could get into that auditorium. But instead I smelled old shoes and heard a scratching noise that meant only one thing. A brush hit Rita's face and she exclaimed. Through the thin walls an orchestra tuned up.

'Don't forget us,' I pushed my head out at Connie, but was presented instead with an uncaring back.

'Don't worry, nearly everyone has passed through,' she grinned back. Trying to straighten up, Rita kicked a mop-bucket this time, sticking it into my shin. Maybe she'd quieten down if we talked about how to rescue Eileen and Fidelma.

'We shouldn't have come and left those darling children,' she muttered as if she'd read my thoughts.

'*Tu? Tu? Tu? Piccolo Iddio!*' the diva's voice travelled into our dark hole. I imagined a porcelain complexioned Cio-Cio San, rejoicing that her American sailor had come back to save her and I sank back enchanted. Even if we were in a broom-cupboard it was a stroke of luck to be here. Soon after, through the same thin partition, a scene of heartbreak began to unfold and Margaret Burke-Sheridan flowed on effortlessly. Opera fanatic Moyra would give anything to be here. Rita interrupted my thoughts by pushing a hand in front of my face.

'What do you think was the cause of that dancer's death that we read about in the shop?' her fingers jabbed my nose.

'She got pregnant, the same as happened to Madam Butterfly. What else?' I had snapped at her for destroying my concentration but then I stopped dead, appalled at my own words.

'Keep the noise down. You can be heard out here.' Poking her head into our cubbyhole, Connie broke the tension. 'I just have to hang up the final coat belonging to that woman, Nurse Kennedy, you know, the one who was arrested for the murder of the dancer? She's out on bail but she has the nerve to turn up here. Everybody in the entertainment world is appalled at the death of Rosy Ryan,' she said crossly.

Nurse Kennedy, I put my hands to my ears. There was that name again and the word pregnancy hung in the air, unspoken. Rita was elbowing past, making a gap in the fur coats to have a look, not caring. It allowed us both to see the back of the late-comer, an elegantly dressed woman dipping out of sight towards the concert entrance.

'Imagine the terror of poor girls having to go to her, because if not they'd never survive themselves,' she whispered loudly.

The concert passed like a dream after that and arriving home hours later I spied a letter to Auntie Terry stuck behind the hall table. It must have slipped down during the excitement after the burglary and remained unseen. The handwriting was my sister's. It would be all about Theo I decided and what a lovely fellow he was and how she was going to bring him up to meet her favourite aunt. Sooner or later Moyra would have the whole family on her side. Turning it around indecisively, I shoved the useless thing into my bag. Guiltily, before going to sleep, it begged to be read.

Dear Auntie Terry,

Expect a visit from somebody called Andrew but pay no attention to him. His intention is to get Theo, the American staying with Ned, to enlist in the Allied Forces. Theo is part of the Irish Auxiliary Force now and much needed. I know the war is devastating Europe, there is a genuine fear of Hitler taking over, and Theo feels he should play his part but as far as I'm concerned he's needed here more. I've told him he will always have a place with us. If you want to know more, ask Lily. She knows all about being protected, from her last trip home.

Your loving niece,

Moyra.

The following morning conversation started about how I'd missed a Yank called Andrew who had paid a visit just after we left. Somebody said the same charmer was a recruiting officer for the United States Navy, that Annie had taken a shine to him but that everyone knew he'd smooth talk her and then leave her. Annie came into the basement during the gossip and shook her head and laughed, staring at me pointedly.

'He can recruit who he likes for all I care,' she said. 'As long as Lily brings him here again.' Then she raised her thinly-arched eyebrows and left with a flourish.

Chapter Twenty-one

It was two days later and this Andrew still hadn't turned up to explain himself. I stretched to keep awake sitting on one of the benches in the main entrance hall of University College Dublin. The concert tiredness wouldn't go away. To compound matters, a lecture delivered by Auntie Terry the morning after our trip to the Mansion House was still revolving in my head.

'Why were you so late? I'd hoped we could sit down and talk about your studies. Miss Hourigan has been in touch about your lack of progress in your History of Art classes. Gallivanting will be the ruination of you,' she'd said.

'I would have come home but the Legion of Mary was looking for volunteers to do an all-night vigil for the Sacred Heart.' Of course it was a lie and I regretted it when I saw the hurt look on her face. She knew it was a fib and now, as I shifted on the seat in the Main Hall with *Gulliver's Travels* open on my lap, a song sheet of a ballad slipped out. The words *Let him go let him tarry, let him sink or let him swim*, fell onto the ground. I was distracted then by the sight of an orange, patterned, paisley scarf draped across the shoulders of a sleek blonde girl. It was the same girl I'd sat beside in the ladies reading room when

I'd opened Moyra's bombshell of a letter. She twirled it about like a mannequin creating a splash of colour and murmurs of appreciation arose from those around her. She was a show-off I decided, enough to put a person off university for life. Burying my head in the book stopped me from seeing Rita until my feet were kicked to one side and she lifted the song from the floor. At the same time she jabbed a St Stephen's student magazine under my nose.

'Don't throw a song away, it might come in handy. I've been reading about a UCD Dublin Orphans benefit concert in the Metropole next week. Catherine Lacy, the lead singer, is sick and they're looking for a replacement. It could be you,' she said with promise and swung my hand in a rhythm. Her corkscrew curls tossed with the movement. 'Rory Masterson will get you in,' she added but her words were drowned out by the blonde before us. Her tapping high heels resounded as she moved off across the floor.

'That's the kind of girl Rory Masterson likes, bright-eyed and shallow. Anyway I don't want to be a singer. It's too difficult.' My bad mood must have come from remembering Auntie Terry but Rita just stood back and mocked.

'You probably wouldn't be picked anyway. Rory might like your singing but a concert like that has a more refined programme.' Then she laughed and swung my hand back onto my lap before dropping it.

'One thing is for sure, I'm not going to ask him straight out,' I said. Having to go cap in hand to Rory really was a reason on its own why I should give up the singing dream, my temper told me again and I lifted my bag and strode towards the canteen, not caring whether Rita followed or not.

Stepping onto the front steps of the university an hour later, my plans not to sing were making me boil inside. It was all tangled up with having to deceive Auntie Terry to get my way and as if the weather was against me too, a cold wind nearly blew me against a pillar. Trying to force myself to go back to study, huddled dejectedly, fingers touched my neck. If it was Rita I was fed up with her efforts to cheer me along but, looking around, I found Rory grinning into the teeth of the gale. His jacket was blowing open and a leaf fluttered in his fingers.

'I was hoping to see you, Lily. This bit of a tree was caught in your hair.' Shoving a tweed cap off his face, wide-awake eyes glinting carelessly, he let the leaf go. He stuck his face into the wind again.

'Marvellous of course, I've been at it since cock-crow,' I said. My tone was so sulky he'd have to notice, but he nodded and began to dance on his toes to get warm, rubbing his hands. Sticking his hands in his pockets, somebody else calling his name made us both spin around.

'Well, look who it is. Where have you been hiding yourself, pet?' a low voice drawled. It was the pert piece with the gaudy scarf. Now she was prowling towards us, swinging her hips. Smoothly brushed hair curled from a simpering face and she linked Rory's arm as if she owned him, looking at me without much interest.

'Hello, I'm Anya. I don't believe we've met.'

'It's hardly my fault we weren't introduced. I've been here all the time. I'm Lily,' I said. She'd brought my temper back. Eyes blazing, I could feel my cheeks glow.

'Lily, this is Anya, a friend of mine,' Rory said smoothly.

'I'd love a cup of coffee, precious.' Anya eyed me coldly and patted his arm.

'Would you like to meet me in Bewley's for afternoon tea at about three? I want to talk to you about a vacancy for a singer that has just come up,' Rory addressed me directly at last. He went around to the other side of his friend, tipping his cap as if she wasn't there and before I could even nod in reply, led her off. If that swank turned up at Bewley's with him I might change my mind about being a singer. It would show him I for one wasn't a walkover. With that thought I sauntered off happily.

As confident as a gentleman at a business meeting, Rory leaned forward in his chair. The afternoon had flown by and we were in Bewley's. The café was crowded and noisy but I just glanced about, pretending not to care. This was the place to be, with one of the leading lights of the Dublin music world.

He lounged back then as if he felt the same and, when a waitress hovered close, raised a finger. There were two English soldiers perched on a nearby red velvet seat, sitting upright in their uniforms. Suddenly they reminded me of Theo. He'd want me to put my best foot forward, I thought importantly. Behind the waitress more high-backed red seats and marble top tables created a cosy feel and dark corners suggested an air of intrigue. Lemon and red light poured from stained glass windows and a generous fire sent out waves of heat. Instead of talking about his proposal straight away Rory took out a concert programme and placed it on the table, tantalisingly near. It was an invitation to look inside but a waitress was standing over us.

'Would you like a cream cake, Lily?' he asked but not waiting to hear, as if he knew what I wanted, Rory murmured an order. It was something to try out with Rita, if all you had to do was wave airily and a plate of buns would appear. I tried not to let him see me grin. With rationing they were probably made from substitute egg powder and sawdust flour, but my mouth watered at the delicious looking display on a trolley beside us.

'I've decided I'm giving up on my ambition to be a singer,' I declared, picking up a jam tart. Saying this made my old moodiness return and Rory lifted a milk jug from the table and banged it down. He thrust his chin out.

'Don't be silly. We wouldn't be here unless I wanted it. If you play your cards right I can get you on the bill for the Metropole. The problem is there's a committee to be got around and they're more interested in *The Bohemian Girl* and Gilbert and Sullivan than an Irish ballad.' His eyes twinkled like sparkling sea breakers to appease me.

'The fact that I want to sing a country ballad is no reason why I shouldn't get an audition. All they'd have to do is listen properly and be hooked,' I shot back.

'*Let him go let him tarry let him sink or let him swim for he doesn't care for me.*' I began to hum the words that were on the sheet that had fallen on the floor that morning. It was going to take a lot of persuading to get me to deceive Auntie Terry again but I could feel my resolve beginning. I studied the jam tart assiduously.

'I might get them to trade letting you sing an Irish song for one of your lovely smiles,' Rory grinned. The boys in uniform looked over hopefully as if they'd sensed a joke and I waved back at them gaily.

'I'm not in a position to talk about it but there is somebody else who would make them change their mind,' I intimated. The hint had come out of the blue. Moyra and I would do our sister act. Slowly but surely I'd win Auntie Terry round. Hardly able to wait for an answer, amazed at my brilliant idea I almost ran from the café, leaving him sitting inside, open-mouthed.

Stephen's Green held a peaceful winter feel, it seemed to me as I walked along one of its paths, not daring to glance back hoping Rory was behind me. He must have decided to ignore my strange behaviour because he reached me at the duck pond. '*Una Bhán*,' he said the name of a song and hummed the air and, pretending to fix my coat, I took a sideways glance. Only a fool would say no to a walk with a debonair gent by her side I thought, even if he didn't agree with my choice of song. So I pointed my toes to walk like a lady and impress, just the way Sister Monica had taught us back in school so we would have good deportment.

He sidestepped as a small girl dashed in front and when she yanked some flowers from a bed and ran off, he picked one from the ground and placed it in my buttonhole.

'*A Úna Bhán, is gránna an luighe sin ort,*' the haunting air was irresistible and the words rose and dipped in the crisp air. Just as well he had pinned the flower on me or I might have been prompted to give him a thank you kiss for the café treat. Instead I tripped on.

'I'm going to see if there's a letter in my flat about the Metropole's final arrangements. They promised to write. I live in Leeson Street, just around the corner,' he said. Exiting at the Earlsfort Terrace end, Rory pointed to an adjoining street.

Warm fingers lingered on mine for a moment as we crossed the road, to pull me back when a motorbike roared past. A few houses down Leeson Street he turned a key in a green door and ushered me inside. There was a high hallway, cluttered with bicycles. Dust-motes swam in a sunbeam from the fanlight and piano notes sounded from the floor above. The man was deliberately standing in my way, I decided, forcing me into a corner. Leaning around to pick up his post from the hall table, he pressed in closer. A whiff of carbolic soap hit my nose.

The confinement of the narrow space was making us touch too and my hand pushed against his face. It was smooth. Transparent eyes deepened to green. Close-up freckles were dots on a speckled wren's egg. Our lips tipped and he pulled back.

'Sorry, I didn't mean to take advantage,' he stammered.

'This doesn't mean you'll get me to sing,' I shot back to stay collected. 'Für Elise' drifted down, as good as our walk in an enchanted garden. To confuse matters more, a knock sounded on the door.

'I have to go,' I said and stepped back. Glancing towards the doorway, Rory pulled a pair of tickets from his waistcoat pocket, gripping them as if they could disappear.

'I got these for the Savoy cinema tomorrow evening. The film is called *The Ghost of Frankenstein*. It's about a man who's trying to lure a girl into his flat and then throw her aside. You might like to accompany me?' He grinned. With a raised hand he touched his head smartly in a soldier's salute. It seemed to me he probably got those tickets for Miss Beauty Queen and she couldn't go. That was when it must have got dull outside because the bad light in the hall gave his high forehead a noble look.

Being clever is no good if a man is a bounder, Rita would say, and I tried to look stern.

'*Let him go let him tarry, let him sink or let him swim,*' That's a song about old lovers,' I announced, 'and since we're just friends, the cinema would be lovely.'

Theo, please don't read my heart the next time we meet, I prayed.

Chapter Twenty-two

The wind sighed through thinly leafed trees and the sound of two attendants came through the railings of Stephen's Green, as I walked towards my date the next day.

'Hide and have a look to see if he's come. You'll make Theo jealous when you tell him,' Rita had grinned when I told her. A whole night had now passed since my meeting with Rory and that was too long, the magic was gone out of things now.

'*Let him go and get another, I hope he will enjoy, for I'm going to marry, a far nicer boy,*' I warbled and tried not to think of Theo's arms when we'd snuggled in the shade of a tree, or hidden in a sunny hollow in Ballyhale.

Trees rustled overhead and traffic growled. Further along the park's edge a Findlater's van rounded a corner. It was my friend Matt and he put a hand up like a policeman to slow me down. Above his head a gaslight created a green hue. To add to the effect the dusk had started to thicken and homeward bound workers trudged past, ignoring us. Matt clicked his horse into place, the harness jingled and he smiled a greeting.

'Good to see you, Matt. I missed you a few days ago. It was when

Sadie went to the garda barracks about the robbery,' I told him and could feel my cheeks redden. It was the wrong thing to say. After what was overheard in their room, I shouldn't have mentioned the police at all.

'Sadie did nothing wrong,' Matt's face darkened.

'That's not what I mean. Only a hypocrite would think she was a bad girl anyway. She's probably sorry now she brought shame on herself and her brother,' I rushed on and began to kick at a stone. This was getting worse. Matt should leave and I could go to Rory like I'd planned.

'You're right, Lily, Sadie is a trusting girl. I was going to tell you about a friend of yours I met, but you won't want to talk to me after this,' Matt hunched his shoulders and before he could be asked to explain, manoeuvred his way into a flow of traffic.

'Come back. I didn't mean it,' my voice echoed forlornly. The stone at my foot glinted. Rain began to fall, creating more misery. Looking at my watch, I knew I certainly wouldn't be singing now because it was too late for the cinema date.

Rory was in cahoots with his blonde friend at a back table in the library when I went in search of him the following morning. They leaned their heads together over the same book, as if there was nobody else in the world. When he did look up and notice me he frowned, trying to stare me out of the place.

Let him go, let him tarry, let him sink or let him swim, for he doesn't care for me and I don't care for him, the song fluttered inside.

'I don't like the look of him anyway,' I'd tell Rita later. 'His lofty forehead has nothing to do with being a brain-box. He's a baldy old man.' I gulped back a wave of disappointment.

The following day a new notice was tacked over the old one on the board of the Music Society. It read: 'New Concert Date, Miss Walden to sing in Metropole Charity Concert'. Anya, Rory's pin-up girl from the famous Walden music family, was to be the new singer, a publicity picture alongside showed. If I went along and spoke to him, I could straighten things out between us and maybe sing in the show after all.

'Lily O'Donoghue, I want to talk to you about some plans for study I've made with your aunt,' Miss Hourigan called crisply as I set off to find him.

'Welcome to UCD, Mainie Jellett,' she exclaimed then, brushing me aside as a trim lady in a black suit ran towards her.

Chapter Twenty-three

'For he doesn't care for me and I don't care for him, Let him go and get another, I hope he will enjoy,' I hummed whenever I saw Rory for the next few days. If thoughts of him were to be kept at bay from now on, all my energies had to be concentrated on study. More importantly there was a tutorial meeting coming up for History of Art and if I didn't hand in an essay on Aesthetics in the Dada Movement I'd be made an example of in front of everyone.

Walking into the library I glanced about at all the heads bent over long tables. Apart from the shuffling of chairs and a few murmured conversations, silence prevailed. The copybook of the student beside me was crowded with notes and out of the corner of my eye I saw Connie waving from behind the library desk. She might keep my mind off the faint-hearted piano player so I picked a finished book up off my table and strolled across. She was organising copies of the *Capuchin Annual* which were stacked beside her and paused to push a badly printed piece of paper over, exclaiming over a masterful drawing of an *uilleann* player in an annual page that fell open at the same time. The announcement caught my eye: 'Exhibition Launch, White Stag group of Painters and Mainie Jellett, The Acorn Gallery,

Lr. Baggot Street'. The name Mainie Jellett leaped into view. I should go to the exhibition; the artist might see me and tell Miss Hourigan what a keen student of art I was. Connie must have noticed my interest because she pushed the drawing of the piper away as if she might be interested too.

'The invitation has been around for a while but it's actually on today. I thought it might appeal to you,' she waved it in the air.

'How did you guess it would help? I can use it to impress Miss Hourigan.'

'You can't go on your own. You'd be lonely.' She looked sheepish.

If I got an interview with Mainie Jellett for *St Stephen's Magazine*, it would be an even better way of showing Miss Hourigan my hidden talents. I had a second thought. Taking a pencil from the desk a geometric head on the invitation called out to be copied. I could talk about new developments in art and the significance of the Irish White Stag Painters.

'If you really have to be at it, I can join you there,' Connie was still speaking. 'Somebody who knows you wants to walk me out. His name is Matt. He had to deliver a crate to store library books here because the boy who usually does it is sick.' She paused. Her hands flew to her face to disguise a creeping red. This was the girl that dark horse had been talking about when we met beside the park and I whistled under my breath.

'It's no wonder he wants to meet. You're a pushover for good looks Connie,' I offered, linking her again, and her flush deepened. I would go the exhibition. At least it would be a chance to make up to Matt for what I had said to him. A colleague of Connie's padded out to answer a query just then and there was a whispered conference. The *Capuchin Annual* she had left aside slipped off the pile and the piper illustration disappeared.

Arriving at the exhibition address, figures moved about in a basement. Heads bobbed behind a grimy window and I clambered down steep steps. There was a press of bodies as soon as the door opened and voices surged out.

In an inner room canvases with dark lines and flat planes of colour were barely visible between craning heads. The name of Mainie Jellett flew about. There was the flick of an eye in my direction and then a glance passed over me. This was the kind of crowd that could ignore you forever.

A lanky-haired man made an arc with a cigarette, nearly stabbing me in the face and then a bony-looking girl dressed only in black swung a tray into my chest. It was loaded with glasses and a bottle labelled 'Dandelion Wine'. I lifted one glass and then another. Laughter burst out nearby. If Connie was here at least we could have a giggle and then I saw her standing in the doorway of the main exhibition area, glowing prettily. The man with the cigarette winked at me as Connie floated over.

'You've been drinking,' she said and my wine glass dipped precariously. 'Sorry I'm late, Matt wasn't on time to collect me. He's charming isn't he?' Her dimples appeared. 'He's interested in books as a matter of fact and he was telling me about an antique books sale in the Phoenix Park next Sunday.'

There was no time to discuss Matt because the ancient-looking painter was getting closer and I pulled my coat tight. He'd probably spied a bit of flesh underneath and I gave him a flash when he least expected it. He was one of those free-thinking men Father Tierney described in sermons, the kind girls were supposed to avoid like the plague. Before there was time to back off he'd flourished a sketch pad in the air, elbowing Connie aside.

'Excuse me for interrupting, darling. I'd like to introduce myself. My name is Larry Foley. I'm an acquaintance of Rory Masterson.' Empty green eyes made an effort not to blink, shining like a cat's to draw me in. 'I saw you perform in the Shelbourne some weeks ago. It's an unexpected treat to meet you here. But then again, we artistic types are drawn to each other,' he squinted. Letting go of my arm he began to sketch on the pad. 'Marvellous breasts,' the words could be heard by everyone. 'I won't let you move until you say you'll come to my studio and be painted.'

'You're confusing me with someone else,' I said stonily and Connie giggled behind me.

'Delights of the body,' the dried up lips smacked nearly touching my face.

'How much would you pay?' Connie said. She was having him on and I gave her a dirty look.

'A pound per sitting, beginning next Saturday,' he beamed.

'She'll do it so. That'll be the easiest few shillings you'll make in a long time,' Connie smirked and the goat would have smothered me in his arms if a blast of air hadn't hit us when the door opened. It was Mainie Jellett, the only reason I'd come here and stepping past she distinctly said Larry Foley's name, drawing him away. The intervention came just in time and I made a bolt for the door, tumbling up steps with Connie, I began to choke with nervous laughter.

On the street above there were helpful railings to lean against and a soft mist to help us clear our heads. Beside us an overflow of people chatted loudly.

'I heard thousands of Jews are being rounded up and transported to gas chambers. Those Nazis are animals,' some English tones proclaimed loudly.

'None of us know how bad the war in Europe really is,' I broke in, attempting not to slur the words, tapping the speaker on the shoulder. 'It's terrible to be so helpless, not to be able to relieve such awful suffering.'

Distracted by the declaration I didn't see smelly Larry standing behind us until he flung one arm around my shoulder. Squirming away, he dug a hand into my waist. It was worse luck that his attack took my attention from the street.

'Don't look, it's Rory Masterson,' Connie hissed at me.

Strolling as if he was only out for a constitutional, Rory was heading for the exhibition. There was a sound of material tearing. The shoulder of my coat had caught on a spike and made a ripping noise.

'Come and have a chat with us, Rory,' the artist beside me called. Without even waiting for permission, Larry leaned and kissed my mouth. Catching me in a direct gaze, Rory moved past. He'd found me out rightly and I stared at his stiff back and yanked myself uselessly out of my captor's grasp.

Twas down by the Glenside, one bright summer's morning, one of

Dinnie's favourite songs flowed inside me while traipsing back over Baggot Street Bridge later. Somehow my thoughts had turned to Moyra. Whatever she had done, I needed her arms about me. Staring up, even the stars had a dispirited look.

'That's a beautiful song, Lily,' Connie said.

'It's not bad for someone who lets the whole world laugh at her like a clown.'

Mist seeped through the air and I staggered and fell. There would be no invitations to sing from Rory from now on.

'Matt will wonder where I am but I had to come with you,' Connie shrugged. I was upsetting this good friend too, taking her away from her new beau and I wrapped my arms around her, nearly pulling her down.

A curtain was drawn back from Rory's window as we passed his flat. Moyra's betrayal would have to be forgotten because through the lace curtains, two shapes had flitted across the room. It had to be Anya and my feet attempted a shaky waltz. 'The O'Donoghue singers' here we come, just you wait and see, my mind raced. It was the only thought that could save me.

The minute I got to the hostel I'd send a telegram to my pushy sister. *Hurry to Dublin for Sisters Act*. That would get her guessing. As soon as we got the better of Rory I'd find out the tricks of the trade I needed for stealing back Theo.

Chapter Twenty-four

It was a rollicking walk home after the Rory debacle. Connie and I giggled a lot. To cheer me up she waved an imaginary cigarette in the air.

'Keep away from my wrinkly skin, darling, I might turn into dust,' she growled as if she was Larry and then began to paint pretend brush strokes mocking me as if I was captured already in his lair of a studio. She was happy because of Matt, I knew. I'll have Moyra up here soon, we'll thrash everything out and be friends again, I told myself but now the memory wouldn't leave me of the pained look on Rory's face when the artist kissed me. Reaching the hostel, Connie barely stepped inside the door.

A vase on the sideboard had been filled with chrysanthemums and their pungent odour drifted towards us. The green edge of a telegram with my name printed on it was peeping out as well, as if it was written by me; as though it was the same one I'd been thinking of sending to Moyra and I stared, confused. It had to be from her. Down in Ballyhale she'd sensed my situation and wanted to help out. The flowers hovered in the air like something set adrift. The effect of the wine was worse than I thought and I blinked stupidly.

'Stand up straight or your aunt will guess what we've been up to,' Connie shifted uneasily poking me in the spine and placed a hand on the latch, ready to run out. A smell of mothballs from a coat on the hallstand drifted over and it was enough to make anyone sick. In the reception area the phone rang and Sister Angelica's barking tones rang out.

Dado probably sent the telegram, I thought, he'd done it before. I shook my head to clear it. More raised tones came from the reception room, as if the person on the other side of the phone was deaf and before the nun could come out and ask to see it, I flipped the telegram open. My father's name sprang out. Miss Hourigan had written to Ballyhale to complain, the thought stuck.

Urgent, Family Conference. Meet Clarence Hotel, Friday, the message declared.

'Stay for a while Connie, we need to talk,' I waved the telegram about. There was no time to say anything more because now Sister Angelica had poked her head out of the reception. She began to purr.

'My friend is on her way home,' I said and throwing pleading eyes at Connie not to give us away I shoved her out the door reluctantly.

After that I sat on the stairs heavily, too tired to move. Rain hit the fanlight outside, making a soothing sound. I should run after Connie with an umbrella and beg her to come back and we'd go and listen to some music, I thought but I stayed put. She'd be flying along. She was going back to her flat to see if Matt had left a note to ask her to meet him. At least one of us was happy, I decided mournfully. There was no time to get up because Auntie Terry arrived with a clatter. She'd banged a tray of dull-looking knives and forks on the sideboard. I straightened them carefully.

'I'd like your help to clean up these.'

The rattling tray made my head thump. Somehow I managed to walk a straight line. Auntie Terry had led me into the nuns' parlour but then seemed to have forgotten why because the cutlery tray was left outside. Her hands began to sweep about and she moved to the door, looking out to make sure no-one was coming.

'You don't have to tell me about the telegram, your father never keeps me informed,' she complained and I shoved it forward, glad of something to do.

'Dado wants to meet me, but he used the word urgent. He's never said that before.'

She darted an icy look as if it was all my fault.

'I'll be going on a retreat to Waterford. You can tell me what happened later.' Instead of giving out more, her eyes began to soften. Beyond us the tapping of a typewriter halted and I imagined Sister Angelica had her ear to our door.

'*Let him go let him tarry, let him sink or let him swim,*' I hummed my anti-Rory song to put her off the scent. 'If you still want to have the cutlery cleaned I'll do it tomorrow. My friend Connie has asked me to give a hand to serve food to the destitute in the Legion of Mary Kitchen in Temple Bar tonight,' I said loudly.

'Whatever you think, Lily,' Auntie Terry shrugged. 'Just remember you can count on me if your father is in opposition to you becoming a nun. You're as good as being one of us anyway.' She put her finger to her lips. She was playing a game of her own but she was just in time before Sister Angelica walked in.

For the next hour as I lay on my bed, sleep was kept at bay. Auntie

Terry's words kept going round in my head. She was only half in jest it seemed to me. Eventually I fell asleep and it must have been shortly afterwards that somebody pulled the bedclothes up to cover me. In no time it seemed, the following morning had arrived because I was turning painfully in the bed. Sun poured in the small window, making me rub my eyes. About to ask Rita if she remembered how I'd been looked after, I saw how she could be depended upon. Keeping my telegram safe from prying fingers, it peeped now from under her pillow, as she turned over.

Later that morning I stood at the door of the hostel as a gang of barefooted children skipped past barely glancing at me as they headed into the school next door. I breathed in deeply. It was time to get away without any more heart-to-hearts with Auntie Terry. Beside the steps Sister Angelica's bike was leaning on the railings. The black Nellie pointed towards me invitingly. She won't need it for a while, the words whispered dangerously inside and before I knew it I'd grabbed the handlebars and sailed off. Taking the corner of Parnell Square sharply children clapped and peering back I could see Sister Angelica was waving me back from the hostel window. It was more important to get to college on time, I'd tell her later, and I pedalled on.

Soon the buckled front wheel had a mind of its own, veering towards footpaths. Overhead the sun began to shine through thinning clouds. Maybe the telegram meant there was a celebration. Mamma's birthday was next week and Dado had probably planned this as a surprise, I decided and began to whistle '*I was told by my aunt, I was told by me mother, that going to a wedding would bring along another*, Rory could go to hell. If Matt was here I could give him a race but a bus pulled out in front of me making me slow down. Exhaust fumes bellowed and I'd reached the O'Connell Monument before it was possible to belt on again. It was a pity I'd picked up speed because swooping past like a bat on his own bike, Rory shot across the front wheel. A peaked cap turned sideways gave him a carefree air but he didn't fool me because his chin stuck out angrily. Larry Foley is a right gom to make such a fool of me, I thought. My rusty crock turned crookedly.

'Rory, look behind you,' I called but the wind swallowed my voice. Stay out of sight, I said to myself then and I slowed to a snail's pace.

Slowing down too much made the bike nearly fall over but reaching O'Connell bridge, the way ahead for Rory was clear and he could have shot ahead. Instead, unlike the brown Liffey surging swiftly beside him, he got off his bike. As soon as I thought of whizzing past an elderly man hugging the edge of the footpath stepped onto the road. The brakes squealed. I gasped and closed my eyes. Tinkling a weak-sounding bell was no use and the bike tilted into a fall. A cry escaped me. Rory leaped onto the road. The wheel of Sister's Angelica's bike whirled round like a numbers board but Rory had stretched a hand out and keeping my gaze down, I had to let him pull me up. To add to my embarrassment, a string of pearls that I hadn't fastened properly in the rush to get out of the hostel fell in a creamy pool on the ground and he swooped low.

'Imagine meeting you here,' I grimaced, stooping to pull the bike away from the traffic.

'I believe you lost your necklace, Madame,' he reached over with the beads, ignoring my remark. Before I knew it, the glowing circle nestled in my hand like a gift and I hobbled about, pretending to rub an ankle.

'I'm most grateful, sir, that you spotted my trinket,' I said proudly. It was hard to keep this up because my eyes had lifted and my mouth insisted on smiling.

'I'll be in the music room in Newman House this afternoon to practise for a singing session in the Irish Club on Parnell Square on Saturday week, if you have something you'd like to work on,' turning to retrieve his own bike he stared at me directly.

'It means cancelling other appointments. I'll see what I can do.' The words drifted light as butterflies on a breeze. It was time to get away before I changed my mind. Leaping on my bike and looking back I could see the Liffey wind lifting his coat like a Galway hooker.

Later on in the college main hall, as though he'd sensed my reluctance, instead of coming to speak to me in the throng, Rory drifted over to Rita. She had seen me too, but chose to ignore it. The pair began to converse like the best of friends. Rita was probably explaining to him about Theo, getting a dig in at him because I'd told her about the blond in the library. I tried to attract her attention when Anya came to join the three of them and kissed him on the cheek, I closed my eyes imagining my American beside me.

Chapter Twenty-five

Newman House was separate from the rest of the college, standing beside University church and overlooking Stephen's Green. I ran towards it, late for my singing practice. As soon as I arrive I'll have to tell Rory to forget anything Rita said about Theo because it's all over, I said to myself.

That has nothing to do with now, another voice said and I lifted onto my toes and hurried on. Outside the church a chatting crowd had gathered as if a party rather than a mass was about to begin. It would be easy just to follow the crowd and go with them into the church but I leaped up the steps beside it, before the thought took over.

'*If I were a blackbird, I'd whistle and sing and I'd follow the ship that my true love sailed in,*' I hummed. It was the song I was going to suggest to Rory to practise and I pushed the door in. We'd start with that choice and go from there. Nothing might happen, I warned myself, but goose pimples of excitement rose. At least I'd get another concert opportunity out of it. I smiled doubtfully at the thought.

Inside a spacious entrance hall a porter barely glanced up from his *Independent* newspaper. A chat about the war should make my love for Theo more real, I decided, even if he wasn't enlisting.

'Are there any new developments on Montgomery and the North African front?' I paused and asked him. The question must have sounded knowledgeable and the porter's eyebrows came together, peering over his paper.

'The Axis forces are being kept at bay by the arrival of Americans. I don't know how those soldiers stand the sun,' he said and pallid figures struggling in the grip of white heat rose before me. For a second I saw Theo, leaning into the shade of a palm tree smoking a cigarette, the last one before going into battle.

That was what Moyra meant in her letter by standing by him. I was to go to Ballyhale and persuade him to stay in the Irish army. Well she'll have to decide herself what to do, I shrugged and bounded up the stairs. The porter's tinkling bell, signalling he wanted to close up, followed me all the way.

Walking up and down the first floor a few times, it was difficult to find the music room as the bell continued its warning signal and I pushed open the first door. Looking insignificant in the large space, an upright piano stood against a wall in the airy room. Everything else was untidy because sheets of music threatened to tumble onto the piano from a shelf overhead and music books lay in heaps on the floor. Light from a window fell onto a poster of the singer John McCormack, giving his eyes and hair a gilded appearance.

'The Olympia Presents Ireland's Favourite Tenor, Admission 2/6d,' the poster declared. Engrossed, barely remembering Rory, there was a sound of papers shuffling and I turned. The slowcoach must have forgotten about me standing in the doorway, pushing sheets of music together and staring as if he saw a mirage.

'You managed to make it,' I said and my nervousness started to leave me. This mightn't be as difficult as I'd imagined. It was only a music practice after all and I flopped onto the piano stool.

Rory must have thought he was still out of doors too because he was wrapped up in an old army coat. He swung a hat off his head and placed it on a small table. I noticed that one of his ears was smaller than the other. Sometimes that kind of thing made me giddy with laughter and the notes of 'The Blackbird' came in handy, to smother a cough.

'Glad you could make it Lily. I know the song you're humming. Maybe we should start with it,' he said pleasantly. '*If I were a blackbird, I'd whistle and sing*,' he began, but his voice was too light and I joined in. Maybe he was the one who should be getting lessons. My spirits began to rise and I gave him a cheeky smile.

Concentrate on me, Theo, wherever you are, I thought then because Rory's willowy figure was having an unsettling effect as he bent to look through some music. Dust had lodged on the corners of the piano and I flicked with a finger to collect myself. 'This place is a mess. Nobody must think of tidying up.'

'So, are we ready to play?' he looked at me mildly. His eyes were twinkling as if he was trying to stop a smile and then they turned serious, muddy-looking, like a duck pond flecked with feathers.

'Come and sit down, it would help. '*I'll follow the ship that my true love sailed in, and on the top rigging I'll there build my nest*,' my words came out more smoothly than I'd hoped for. There was a sharp cracking noise like a gunshot which distracted us both. It sounded like it had come from the grounds of the Iveagh Gardens at the back of the building.

The last time Moyra and I really had a chance to be alone together was in that green backwater. She'd sing with me now if she was here. The thought had a more unsettling effect than I'd imagined. Maybe I didn't want her coming in between Rory and myself. She might try and steal him too. I was about to apologise for not making the cinema date but it was too late because the porter was at the door. His face was red as if he'd puffed up the stairs and he rasped harshly, throwing his hand in the air and smiling apologetically. As if he expected something was wrong, Rory leaned towards me on the piano stool. His side brushed mine.

'I'm sorry I'll have to ask the two of you to go. Word has been sent round that I'm needed in the main building and I have to lock up here,' the *amadán* porter blustered.

'That's a pity. Perhaps you could give us a few minutes more,' Rory looked stern but a finger lay on mine. He had left it too late though. The porter had caused the picture of the soldiers in the desert to return to my memory.

'We can come back another time,' I attempted to stand up.

'I'll put the catch on the window to give you time to get organised,' the porter paused. Passing by, he tugged at my sleeve.

'Maybe you could sing one song,' he said. 'Do you know, "The Blackbird"? It's about a girl who can't forget her sailor. He's hundreds of miles away where the sea is blue as peacock feathers and he isn't coming home.'

I shot him a grateful glance. It wasn't fair though. Warmth from the man beside me had gone down as far as my knees and I had to rub them furiously. Glancing at the porter for more help, he winked.

'That's what I like about songs. They can let us forget our troubles. There's nothing like young love,' he declared and before he could be stopped, put a hand on both our shoulders, pressing them down.

'I don't have a boyfriend, we only came here to practise,' I said. At least I'd kept my bond with Theo safe, I thought, forgetting about the request for a song and joining the porter by the window to look out. Rory had taken up a music sheet and was staring at it intently when I glanced back. The gardens below offered a vision of green but I saw something else. The green had disappeared and the heat of a desert flooded up.

'It's too hot outside,' I croaked 'We need to stay,' because down below an oak had become a palm tree and Theo was beckoning me to try its shade.

Chapter Twenty-six

I'll ask Moyra to come and sing in Dublin. It will keep her away from Theo and Rory won't be annoying me either, I decided. The day Dado had asked for us all to meet had arrived and I stood in the lobby of the Clarence Hotel. Red wallpaper glowed, giving an opulent feel and I shifted, taking the telegram out of my bag again to make sure I had the details right. I had done battle against a bitter wind blowing down the Liffey on my way here but gradually the shivering was subsiding.

My parents would walk in the door any minute now, looking like skinned cats from the cold and with long pusses on them ready to give out. Moyra would probably come in last, hugging Mamma as if they were the best of friends and I glanced around, suddenly determined not to stay. A passing bellboy smiled and nodded, and I relaxed. Glowing heat from the fireplace meant the place was cosy and there would be a good dinner ahead. Dado would make sure of that. The wind rattled the door each time it opened and the noise of passing traffic came in. Once I definitely thought it was Dado outside and I prepared myself for an assault, standing stiff as a soldier on parade. It was only a man wearing thick glasses who looked familiar to me. I had seen him a few times at the university.

'Welcome Mr Kavanagh,' the bellboy rushed up to him and took his coat.

The newcomer was definitely Patrick Kavanagh, the poet who'd addressed the Literary and Historical Society the only time I'd been to a meeting. Now he was scowling and peering about as if annoyed. Turning around to follow his progress a strong smell from the Liffey arrived, catching me unawares and at that moment my parents came in the door.

'Hello everyone, if you think I'm in trouble there's an explanation for everything,' I said breathlessly. The words were out before I could stop myself. They were decked out in their Sunday best. Out of the corner of my eye Moyra was grinning at me uncertainly. I'd noticed that she'd borrowed one of my Spanish combs. There it was, plonked on top of her head. It was my favourite one too.

'Control yourself child. We're only in the door,' Dado said grumpily before I could act and Moyra smoothed back her hair and grinned loftily. She grabbed at the tiny head of a fox acting as a clasp for a fur stole and pulled it off, fiddling with her coat next.

'The whole world knows you're barely keeping up in college Lily,' she said smoothly, 'but don't worry, we're not here because of you. I'm the one in the dock today.' She couldn't upset me too much though, because Mamma's arms stretched out pulling me close and I winked over at her smugly, above clinging shoulders.

'Sorry everyone but I can't stay for very long. There's an essay I have to get in for tomorrow and I want to make sure it's right,' I said loudly.

After freshening up in the powder room we ladies moved

together to the hotel dining-area. A tic appeared under one of Moyra's eyes, as if my words were an attack or maybe she was hoping that I would take her side when the real business of the visit came. With that I threw my head back in the air carelessly. She was getting some of her own medicine now.

Our table was partly hidden by a pillar for privacy and was close to a window at the back of the restaurant. A subdued clatter of silver serving dishes filled the air and waiters glided about. Looking towards the street, I imagined lamplight on the Liffey making faint pools. Only a few diners dotted the stylish room. Not caring who might hear, Dado spoke loudly about bad weather and a poor harvest. Moyra tapped me with a foot under the table and then Mamma took our attention, craning her head to see who was looking at her. A waiter pushed a serving trolley past, on which floury potatoes made a pyramid as a centrepiece. The rich smell of roast beef wafted by and Dado waved to him to stop.

'Steak for all of us I suppose?' he looked around, Mamma nodded for everyone and he flapped his hand, dismissing the waiter and shaking out a napkin. A silence grew. I smoothed the tablecloth and began to push the cutlery about, lining it up neatly. One way of helping Moyra would be to suggest that she come and stay in Dublin for a while. Looking across at her, I could see her face had a distracted look, like somebody in love. I shrugged.

'Auntie Terry asked to send her apologies for not being here but she had to go on a retreat.' Before I could chat on, my knife dropped to the floor.

'I'll get it, I can look after you,' Moyra dived under the table.

'You'll want to know what the telegram was about, Lily,' Dado's voice boomed above her and she struggled up slowly. Pink had tinged her cheeks from the effort but her eyes were smouldering. Facing the blade of the knife up, she banged the table. 'There is some news we thought you'd better hear, Lily. It concerns your sister,' my father went on blandly. He'd lifted a corner of the table cloth to smooth it and a jug of milk wobbled.

'Maybe you should ask Lily about her evenings off and how she spends them. I believe she's hardly ever in the hostel,' Moyra said. It was an obvious distraction and I kicked her under the table. At this point Patrick Kavanagh created another diversion by passing by, veering towards a place by the window and taking out a newspaper. But Dado wouldn't be put off.

'*If I were a blackbird I'd whistle and sing.*' It was the song I'd wanted to sing for Rory and now it was coming back. It was perfect to keep their minds off whatever was about to come and I began to hum louder. Maybe I should help Moyra and make her grateful. I'd tell them about the mess in the music room and make it funny.

'Moyra has agreed to go to Limerick to do a commercial course. Your mother thinks it best,' Dado declared, ignoring my starting notes. His brow furrowed and his face grew hard. Mamma caught Moyra's hand and pinned it down and darted a warning glance at me.

'Theo is the reason I've been ordered to go,' Moyra's lower lip trembled. 'I might be twenty-one next month but I have no control over who I meet. According to Mamma, he's not good enough for the family.'

'He lied, Lily. We all thought he was a cousin of Ned's. It turned out his mother is a gold-digging Lloyd.' Dado banged the table then, grimacing at my mother as if it was all her fault. 'As if that wasn't bad enough we wouldn't have known anything if Miss Mahon hadn't seen his birth certificate. The gloating face of the same woman talking about it would make you sick,' he growled. 'The only reason Theo courted you girls is to get the farm for his penniless family. The next thing your mother and I will be homeless.'

'Theo is honourable. None of you know him like I do.' I stood up. A small pulse began to beat in my neck.

'Show some respect. It won't kill Moyra to go to Limerick.' Dado's voice softened unexpectedly. 'We're only thinking of her,' he thrust his face into mine, forcing me to sit down.

'Moyra has to make up her own mind. Unless she'd like to sing with me,' I asked. It was my desperate measure to solve the situation at last but it was too late because Mamma began to cry softly. She looked at me with soulful eyes.

'You were always foolish, Lily. Think of others beside yourself,' she whimpered.

'All they care about is the farm. Well I know somebody told the American authorities of Theo's whereabouts. There are people who'd sell their soul for a bit of cash,' Moyra said. The trolley arrived to interrupt her. Smells of food drifted strongly, hinting at a feast, and my mouth began to water.

Before there was time to be dragged into some sort of a deal to get Moyra to leave, the poet was on the move again. 'Have you forgotten my drink?' he called out as he reached our table. He was probably one of Rory's arty set too, but it was a good enough excuse to let me get away from this madness and I called out his name, to try and engage in a conversation and leave.

'Keep your voice down. It's enough to have one daughter making a fool of herself in public,' my father said sharply.

Chapter Twenty-seven

'Opportunities For Singing Duos, First Prize An Audition For Radio éireann, Walden's Programme.' I saw the poster outside the Irish Club on my way home. It could be made for Moyra and myself. From the conversation in the Clarence, the only thing my parents cared about was the farm and maligning Theo. If I was to go to the Irish Club every night of the week and neglect my studies they wouldn't care so long as he was out of the picture. I gazed longingly at the poster, finally forcing myself to keep walking.

Walking out of the hotel I'd never felt so alone and now, shivering as if still beside the cold Liffey, Moyra's upset face came back. She didn't give a fig about me really. The only reason she was playing on my feelings was to get me to invite Theo to Dublin. Then she would arrive and pounce on him for herself. The wind blew my hair out like a clump of gorse. As I left the poster behind me I had another thought. If both of us entered for the show Moyra would steal the limelight. As soon as I got back to the hostel I'd better dash off a note to apply. Any time spent thinking about it would make me change my mind.

Sister Angelica was standing inside the door of the hostel a few minutes later. It was obvious that there was something up because her head shot forward like a hen spotting a juicy grain and she smiled sweetly.

'Your aunt sent a card to say she's extending her retreat with the Brigidine Sisters.' She wrinkled her nose as if the smell of dinner in the Clarence wafted in the air. Then she thrust out Auntie Terry's postcard, jabbing it in the air.

'That's good news. Pity she missed the family scandal,' I said smartly and before she could stop me I ran towards voices in the basement. Rita would help with a letter to Moyra. She'd be good at explaining that all a duet needed was a combined effort, not a show-off act.

'We'll have a chat about your family again,' Sister Angelica called after me loudly.

The following morning I was the first to greet the day. It was too early but it occurred to me that maybe I could drop that request into the Irish Club to apply for their act before Sister Angelica asked where I was going. All around me girls slept and I stretched and slipped out of bed, lifting a notepad from the locker to write quickly.

A glass of water was needed straight after the effort of composing and, letter in hand, I padded down the stairs. In the hall, Auntie Terry's swing style coat hung invitingly. It could be slipped over my nightdress. Pulling the door open a few minutes later it looked as if I wasn't going anywhere because a policeman was walking up the steps, smiling as if he knew my face.

'I'm looking for a Terry O'Donoghue,' he spoke crisply and I pushed my note behind me. He must have been sent by Miss

Hourigan to keep a friendly eye on the university girls and used the excuse of looking for Auntie Terry. Then another thought took hold. He might be here about that dress stolen from Clerys. A keen gaze went past me into the hostel hall. A bunch of letters was clutched in his fist and he brought them to his chest.

'We were informed there was a robbery here some weeks ago and we have reason to believe these objects were amongst the items stolen. They were retrieved from a young man who confessed where they came from.' The letters were pushed in my direction and he lifted his hat back to scratch his head.

Ballyhale Manor, Ballyhaunis, Co. Mayo; an address on a bulky-looking envelope stood out. There was no stamp either and the flap was torn across. They must be Auntie Terry's stolen letters. Bringing them to her would put me in her good books.

'She's away but I'm a relation of hers and can keep them for her,' I reached out. The policeman hesitated and I smiled winningly. It would be just my luck if Sister Angelica came down the stairs with the stolen dress draped over her arm.

'Well, if you could accept responsibility for them Miss, it would be a great help. She won't have to come traipsing down to the station later.' The policeman handed the letters over and, it seemingly not occurring to him that I might be a thief, retreated down the steps without a backward glance.

What's all the mystery about these letters Auntie Terry? Maybe I might be able to use them to persuade you to let Moyra and me go to the talent contest, I thought that evening. I was in the dormitory, more plans were going through my head about getting Moyra to

Dublin and Annie was laughing outside on the corridor. There was a flash of red as a scarf billowed round the door. Auntie Terry had stayed away an extra day. Hidden at the back of a shelf, my fingers touched the letters. Somebody called a greeting to Annie on the landing, making me hesitate. They probably contained nothing, just commonplace thoughts you couldn't use against anyone and I drew them out.

Sitting on the bed and turning the first envelope over, Auntie Terry's disapproving presence seemed to hover and, opening the flap, yellowed paper peeped up. Out on the corridor more girls had gathered because there were peals of laughter as if Annie had told a joke. My fingers edged out the corner of a newspaper cutting. This was a news item I'd often seen because there was my sister, tripping down a street in a long dress with a rosette pinned on her front. 'Winner of the Claremorris Toddler Show', the headline announced. The whole outfit made her look like an old-fashioned doll and I could see myself peering out of a pram behind her. Faded writing caught my eye.

Lily is so forward, before long our little orphan in the pram will want a share of the limelight. It was my mother's hand and I frowned. There was something fishy about this. Maybe I could get Mamma on my side, talking about it. I'd tell her that from the beginning Moyra was the one trying to steal the show from me.

My own Lily Marlene. The girls on the corridor started to sing and I began to hum to stay calm. A letter had lain between the folds of the cutting. Maybe I could put a little pressure on Auntie Terry first. Imagining Rita and I sailing out to the Irish Club, I opened the sheet out.

Dear Terry,

I hope you don't mind me calling you by such a familiar name. For reasons we both know, I feel as close to you as if we have been friends for a considerable time.

I hesitate before sending you this cutting in case it causes pain, but perhaps the joy that this little girl brings me might cheer you up too. You did your best regarding baby X. As you know she is much loved. Forgive me for breaking your silence in this matter but in the circumstance I'm sure you'll understand.

A board creaked outside, stopping my reading. Sister Angelica had probably been out there all along. Backing onto the bed to sit down I pushed the letters underneath and then rolled over and pretended to be asleep. *Lily Marlene the soldier's friend,* I thought, to stay strong and even when Sister Angelica came in and breathed over me I kept my eyes shut tight and covered the letters by spreading out.

It was an hour later when Sister Angelica finally waylaid me. I was propped up with my pillow, trying again to make sense of Auntie Terry's letters and had just bundled them up when she glided into the dormitory. A bed had been vacated by a girl leaving her job and she thumped at the mattress before putting some fresh sheets down.

'Can I give you a hand?' I pretended I'd just looked up and she simpered.

'Not at all. I wouldn't want to disturb you. I'm being told a policeman came to the door yesterday and gave you some letters. We wouldn't want somebody like Father Lonergan to find out there is a deceitful girl here. It would go against her in my reports. It's my job to nip things in the bud before somewhere like the Magdalene Home has to be contacted.' Her face began to look like a martyred saint and she sobbed and took out a handkerchief. 'I believe you have Auntie Terry's letters,' she murmured. 'You know all about the death of baby Mary I suppose? Terry told me a long time ago.'

She began to slap out sheets making them flap gaily like swan's wings.

'God keep the angel safe in heaven. Your aunt told me they barely got the baby christened before she died. May she rest in peace, the poor mite,' she paused then to lift a crucifix that was on a long chain around her neck and kiss it.

A penetrating glance met mine to see if her words had got through and she blinked tears away. A smell drifted in the air. It was the same scent of mothballs that had been in Dado's coat with the photograph, but this time it was Sister Angelica's shawl. A shifty gaze met mine. Flicking out her shawl she'd flung it over her shoulders.

'You'll have to chat to your aunt. These things can run in the family. Although in the circumstances perhaps it wouldn't be a good idea. You don't want her to find out you read her letters without permission.' She straightened and touched up eyes that had dried mysteriously and when she thought I was off my guard, dived a hand under my pillow in case the letters were there.

The following night Rita and I went - without permission - to the singing session in the Irish Club. There was so much going on in my family I didn't want to know any more. If Moyra was trying to follow her own path then she'd need more than the trick of getting Theo to Dublin to have her way.

'It will be Christmas soon,' Rita said as we left the hall hours later. We had danced all night. Frost glittered on the footpath but my feet were sore from high-stepping and I kicked off my shoes. 'What did you think of the boy with the red curls who asked me to dance?' she questioned shyly as soon as I opened my mouth to complain.

'I don't care about any boy so long as we can have fun,' I said laughing and swung her around making my feet sting with pain. But that wasn't how I felt. Watching the two of them together I'd begun to think of Theo's kisses.

Chapter Twenty-eight

Rita was right about Christmas, because it seemed to come overnight. Along Henry Street a colourful array of stalls selling everything from paper decorations to cheap toys spilled over into the fruit and flower sellers of the cheaper Moore Street. The usual food shortages might have gripped the city, making the lives of struggling Dubliners even more miserable in a festive season, but here all was colour and delicious sights.

'See you at the Christmas Toy Fair, McBirney's, O'Connell Bridge, Dublin. Lucky Dip, 1/' announced a new board held up on the GPO corner as I passed on my way to college.

I thought of Eileen and Fidelma, the two little girls from Matt's building, and how this would be the worst time of the year for them and how I'd never gone back as promised. As if they wanted to prove my guilt, I saw the two of them emerging from the doorway of Woolworths as I took a sharp turn into the shopping street towards them. The older sister carried a bucket of slops. Potatoes floated in a grey liquid and I managed to slip a shilling into her pocket and step back. Staring towards O'Connell Street, I worried about my studies. I saw a group of men who were out of work, thin as scarecrows, leaning dejectedly against a wall. They were begging for alms, but spying a stall with a row of dolls I called out to Eileen. Her glance was hurried but she smiled, probably fearful that I'd ask her about Nurse Kennedy, she disappeared into the crowd.

There was a party atmosphere in the university when I finally arrived. Even if it meant missing a lecture I'd stopped to buy Christmas presents for everyone in Ballyhale. Rita would fill me in with her lecture notes and I was sure she'd love to see the star-shaped glass decoration I'd bought for Mamma and tucked away carefully. About to chase after her figure spotting her going into the library, I heard Rory's voice calling. Anya was stuck to his arm like a limpet.

'I'm playing in the orchestra of the Christmas pantomime in the Gaiety.' He drew a deep breath and prevented me from veering away, standing stiffly as if he was delivering somebody a message. 'I can put a word in for you to get in the chorus if you like, but you'll have to shorten your Christmas holidays to attend rehearsals.' He scratched behind an ear and shuffled.

'I'll think about it,' I nodded solemnly. As soon as he said the words a smell of greasepaint entered the air and I had a sudden sensation of stage-lights. I had to stick my feet firmly on the ground not to jump for joy.

'See you outside the theatre at five o'clock on Stephen's Day so,' he smiled. Anya murmured something about wild country girls and their free spirit as my whoop of delight broke out. Whatever they'd choose to believe, music was my life and I waltzed away.

'Can my sister come too?' I should have asked and added, 'she's a great singer.' It would be a perfect opportunity to get Moyra in my clutches. There'd be no problem persuading Mamma to let me leave for Dublin early, because as soon as Moyra arrived Auntie Terry would be all over us.

Later on that day I dropped a note in Rory's letterbox.

Expect a surprise visitor when you see me at rehearsals, but don't forget I'm the one who wants to be a singer.

This could be the perfect opportunity for Moyra to get Theo to Dublin, I thought, just as the envelope left my hand.

Chapter Twenty-nine

'Moyra won't believe her ears. I'll hardly be in the door before shouting out about the pantomime and then as soon as she comes to Dublin I'll tell her about the request for singers in the Irish Club,' I gabbled away to Rita, brushing my hair in the dormitory the evening after Rory had given me his invitation. She lifted a tasselled scarf I'd bought as a Christmas present for my sister, sending it swinging out like a girl in a dancing line.

'What about the can-can? You'll have to practise when you arrive with Theo. She won't like that.' Rita hugged me then and kicked her legs in the air and we both jumped over and back on the beds for the fun of it, falling between them and shrieking.

'If I told my parents I was going to be doing a knickers fling like that they'd get the parish priest after me,' I laughed.

'Your father wouldn't care what you do if he thought it would distract your sister,' Rita said, but made a face as if she didn't really believe it and nodded slowly. As sure as anything, the first thing he'd mention before I stepped off the train would be the Clarence and how I should influence my sister to accept her fate.

A fortnight later I recalled Rita's words as I woke up after a doze just as the train pulled into Ballyhaunis station. All was going to be doom and gloom if Dado picked me up.

Stay at the station and wait for a lift, he had written before I came and I stood up stiffly. Rubbing my eyes before jumping off, I had to stare again because Theo was waiting by a weathered station door. A minute later it was more like a dream because the platform was empty. Pulling my case off the train I looked around for the absent figure. The noise of a trap bouncing along could be heard and Strawberry appeared over a low wall with Dado waving a whip. I was in trouble because he wore a frown of concentration and was scowling. Miss Hourigan must have issued a warning that I wasn't behaving well and needed to be observed. She probably told him I was to be locked up to study. He wasn't going to let me out of his sight.

By the look of pleasure on Dado's face when he stepped on to the platform, his bad humour was gone. The train had puffed steam, a fresh group of passengers alighted and rushing forward to pick up my case he rubbed his palms together as if he'd never been so pleased and took one of my hands and shook it.

'*Oh Danny Boy, the pipes the pipes are calling,*' he hummed through the noise of the engine.

'We'd better get home. Your sister has the oven stuffed with good things to eat,' he hoisted the case to his waist.

'Moyra only makes her cakes for you. She can't wait for your approval. The best of it is the way you manage to get sugar and flour when everyone else is scouring the country without success,' I buttered him up and plunged on. 'Auntie Terry was thinking of asking the both of us up to Dublin for a few days to help with a Christmas party.' The fib came out smoothly.

'It's a fact. Moyra thinks she can have her way with anyone she likes,' Dado said crossly as if the Clarence Hotel conversation had never happened. He shook the case in the hall in a threatening way as if he could really kill my sister and dived past the station master. Reaching the trap he flung the baggage on. The harness gleamed and I pulled a tartan rug over my knees. Dado bunched the reins in a knot and slapped the side of the trap making Strawberry dig her feet in before moving reluctantly. This was some welcome home, I fumed inside. All he cared about was Moyra. Soon there was a brooding silence and dank winter hedges rolling by and a cold wind over a lonesome bog.

'Goodbye Pat and goodbye Jack and goodbye Kate and Mary. The anchor's weighed and the gangway's up and we're leaving Tipperary,' I sang aloud. It was a song I'd learnt that time I'd stolen into the Irish Club with Rita. Just as well Dado liked it because it kept that expected scowl from materialising.

As we drew up to the house there was an impression of a figure peering from Moyra's bedroom window over the front entrance and I waved vigorously. Better to get her excited about a stage debut in Dublin straightaway. I called out her name. Instead of opening up the window her figure disappeared. A warming light shone from deep inside the house. At least Mamma was waiting for me, ready to welcome her daughter home.

Rich smells of baking mingled with wax polish drifted out the front door and Dado heaved my bag into the porch. In the cold hall, holly and ivy festooned corners and I called out Moyra's name sharply. Perched over Mamma's precious walnut sideboard,

Christmas pine clung to the antlers of Dado's newly mounted deer's head, staring wide-eyed above the stairs. There was an impression of voices but nobody appeared.

With artistic flair Moyra had tipped pine cones tinged with gold from her precious store of paints and displayed them with dried hydrangea blooms and rose-hips. She was going all out to get me in the right mood to talk to Theo to keep him in Ireland. She'd even inscribed 'Welcome home Lily' with soap on the hallstand mirror. There was a flurry of movement, and like a film reel slowed down, she posed on the top step.

'I'm home Moyra,' I was suddenly shy. There was a blur of movement as she descended but with no regard for my homecoming she put her lips to my ear.

'It's been awful here, Lily. They're still trying to push me into going to Limerick but I'll run away first.' Without pausing she'd stepped into the porch as if ready to leave. I tapped my foot impatiently.

'Let's have a chat. I have so much to tell you.' It would have been perfect to link her into the drawing room to be on our own but the talk would have to be postponed because she plucked a scarf from a porch chair to go out. She straightened her back and increased her pace, walking away as if she couldn't care less, like some sort of stranger.

A delicious smell of baking came into the corridor from the kitchen. A few sprigs of holly adorned the cosy place and brown paper parcels lined the top shelves of the dresser, gifts for the poor of the parish my mother always collected together at Christmas.

I wondered if she might be too busy to notice me. I was beginning to have second thoughts, but then I knew Mamma had missed me, because she looked up when I entered, flushed from turning dough on the scrubbed table, before extending her arms for a hug.

'There you are darling. It's lovely to have you back, Lily. Would you look at those shining eyes. I told you university would give you something higher than being a singer to aspire to. You're skin and bone *a stór*,' she said and placed a kiss on my cheek. 'You've been studying too hard. Auntie Terry mustn't be feeding you at all.' She shook the flour out of her hands and placed them on her hips.

'Don't fret Mamma. I suppose Auntie Terry told you I'm going back to Dublin on St Stephen's Day for a wonderful feast the hostel is preparing. They've invited Archbishop McQuaid so there'll be plenty to eat. She wants me to serve.' The words came out despite myself and I bit my lip sensing her disappointment too late. 'I might sing in a concert too,' I said lamely. I'd fished the Christmas star quickly from my case in the hall and now it was grasped too tightly behind my back. If I was being unfair to Mamma she'd soon let me know and catching her by the waist I clung on, placing the star on the table, to soften her up more.

It was the following morning before a chance came to ask Moyra to come to the rehearsals. I'd gone into the backyard and she was holding in her arms a squirming sheepdog puppy that had escaped from a shed and she pretended not to see me. It was obvious she was embarrassed about how she'd disappeared the day before because she kissed the pup on the nose and pushed the squirming thing into my arms.

'Did you ever think of living in America? Lots of newly weds are emigrating there,' she said suddenly as if her mind had wandered off and then she clapped her hands in the air and laughed.

'*Goodbye Pat and goodbye Jack and goodbye Kate and Mary. The anchor's weighed and the gangway's up and we're leaving Tipperary,*' I sang my new air. Maybe she was getting married to Theo. The thought made me reel. The rehearsals would be put on the back burner if that was the case.

A bright winter sun lit up the cobblestones and hens scattered.

'You'll never go Moyra, you like it too much here,' I kept my voice steady. One rowdy pup was twisting about at my feet and I concentrated on capturing the scamp to hide the lightness in my head. She'd better not go or I'd be over in America after her, looking for another singing opportunity. 'Don't forget to invite me to the wedding, unless you're afraid he'll leave you at the altar and marry the other sister instead,' I smiled triumphantly.

Fuel shortages here bore no resemblance to Dublin. There was turf aplenty and a fire glowed in Moyra's bedroom grate when I went to my sister's room later to have it out with her. She must have just left the room because the double door of her wardrobe swung ajar. The eiderdown on her bed was thrown back and there was a cuff link, probably one of Dado's, on the floor. The look of the bare bed made me want to lie down and pull that warm quilt up to my ears like I often did, jumping in beside her on cold nights. A distant tapping sound drew me to the back stairs and the old dressing room meeting place. It had to be her and, peering in, I found Moyra sitting sideways to the window, gazing out. Closing up a notebook that was very like my old one she placed it beside her on the makeshift table. A choking smell of mouse-droppings reached out.

'Lily, where are you?' my mother's singsong voice made me pull back. Moyra drew a typed sheet of paper from the machine and I saw lines of a verse. She'd typed up one of my love poems to Nellie the pony, one I'd written years ago. What she did next stopped me short because she pulled out the sheet, dipped one of her old school pens in ink and, writing 'Ode for Theo' instead of 'Ode to Nellie' on the top, and signed her own name. The look of my sister was more like somebody bowed down by worry than happiness. But before I could accuse her of this fresh deceit, a sharper sounding Mamma called again and I slipped away.

It was impossible to find Moyra for the rest of the day and that evening Father Tierney visited to play cards.

'Take them to bed, Rosie. Do you want to keep us here all night?' he called out when I hesitated in play and before I could answer Moyra had excused herself saying she had a cold and left the table rolling her eyes with mock pain.

'You won't get away so lightly,' I hissed.

'How about a gin rummy? I could play all night,' Father Tierney announced then and Dado poured them another whiskey as if the card playing was only beginning.

'I've a chance to get you to Dublin if you want to speak to Theo without sneaking around. You and I can be in a pantomime together,' I blurted out to her the following day. If I didn't say it now I'd be going on my own and my heart began to beat fast. A mixture of leather and horse manure rose up. We were in the stables grooming the horses, I was trying a new saddle on Nellie and I sniffed the used straw smell appreciatively.

'I know what your game is. You're trying to get between Theo and me. You don't care if he goes off to war and gets killed,' she blazed.

'You're a sneak,' I said. 'You had no permission to open my notebooks. I'm going to Ned's to tell Theo the poem you typed wasn't for him. You deserve what Dado is doing,' I added as a parting shot and jumped onto a surprised Nellie. It's your fault, Theo, breaking up two sisters, I moaned inside and imagined his brown eyes shining for me only.

Chapter Thirty

Dashing towards Ned's to get away from Moyra, the cold wind rushed past and rain stung like fine needles. Nellie lengthened her stride. Back in Ballyhale, Moyra must have saddled Strawberry because soon her hooves thundered behind. Crossing some clumpy fields, Nellie's hooves dug in. Dismounting to open a rusted gate, my sister went soaring over a ragged hedge beside me and her face flamed like a rose. Then she reined in Strawberry, letting me come up close.

'You continue to Ned's and I'll follow you on,' she declared and before I could apologise or bring up a singing date, she twisted away.

Every minute I was with Ned I dwelt on what Moyra said about me wanting Theo to go to war. Coming across the peaceful fields, land mines had seemed to explode before my eyes and I saw bodies writhe. Later at the farm Ned had sensed my unease because he pushed me strongly on the swing until I laughed and begged to be let down. We sang songs, chasing around the hay barn. I asked him how Theo was and he said he was too nice for his own good. He was staying in Ireland for the sake of a girl he didn't love because he couldn't let her down but his duty was telling him to fight with his country.

'Moyra is the one who wants to keep him here,' I said.

'Your father and the man called Andrew will make sure he does enlist in the end,' Ned shrugged.

Afternoon shadows lengthened and a setting sun dulled the ivy on Ned's farmhouse when Moyra returned and I ran towards the dim figure leaping off her horse. Nothing had prepared me for what happened next. Ned had gone into the farmhouse, as if at a signal, and Theo stepped into the yard. It seemed to me it was only days since I'd seen him because he was in the same Irish military uniform as he had worn outside Murphy's Hotel. His brass buttons glowed dully. Drained of colour, a robin sang in the deepening evening. Theo's breathing was shallow and he reached out.

'Hello Theo. Is this some kind of a trick to impress a girl? You're not on duty now.' I said brightly before he could take my hand and his shoulders slumped. 'Did you like the poem Moyra gave you?' I added and his head shook rapidly, like Nellie getting rid of a fly.

'Your sister has been trying to keep me in the Irish forces but I think I should enlist for the war. Unless you'd want me to stay here Lily,' he said abruptly. Attempting to hold my eyes he lost and picked up a stone to skim it through the air. A series of sharp explosions rang out, most likely the IRA on secret manoeuvres and I took his hand at last and swung it over and back. He pressed my little finger.

'Moyra won't be here to bother you anymore. She'll be coming with me to Dublin to sing in a theatre. After that you can marry me ten times over because I'll be a Gaiety star,' I grinned foolishly.

Grey wreathed Currach Hill on Christmas Day, not long after the rendezvous with Theo, and a chill wind brought roses to our cheeks.

'The sky is full to the brim with snow. If them clouds have their way we won't be able to stir out later on.' Dinnie shaded his face, staring at the horizon. Down the avenue between the bare limes Croagh Patrick Mountain, white as a sheet of icing, rose against the skyline. As Dinnie spoke thin flakes began to fall, swirling and drifting like feathers and I managed a glassy-eyed celebratory smile at my sister.

At mass in St Patrick's church in Ballyhaunis after a freezing family journey in the trap, our teeth chattered. A few candles flickering on the altar were supposed to heat the place and a single oil lamp cast a shadow on Father Tierney's face. Moyra sat beside me keeping her face averted and I heard a loud whisper.

'Protestant hussies. First one sister walks out with the American and then he picks up with the other wan. They're a bad lot, like Michael O'Donoghue, up to his oxters in debt and marrying into the other side. It's only to keep in with Protestant nobs that Alf Murphy has to rent a useless butcher's stall from him.'

I knew that voice and before Moyra could stop me, turned round and stuck my tongue out at a startled Miss Mahon. Dublin here I come, I said to myself.

'A special prayer for the victims of war, especially widowed wives and children without a father this Christmas,' Father Tierney intoned.

I must have hit against Moyra swinging back to make a face at Miss Mahon because she had daggers in her eyes. Soon I saw another reason. A trilby was lifted from a head directly in front of us. Dado must have made the arrangement to have a chat afterwards because it was Andrew, ahead of our pew.

'*Goodbye Pat and goodbye Jack and goodbye Kate and Mary, The anchor's weighed and the gangway's up and we're leaving Tipperary,*' I hummed my departure song to keep calm. My hopes were dashed. Instead of Dublin the sights of Ballyhale were forming a tight circle to hold me back.

There was a note on my pillow that night when I went to my room.

Lily, Theo has made his mind up since speaking to you. He is going to Belfast to enlist. The thought of the fighting to come won't let him rest. He is drifting away from us all Lily, and needs desperately to feel connected to the real world. I've tidied up a room in Granny's Lodge where we can say goodbye. He asked me to bring you to meet him but I believe you don't want to hurt him again. I will tell him to imagine that I am you because we've always been inseparable. He won't want to make love to me but he is not in his right mind now and I know I can bring him comfort. Don't blame me for this.

Your loving sister,

Moyra.

It might be too late to stop her, but rushing down the stairs and pulling open the dairy door, thick snow padded the yard. Theo was standing under the boughs of an oak tree drooping over the back wall.

'I've committed myself to Moyra. Tell me you love me and I'll cope with anything,' he stepped near.

'Order her to come to the Gaiety and I'll see then,' I said helplessly.

Chapter Thirty-one

Sunshine was fitful in Dublin and I shivered after a long journey in a cold train. Somehow I'd managed to convince Mamma to let me go and now Rory wasn't here and I leaned against the Gaiety Theatre. Moyra, you shouldn't have done this to me, I thought, but a busy city cranked all around and nobody looked or cared. My head throbbed. Soon there was a decent splash of sun and I sank against the theatre gratefully.

If you're thinking about going to America, we have a chance as a duo to audition for Radio éireann. I'll put a good word in for you in the Gaiety first. As soon as they hear me sing I'll mention your voice. A letter to Moyra worded itself inside my head. She didn't deserve to be included after her carry on, of course. If she didn't agree to come I'd soon tell Dado everything, I brooded. Most likely she had stayed in Granny Lloyd's until she was sure I'd left and then gone home with her head held high as if I didn't exist.

As I tried hard to forget the night before, an unexpected heat started to dispel the clouds letting me lift my face upwards. For some reason too, my cheeks blushed thinking about Moyra's actions and I pressed my cold hands against them. I was about to have the greatest fun of my life and my sister was haunting me like a ghost. I braced myself to look happy. Any minute now the theatre door would open. A girl walked past pushing a pram, shaking it to stop the bundle inside crying, and the sight made me glance away quickly.

'*I am a young maiden and my story is sad, for once I was courted by a brave sailor lad,*' the words of 'The Blackbird' came out softly.

'Mother Goose, with Jimmy O'Dea, Star of Stage and Screen,' a poster beside the Gaiety entrance announced. It was pinned inside a display box and showed a dapper man dancing with a cane and smiling from ear to ear. Jimmy O'Dea spends all his life on radio and stage, he's the best person to help a struggling newcomer, I thought but instead I stared at a photograph of a redhead. She was the image of Moyra. There were reminders of her everywhere. She had to have her own way and now it could take her from me forever. A line of showgirls was pasted beside the redhead and I tried some feeble steps. At least this was the place for me. It would serve Moyra right if I got somebody else to sing with me, I frowned.

Rory must have been watching out of sight because he stepped suddenly from the passing crowd. He saluted cheerfully. At the same time a trumpet blared deep in the theatre like a clarion call.

'Thank you for arranging this, Rory,' I bobbed. 'My sister Moyra will be here soon,' the words were an afterthought and I shrugged hopefully.

For once she was courted by a brave sailor lad. He courted her truly by night and by day, the song came back and, aiming a foot vigorously, I imagined Moyra flying through the air like a well-kicked ball.

Rory's arm linked mine and he ushered me into an auditorium behind a high stage. There was a whirlwind of activity. A cacophony of noises came from a faraway platform. Scenery was being hoisted and girls called to one another loudly.

'You'll need to have your wits about you in this place. Wait until you meet Beatrice Sweeney, the chorus mistress. They call her The Killer and you'll soon see why.' Rory drew me forward. 'It looks as if the rehearsal is going to start with dancing.' As I turned to answer him, he seemed to have vanished.

Moving across the stage a small figure with a moustache and the ugliest, caved-in looking face I'd ever seen whipped a long stick through the air. I was about to duck behind a seat when she called my name.

'Thank you for inviting me to come along Mrs Sweeney,' my voice seemed to bounce over the front row of seats. By the time I was half way to the stage people began to separate and approaching the woman in charge stared down a pug nose.

'I'm too tired to dance today, would it be all right to sing?' I'd said crisply as soon as I clambered up. At that point a dancer beckoned me to her side whispering that her name was Sheila. She was an even bigger lump of a girl than me, so there was no need to worry about being awkward. She put her finger to her lips. It looked as if she'd saved me from the tyrant Sweeney. Linked by my new friend, I tried a clumsy twirl.

Eyebrows nearly meeting her moustache Mrs Sweeney tapped the floor with the cane.

'Keep your head down at the start or The Killer will ate you alive,'

Sheila whispered. As if we'd started a mutiny, a venomous glance from The Killer pinned us to the spot.

'Get into position, girls, we haven't all day,' Mrs Sweeney pirouetted around. The stick prodded into my side. My next thoughts emerged as a series of yelps because my feet were sliding all over the place and drops of perspiration rolled down my back. Glancing back a lithe girl in front smiled reassuringly. Dancing up and down in a line the orchestra pit loomed. Miming 'The Rose of Mooncoin' I signalled to Rory on the piano but his gaze was averted. At that moment a roly-poly man with a limpid gaze who was as light on his feet as a mountain goat darted onto the stage. Jimmy O'Dea moved before us. He'd hardly have time for an out of breath dancer with a turkey-cock face but there wouldn't be such a chance again to get his attention.

'Lovely to meet you Jimmy,' I shouted and Mrs Sweeney glowered.

'I see we really do have to hide our country clod-hopper,' she darted a poisonous look at me but the dapper man bowed in her direction.

'Good to be back, Mrs Sweeney,' he lisped. Our angelic dance mistress was posing as if she was the prettiest thing in the world and she simpered. An order floated in the air.

'Get into line for the opening number, lovies,' she stretched her arms towards the newcomer but, taking a bow and brilliantine glistening in his flattened hair, Jimmy O'Dea took my arm. He swooped low and pirouetted a greeting. I'd try an air on him soon, even if it meant being sent back to Ballyhale, I vowed.

For the next few hours Sheila pinched and pushed to keep me in line. Down below us a scrawny Rory looked so slight a good wind would toss him away. He deserved some thanks for getting me here, though, and I blew him a kiss. Maybe he'd play the accompaniment, singing for Jimmy later.

'You dolt, lift your arms, at least pretend you can dance,' The Killer barked. It was close to the end of the rehearsal and I forced my aching bones into action. Below us, Rory grinned and mimed a closed fist at Mrs Sweeney but it barely registered. The edge of the stage was shifting through tiredness. Theo might bring Moyra up, I convinced myself, to keep awake. As soon as he did he'd get a piece of my mind and I'd snatch her away.

Ages later, the cast clattered up the stairs and I wandered into a damp alleyway. A mist drifted and I rubbed aching ankles and groaned. It was more likely that Moyra was in Ballyhale making another rendezvous with her lover and I leaned against a wall and closed my eyes. A faint footfall sounded. There was an unfamiliar scent like Christmas spice.

'Is that you Moyra?' I called out but my heart beat loudly. The effort had caused a throbbing head too, but my arms lifted, as if her hug was just around the corner.

'It shouldn't surprise you if Moyra was here. Your sister has a habit of turning up in unexpected places,' lovable American tones called. 'She'd come in return for your aunt putting in a good word for me in Ballyhale,' Theo's face was drawing close.

'Forgive me for interrupting a lovers' *téte a téte*,' Rory spoke up too. He'd crept up behind us. Twirling a props hat with a feather he kissed my hand, as if it was *he* who was the visiting mysterious stranger, leading a lover's scene.

Chapter Thirty-two

'We can't keep you on,' Mrs Sweeney declared as soon as I walked into the theatre the next day. 'Our girl has returned,' she was leaning languidly on the rear end of a stage cow just in case Jimmy O'Dea happened to pass and any thoughts I had of Moyra vanished.

'It doesn't matter. I have other business to attend to,' I drew in a deep breath and before she could see how badly I really cared, I walked away.

It looks as if this is my last chance in the theatre world, I thought, looking around moodily. Mrs Sweeney had disappeared and Sheila and I were side by side in a crowded dressing room before the evening performance. Here everything was rushing ahead at a whirlwind pace. Hemmed into a tight space girls sang the first chorus number and swayed. 'Ten minutes to go,' somebody shouted and the frenzied activity all around increased. Forgetting about modesty, pulling clothes off to struggle into costumes, everyone pushed to get elbow room. It was just as well I had invited Rita and Connie to the first performance or they wouldn't see it. There is always a chance I could talk to Jimmy O'Dea and with that in mind I smiled into the make-up mirror to cheer myself up.

'Give them a good display,' I blinked solemnly. A smell of sweat and cheap perfume thickened.

'Have you got a number five make-up stick? Can you do my lips?' Sheila shrilled. 'Throw me the carmine,' she said thrusting reddened cheeks forward.

'Time up,' another command followed promptly and, casting a last, startled look in the mirror at my jezebel face, we hurried out. The Killer hadn't gone away because she was ready to ambush me in the narrow corridor and when she poked her pointer at my leg an old bruise began to throb.

'Blend in. I can see you're going to let the show down. Pick your feet up and don't slouch.' Her eyes bored through me. She couldn't stop a girl from enjoying herself and I breathed in sharply. She didn't bother to watch this new recruit troop onto the stage like a frisky foal either. Jimmy O'Dea will see the height of my kicks, I'll be back again, even if it's to get Moyra on board, the thought became a spur.

After that, each routine went like a dream. My feet had wings and we flew along. Waves of approval flowed up from the rows of seats. Between drops of sweat, flitting over and back, Rory could be glimpsed straining in the orchestra. If my singing wasn't as good as it should be Sheila nudged me and the words jerked out. There was no point in trying to impress Miss Sweeney though, because she spent all her time being mesmerised by Jimmy O'Dea, staring at him from the wings. As soon as the show was over I'd get him to sit down in a corner to discuss Moyra. If she did come to Dublin, all she needed was a chance and the killer would be smitten by her good looks. It would be the end of that other girl coming back.

'There's a birthday party that's to be a surprise for John Dunne our leading man. It's in the Green Room beside the auditorium and you and any friends in the audience are invited,' Sheila offered an extension to my stay, hugging me with the news after the show. This was a last chance to prove myself but I stretched tiredly.

'There'll be a cake,' Sheila licked her lips as if she could taste it. It was all right though because 'Down by the Glenside' had started to float into my mind. It was a song I'd talked to John about the previous day. He might ask me to sing it as a party piece. It should be easy to have a word with him as soon as the party started. The show wasn't over yet and with that thought I put on an appealing smile.

'Wait for me in the lobby after the curtain goes down,' I said to the girls. After what seemed like ages since Sheila's invitation they appeared behind a group of children. Pulling away from their pats and kisses I dragged them into a corner.

'We're all invited to celebrate John Dunne's birthday after the show. You'll have to come. It's my last night here,' I sucked a breath in and then exploded with nervous laughter.

'It sounds lovely but Matt is working late and wants to have a chat,' Connie shrugged.

'I didn't know you two were so friendly,' I pretended to look stern, 'bring him if you have to and make sure he gets his fiddle from the van.'

'*Twas down by the Glenside I met an old woman, a plucking young nettles nor saw I was coming*,' I hummed. Matt could get the party crowd quiet by trying a tune, in time for me to break into song.

Word of the birthday party had gone around like wildfire. Snug in the Green Room John Dunne waved an elegant hand at Connie and Rita. Mirrors glittered behind a mahogany counter and bunting crisscrossed the ceiling. Some of the actors had changed to their street clothes for the party but some vestiges of stage paint remained. The purple plume of an ornate hat waved above heads and a stuffed parrot sat on a shoulder. There was champagne for everybody and plates of sandwiches crowded out a bar counter. Smoke drifted to the ceiling and cheerful voices called out their dialogue, addressing each other by their panto names. Emerging from a group of devotees surrounding Mrs Sweeney, Rory was here too and made his way towards us.

'There's Maureen Potter beside the picture of Jimmy O'Dea,' Rita dragged me away to a wall of portraits. 'You'll become a star too Lily.'

'Of course, this is only the beginning,' I laughed. Beyond our group, Mrs Sweeney was frowning. Rory leaned to take a sandwich from a plate beside us.

'You didn't bring your boyfriend up for the first night,' said he, peering into a sandwich intently.

'You were enjoying the adoration of your fans too much to notice anything,' I stammered, gazing at the pictures as if I was riveted to the spot.

'Matt will be waiting for me,' Connie tapped me on the shoulder and, getting no further response, Rory walked away.

Up at the bar, there were calls for quiet. Ahead of us, John Dunne had already thrown his arms out to embrace the audience.

'*It was down by the Glenside, I met an old woman*,' melodious notes beguiled. The party man had chosen my own air to sing. There'd be no chance to perform now and I sat down heavily.

'Connie told me to bring my fiddle,' Matt had arrived by my side. A strong smell of horse dung rose up. Connie had brought him in without thinking, his shirt hung out and the stench was off his boots. Before he could be asked to melt into the background Mrs Sweeney strode towards us. She'd seen the intruder and I picked up my bag ready to grab him and pull him out.

'Talk about making a disgrace of the show. Get out of my sight, Lily O'Donoghue and don't bother coming back,' she thundered, reaching for her cane.

'Lily has a sister who can play too. She told me all about her,' Matt piped up in an effort to help. Behind her back Jimmy O'Dea shook his head as if to say there's nothing can be done about this mess-up.

A plea for help froze on my lips as we were escorted outside.

Chapter Thirty-three

From the beginning of the second term, Miss Hourigan had begun to shadow me. Any moment now, I told myself, Moyra will be up in Dublin. She'll apologise for her bad behaviour and we'll sing in the Irish Club. But time flew and nothing happened. If she wasn't going to make any moves I realised I'd have to do it myself and one day Miss Hourigan provided the opportunity. It was Rita who pointed it out to me. College was in full swing and I had walked into the ladies reading room, looking for a notebook I'd left behind the previous day.

'See this, Lily,' my friend had looked up from a newspaper her nose was stuck in and jabbed excitedly. 'Miss Hourigan has just gone out and left this behind.' 'Talent Contest in St Bernadette's Hall, Rathmines'; an advertisement leaped up at me from an opened page. It was the *Catholic Standard* and no doubt Miss Hourigan had put it beside Rita deliberately, knowing she'd see it and show it to me. The picture was pretty clear. She wanted to set me up as an example of bad behaviour to the other girls. I was dropping behind and not doing well in tests and because she must know all about my love of singing - the files she had on every girl proved that - she wanted to catch me out.

'The winner gets twenty pounds. I'm going in for it,' Rita grinned.

'Miss Hourigan left it there on purpose to trick us,' I tried not to stare. The prize money was in large print. If I offered even half of it to Moyra she'd fly up.

'The show is in the evening. Miss Hourigan has nothing to do with us after we leave the college. It's not like you to ignore such an opportunity,' Rita looked at me uncertainly.

'All right if you insist, I'll come along, but that's it.'

She shrugged at my sceptical look and laughed.

Setting out like adventurers on a dangerous mission, the following Saturday Rita and I boarded the Rathmines tram at Nelson's pillar.

'Promise me you won't let me get up and sing,' I said to my friend because temptation was beginning to assail me and I had to stop myself humming. It was a bright evening. Over a jumble of buildings an orange sunset seeped from behind clouds.

Cold had set in early. As I tried to get comfortable the thought occurred that all of the Dublin tram fleet were falling apart, like everything else during the Emergency. There was no money for repairs, my aunt often said. Even if it was marked and scuffed and had worn seats we managed to snuggle in. It shuddered before setting off, creating sparks and there was a screeching sound as the wheels grated. Pausing at the O'Connell Monument an old lady boarded, bundled up in coats and a dowdy hat that hid her face. Despite her age she moved quickly to get a top seat.

Rounding the corner from Harcourt Street, on the skyline, the green dome of Rathmines Church blended into darkness. The smell of a slaughter-yard swept in. When a broken-down tram ahead of us caused ours to grind to a halt the muffled woman in the top seat stood up and tapped at the driver's partition, stepping nimbly onto the street and out of sight. Straight after her, the driver clambered out for a consultation. If we didn't move quickly we'd miss the start of the contest.

'*Come single belle and beau, unto me pay attention, Don't ever fall in love, it's the devil's own invention, For once I fell in love with a maiden so bewitching, Miss Henrietta Bell out in Captain Kelly's kitchen*.' The tune was called 'Courtin' in the Kitchen' and I sang it to pass the time and Rita clapped.

'It's funny and light-hearted, the kind of street-ballad Mamma says I'd be made a laughing stock of for singing in public,' I shrugged.

'Just as well your mother is not doing it so,' Rita was looking through the window, seeming to find the gesticulations of the driver so funny she giggled in appreciation.

'St Bernadette's Hall,' the conductor's voice rang out and the tram drew smoothly to a halt.

'If you call me up from the stage after your act and get me a glass of whiskey I'll sing 'Oft' in the Stilly Night'. That's the way Dado performs it to give him courage. It's the only kind of air that would go down well here,' I joked as we clambered off.

Walking round from Rathmines Road to our destination we could see that a small crowd had gathered outside a red-bricked building set back from the street. St Bernadette's Hall had a poky entrance and a sign beside the door said 'Fundraising Variety Show'. Barely stepping into a musty porch we were trapped against a wall. A burly man with a toupée came rushing down the stairs and grabbed Rita. He shook her hand as if he'd known her for years.

'Liam Purcell at your service, and from the description I got, you must be Rita,' his eyes twinkled and spit sprayed the air.

'You're right Mr Purcell,' Rita simpered. 'I'd like you to meet Moyra O'Donoghue from Mayo. She's a beautiful singer. Say hello to the man in charge of the competition, Moyra.' Her next words made my heart jump in alarm. She had stumbled over my sister's name but nodded her head slowly to make sure I'd taken it in. The man's hands fastened on mine.

'Tell him it's not true,' I turned to Rita but the girl had gone. There was a clattering noise on the wooden stairs beside us. Mr Purcell was disappearing too. The mistake had to be rectified and racing after him I found myself in a cluttered dressing room. A vividly made-up girl with a black fringed shawl paced up and down.

'Have you seen the boss? There's been a mistake,' I called, but she was too preoccupied muttering some lines and then a cut-out tree nearly knocked me flat. It was being manoeuvred past the actress by a helper. Swinging back her tasselled shawl, the silken thing caught in one of the branches and laughing she let it go.

'If you want Mr Purcell he might be in the hall,' the actress saw me at last. 'Let's have a peep through the curtains and we'll see if he's in the audience.'

Rita would pay for this as soon as I got off. Up close to the drapes voices could be heard in the room beyond and, as if she didn't care about being seen, the actress peered through a chink in the drapes. The place was filling up, I saw, taking her cue. A wrapped-up figure in the front row looked familiar. It was the auld Biddy who had sat at the top of the tram when we got on. Liam Purcell was nowhere in sight though and before I could look for Rita, the curtains swung closed.

'Everybody knows me but it's bad luck for a newcomer to be seen before going on,' the actress imprisoned my arm to lead me away.

If I can't get back into the audience, I'll sit it out here, I thought in despair. Making another search for the missing man I'd opened the door of a storeroom. There were flats against a wall and a deep enamel sink. Snatches of words came through from the stage. The man who'd carried the tree took a false boulder from the room.

Oft in a stilly night, when other shades surround me, the words of Dado's song were like a scratched gramophone record going round and around in my head. I shouldn't be thinking of any kind of singing. There was another door at the back of the room. Opening it, I saw there were steps on the outside of the building, a way to escape and get away from this torture. A garda had been placed there to protect the contestants and I drew back.

There was still time to find Mr Purcell but, as if in the flesh, Mamma appeared to detain me. I'd closed my eyes to shut the scene out and found myself transported to one of her soirées. She had her head back and launched into 'Kathleen Mavourneen', sounding pure as a mountain stream and accompanied by the flowery piano playing of Father Tierney. We are two of a kind, Mamma, I thought and tapped uneasily. The only difference between you and me is our choice of song.

'*Come single belle and beau, unto me pay attention,*' I hummed the line to prove my point. Soon the fantasy scene changed and even though I opened my eyes to try and take it away, a kettle on a range and a bewitching maid making tea made my singing louder.

'Moyra Lloyd, all the way from Mayo,' a voice on stage reached in clearly. Singing to dispel the vision, my voice had reached Mr Purcell and I was caught. Powerless to stop him, the props man was leading me forward. The shawl was still on that branch, I noticed in a daze and I lifted it off and flung it round my shoulders. At least 'Miss Henrietta Bell' would be in the right style for 'Courtin' in the kitchen'.

I shouldn't be singing, Miss Hourigan will find out. Look at the back of the hall. Don't make eye contact with anyone, I ordered myself a few seconds later. The words of the song poured out still in spite of myself. To make matters worse the audience responded, coming alive and eager to hear more. A few laughs came and my voice got stronger.

Soon the air was filling with notes. It was too hard to stop now but my heart was lifting too. Down below somebody thought the song was over and had started clapping slowly. Too late, I pulled the shawl over my head. A figure in military uniform was strolling up the centre aisle. The rig-out was American. Theo had found out about the performance. Seeing my frown he sat on the edge of a row to wait, smiling up at me as if the same Bernadette had returned and he was seeing a vision. The lady in the top row stood up and took off her hat. It was Miss Hourigan.

Time went by agonisingly slowly until the end of the contest. Despite my hesitation on the last verse and my head being in a whirl, in the final reckoning it seemed I was the winner. All through the presentation of the prizes the sense of unreality stayed. I should have known Theo would charm Miss Hourigan as well because the two of them strolled over to watch the prize-giving ceremony. He had tucked the Dean's arm into his crooked one and brought her forward to meet the committee, as if my entering was all his idea and of course I should be forgiven. He even got her to wear a tight smile as the money was handed across.

Outside there was frost in the air as we spilled from the hall. Moonlight made the pavement glitter and cold penetrated my thin shoes and froze my toes.

'We'll get the tram girls,' Miss Hourigan came between Theo and me but then a chatting crowd approached to offer congratulations and she and Rita had to move on.

'Hurry up back there. It's getting late. We'll catch a tram,' she called back. It was a last chance to sort out his feelings for me and I pulled Theo into a gateway.

'You joined the American army. You won't be here much longer,' I avoided looking at the man beside me in case I'd soften up and began to hum my tune to maintain a distance. *For once I fell in love with a maiden so bewitching, Miss Henrietta Belle from the Captain Kelly's kitchen.* His figure remained still.

'Don't taunt me, Lily. As sure as night follows day I loved you from the first minute I saw you. It nearly broke my heart when you went away,' Theo declared softly. A pigeon cooed in a tree in the garden and I leaned towards him.

'It's a lie. You're just a cheat and look where it's landed you now,' I said weakly.

'You're right to defend your sister. It was wrong of me to behave the way I did. You know how sweet and nice she can be. One thing led to another and somehow being with her brought me nearer to you.' Theo shrugged and I saw his fist tighten. It must be late devotions I thought, in a far off way, because a bell began to toll. As soon as this stops he'll be gone and I'll never speak to him again. A cloud edging over the moon plunged us into thick darkness and his shoulder bumped against mine.

'Hurry up back there,' Miss Hourigan's voice arrived with a sharper edge. The envelope with the prize money felt creased in my hand. I was planning to give half of it to Moyra to prove to her what we could do and now I pushed it towards him.

'Take this and you can find a way to stay.' The envelope was damp and stuck to my palm.

'Are you two going to stay behind there all night?' Rita called this time and Theo flicked away my hand.

'Listen. I've got to say this before they come back to us.' His eyes glinted in the dark. 'I've compromised Moyra and we'll have to get married. Enlisting is only a way of putting it off. Your father was making sure I'd join the forces anyway. He never wanted me to have anything to do with your family.'

'*Oft' in the stilly night, Fond memories bring the light of other days around me.*' For some reason he was singing Dado's song so well he could be my father. He took my elbow as if about to dance.

'Take care of Moyra for me, Lily, until I come back. She's a wonderful girl and I'll do my best by her,' peering round, he plunged a hand into a uniform pocket. 'Take this phone number. Even if your father made use of Andrew, he's a decent sort.' I was numb and saw another piece of paper had fallen out, and fluttered to the ground. 'He's agreed you can keep in touch.' A smooth cheek was against mine, soft as a baby's. 'Ask me again to stay, Lily. This war can go to hell.' An old daredevil smile from long ago surfaced. He put an imaginary trumpet to his lips like the jazz-player he knew I'd like him to be and raised it.

'Maybe next time,' I said pausing, if I wasn't careful I'd cry but my feet tapped to a mood. 'We'll travel incognito to New York and you could bring me to those night clubs you promised to show me long ago.'

'Lily, the tram is coming,' Miss Hourigan called sharply. Theo moved backwards.

'Goodbye, Lily. Don't forget me.' The unstoppable figure was starting to fade.

'Wait. You dropped this,' I swooped and picked up the piece of paper. Moving under a gaslight, an obituary notice cut from a newspaper shimmered.

'Hynes, Louise, formerly Lloyd of Mayo, Ireland, sadly missed by her loving husband Gerard and son Theo.'

'Stay and I'll marry you.' The words came out as a squeak, weak enough to send a man I loved to his death. A shooting star quenched overhead and the cold moon glittered.

'Trapping a man's heart like a common trollop, your game is up, Lily O'Donoghue,' Miss Hourigan had arrived and pulled me after her.

Chapter Thirty-four

The day after Theo left I wrote to Moyra and asked her to come to Dublin. I'd have to tell her straight out that Theo didn't love her and that she'd have to give him up because we were getting married instead. It was that or let him fry to death in a war. For the next few weeks I imagined I saw him everywhere I went. He was about to throw himself into the heart of danger and I could have stopped him. I told myself that he had a charmed life, that he would come out of the war safely and I would do the nine novenas for him, just to make sure. Once, just for a few minutes, I changed my mind. I was standing in a sweet shop trying to choose between penny toffees or bull's eyes. He was probably strolling down a French boulevard right now, with a girl on either arm.

'I'll have some of both,' I said to the shopkeeper to take away the shock of such a thought and pocketed the paper wrap greedily. Crunching an aniseed ball I tried to forget him, it was no good. His gloomy looks as we parted mixed with the sensation of sweetness in my mouth. Moyra could have him to get rid of all this torment I thought in despair. It could be part of the bargaining to make sure she took part in our sister act.

The next day, two feather dusters and wax polish lay on my bed. It was mid-morning. I hadn't left the dormitory because Rita and I had decided to do some spring-cleaning. A burst of sunshine had arrived in the room, showing up a cobweb in one corner and I was stretching up to swipe at it when Sister Angelica's voice came up.

'Watch out, she sounds as if she's ready to pounce,' Rita seized the feather stick and flicked at a scurrying spider. 'Tell her you'll give her a good dusting down if she doesn't leave us alone,' she grinned.

'She's angling for news I bet,' I said. I was right because later on as I was walking into the reception area to see what she wanted, Sister Angelica, snug behind her desk, waved at me to sit down. 'American convoy ship lost in the North Sea with fifty seamen feared dead', a newspaper that was laid out on the desk reported. Miss Hourigan has spoken to her about Theo, I had a sudden thought. The nun would love to get me off my guard now and my eyes swivelled away.

'Were you calling me? I was doing some spring-cleaning,' I said coolly. She closed the paper with a flourish and, reaching into a cubbyhole underneath, her smile tightened.

'This letter came just now. It's been posted from Belfast but if I'm not mistaken it has your sister's handwriting on it.' She produced an envelope grandly. It had a Northern Ireland stamp with a censor's mark to say it had been already opened. She was right about it being from Moyra. Somehow she'd made her way to Belfast to see Theo and forgetting to be calm I snatched it from her grasping fingers.

'Moyra is visiting my mother's sister. She lives on the Ormeau Road,' I fished up a lie. Backing out of the room, my palms started to feel damp. There and then a picture of Moyra arose, wandering about

Belfast with a suitcase, thinking she was a romantic but letting the whole world see a single girl chasing after a soldier. At least it meant I didn't have to marry Theo, I thought doubtfully.

'Don't forget we're supposed to be the singing sisters Moyra, now you're putting Theo before me,' I said aloud, halfway up the stairs and then I stopped abruptly. I wouldn't open the letter until I reached the safety of the college. At least there I'd be able to think, where life went on normally.

It was lunch break and the heat of the canteen was beginning to stifle, as I opened the forbidding looking envelope. A buzz of noise filled the air but the queue at the tea counter had begun to die down, creating an oasis of peace. 'She bid me take love easy as the leaves grow on the trees, but I was young and easy . . .' William Butler Yeats was being quoted from nearby. The words reverberated lazily. Separating carefully the folded sheets of notepaper, my sister's handwriting had, in contrast, a rushed look. As if to lure me to read on, the address was Ballyhale House.

Dear Lily,

This letter is for your eyes only. Theo has left and agreed to post it on to you. You know the way our Miss Mahon tries to see through envelopes. I wouldn't put it past her to open it.

Forgive me for bringing it up at this time, Lily, because you probably hate me for what I've done but from now on it looks as if I'm going to have to lead a secret life. Maybe it's just as well I'll be taking a commercial course and learning to be independent.

I have a favour to ask you Lily. Will you look after the letters Theo sends on to the hostel for me and post them here with your own? Over the past few weeks I've had time to understand his position. He says he wants to make the world a better place to live in. There is a terrible conflict raging in Europe and here at home we only dimly know what is going on. He is noble and kind by nature I suppose and it is hard for him to ignore the feelings in his heart. I know those few hours we had together before he left were wrong. Please be kind to your poor sister and forgive her.

All I can hope is that love changes everything and that God understands.

Your loving Moyra.

Putting the letter down the silence around me deepened. During the pause a tray banged and a shaky pile fell on the floor resounding like a bomb. Moyra would never listen to me when I told her Theo didn't love her and if I didn't write to him he might never come back from whatever hellhole he was in. I don't want to marry him but the war is changing everything I thought, clutching the pages miserably.

I must have held onto the letter for ages because the next time I looked, the bunch of people who had been quoting Yeats had moved away and then Rory arrived. Anya was beside him and he strolled across making me fold the letter up.

'It's a wedding proposal if you must know,' I said watching his eyes glance down and they darkened. Let him believe what he liked. Theo was clogging my thoughts and I smiled grudgingly. A chair was pulled out and Anya perched.

'Awfully nice to see you, Lily, we have never talked properly,' she declared. She sat back on her seat and nodded seriously as if she was a perfect student on a much-needed break and then she patted her perfect hair getting ready to show off. There was a real world out there Anya knew nothing about and I was in the middle of a terrible conundrum.

'Lovely to meet you too I'm sure,' I held her gaze. 'Isn't life a dream? While the whole crazy planet of ours goes round as if nothing is wrong, thousands of people are dying in a war.' There was a shake in my voice. Anya looked solemn and closed her eyes and I grabbed my bag.

'Some people have time for idle talk, but study calls.'

'Still the same Lily, rushing about. Stay a while and we'll all chat,' Rory half stood up.

'This is no place to discuss private matters. My life is at a crossroads if you must know,' I said enigmatically and Anya pouted. It was only when I reached the canteen door I realised the letter had been left on the table. Looking back, Rory was picking it off the floor.

'*Come single belle and beau, unto my pay attention. Don't ever fall in love, it's the devil's own invention,*' I hummed to cheer up, walking into the Great Hall. If all came to all the tune would be my wedding song. Let Rory read what he wanted, I brooded then, about to rush back. A few seconds later the song turned into a funeral march.

That afternoon it became impossible not to chat about it all with Rita and I invited her to the Country Kitchen tea rooms. We took the short cut through Stephen's Green and a fresh wind whipped at our skirts. Dead leaves scurried along the path merrily, but I hardly noticed, trying to find a way to begin. Tommy, a park tramp I'd talked to once, was proving to be another distraction. He was huddling in a torn coat and had his cap out for money.

'*Fond memory brings the light of other days around me, the smiles the tears of boyhood years, the words of love then spoken,*' Tommy croaked my father's 'Oft in the Stilly Night'. Ahead of us a group of school children, dressed like peas in a pod, marched crocodile style with their teacher. The wind lifted the beret of a gauche girl and blew it in our direction. Grabbing up the hat her long legs could have brought her back to the crocodile in an instant but she stared at us, forgetting her duty like that curious child I once was who'd left the protection of her sister and didn't care. As soon as Moyra came up to Dublin we'd sing together and all would be fine again, I decided, smiling at the girl until her school companions were almost gone.

The Country Kitchen was really a tea room in a basement and there was a smell of home-baking and subdued conversation when we stepped inside. Painted English rustic scenes adorned the walls and each table had a round embroidered cloth. We chose the only one left, close to the door. A paper carnation in a glass vase adorned the centre and I sniffed, pretending it was real. Close your eyes and imagine Theo, it will fix him in your thoughts I decided and remembered Rory in the canteen instead. I was back, seeing him staring at me fixedly after my marriage proposal remark and pushing in closer to Anya. At least she knew what she wanted. Anya could get Rory to do whatever she liked.

'A penny for your thoughts,' said Rita, jamming the flower under my nose, rolling her eyes like Tommy the drunk and giggling.

'Rory should be here for a bit of fun. He hasn't talked to us properly in ages,' she said then, but she was looking around. Next thing she'd be telling me how much Rory liked me, as if the truth was written on the tea room wall. As soon as she heard about Theo's marriage proposal there'd be a different tune, I thought, but now her eyes were glued to the window. It was obvious she thought somebody else should be here because she took out a piece of mirror and glanced in. Her mouth curled in a know-all grin. A teapot arrived, steaming gently.

'We're not here to talk about boys. Life is much more complicated,' I said moodily but she was beginning to peer around the door.

'What's the matter, Lily? You make things so difficult for yourself,' she said.

This time I might as well not be there, because a foxy-haired boy I recognised as a science student had come in and stretching backwards she gave me a kick. 'Don't look. It's Peadar Glennon.'

She barely greeted him when, lifting his cap from his flaming curls, the redhead saluted her, as if she was a long lost friend. She pushed the flower on the table to one side.

'Would you mind if we talked later, Lily? Peadar wants to show me a painting by Mainie Jellett, you know, that new artist you said you saw at the exhibition you went to with Connie. It's on display in a gallery in Clare Street,' Rita informed us a few minutes later. She'd dabbed her mouth with her napkin as if she was in the habit of inspecting paintings on a regular basis and pinched me in the side to make sure I understood.

'I wanted to talk about Theo,' I said, 'but don't worry, you haven't the time.' She must have touched his hand by mistake because his face went as red as his hair and he lifted her hand awkwardly as they rose to leave.

Instead of staying on my own, trying to get into the mood to study, I followed the pair out of the tea rooms. I watched them head away from the college and turn towards the Shelbourne. Tommy had made his way from the park. He was lurching about, grasping a brown paper bag covering a bottle.

Splashes of rain hit the pavement and Rita and Peadar started to run. Up ahead the swing door of the Shelbourne was circling gently. Rory might be playing the piano inside. Now was the chance to get the letter back but I dithered. As if he was reading my thoughts right then, through the hotel glass door, I could see the same gent appear in the lobby. Fixing a rose in his button-hole he saw me and waved. His fingers dipped into a breast pocket and he took out those revealing sheets left in the canteen and advanced, through the circling door. I could see the same gent appear in the lobby. He'd read the whole thing. Since sisters were alike it meant I was the same easy girl as her, a smug glance declared and I stuck my nose in the air.

'*For once I fell in love with a maiden so bewitchin', Miss Henrietta Belle from The Captain Kelly's kitchen*,' I hummed desperately. A bar of my father's song came in snatches too, from another hotel door lower down. It was Tommy bellowing loud enough to bring Dado all the way across from Mayo and I put my hands to my ears.

'Bordello Lily is easy and she's the girl for me,' Tommy arrived beside us next, grinning. He'd skidded to a halt and at the same time the wind lifted the notepaper from Rory's hands and plonked the sheets in my bosom.

'I don't believe a word this letter says' I plucked it back. 'One minute my sister is deciding to be a nun and the next marry a soldier. She's been playing games like this ever since we were children. I want her to be a singer though and I think I know how to do it.'

Chapter Thirty-five

Moyra has made a right fool of me now I thought, but before there was time to blacken her character any further, a porter had come to see where Rory was and the pair of them disappeared into the Shelbourne.

In the distance a wavering note sounded. A pipe band was coming from Ely Place. It was a noisy racket but better to listen to them than chase after Rory, so I stood to watch. The pipers must have sought me out on purpose, screeching like banshees, because a fresh swirl was like spirits heading for a funeral. Narrowing my eyes against the glitter of the instruments, the band bore down. Beating drums echoed and bicycles and carts drew aside on the busy road. Beside me a man stood stiffly to attention and saluted. The banner over the band bore the name of Sinn Féin and the men bearing it were gaunt and solemn-eyed.

'Fair play to their fighting spirit! De Valera would be out of office if he asked this country to join up with the British!' a stranger shouted above the din.

'He could try but the IRA do what they want,' I called back until another crash of a big drum made me jump. I saw Connie emerging from the crowd. She had been marching with the parade. She manoeuvred past a mother wheeling a pram and stopped afterward to join me. Instead of clapping to the music, she lifted herself on her toes and peered into the distance. Beyond us a Findlater's van was taking a detour around the crowd and driving away.

'Over here, Matt,' she called eagerly. He mustn't have seen her because the coloured van kept going and she sank into silence. Here was the best person to take my mind off Rory, I decided. But, instead of talking eagerly, she only shook her head and took my arm to stroll back towards the university.

'I was thinking of going to a dance tonight. 'The Mick Mulcahey Orchestra' are playing in the Crystal and I'd love to see them,' Connie brought up her boyfriend a few minutes later. There was no sign of Rita and her new admirer walking under the trees of Stephen's Green and she picked up a fallen twig and began to pluck at the leaves.

I had to think of something because I'd just bumped into Matt in the yard of UCD. He was after having a row with one of the storemen there and his eyes were spitting fire. The man said he knew him from his old neighbourhood and wasn't Matt the brother of the girl Sadie, there was some suspicion about. I had to shout out about the Mick Mulcahey band and how we were all going, just to drag him away. It might be our last dance together unless I get him to change his mind. He says he's giving up the job and going to London,' Connie flung away the peeled stick and grimaced suddenly.

'Please come and talk to him, Lily. I'll tell Rory and Rita about the dance. I'm sure they'd all love it.' She shoved the twig gently to one side with her shoe and before it was possible to explain about the letter, wended her way to work.

It wouldn't be right to say I won't stay, I thought, staring in admiration at the glowing cheeks of my friend and her pretty red dress as we queued outside the ballroom a few hours later. Live music filtered through the doorway and our feet tapped. She pinned on the gold brooch I'd taken back from Annie for her and swirled her new dress to let me see. I had decided to wear my blue satin, the one that was bought in Moon's of Galway as a treat for my nineteenth birthday. The weather might be wintry and damp but Rita was in a low-cut dress of primrose-shade and had tamed her blonde curls, tidying them into a neat coil at the back and pinning the rebellious front waves into place with a velvet white bow. We were three girls out to enjoy ourselves, whatever Rory believed. My shoulders went back. *'There are three lovely lassies in Bannion, and I am the best of them all,'* I swished and hummed.

A blast of sweaty heat hit us as soon as we were inside the hall. Connie pulled me into the ladies. 'Matt is looking too handsome for words. Wish me well, Lily,' she breathed and wiped some fog from the mirror to help her see.

When we came outside a few minutes later there was Peadar, Rita's new friend, standing at the foot of the stairs. He must have been waiting for us because as soon as he spotted us he was across. Soon there'd be nobody left but Rory to talk to. He was bound to bring up what he'd read and I began to edge into the crowd. It was too late to say no to her as Connie pointed towards the balcony and nodded. Skipping up the stairs the man I wanted to avoid was talking to Matt, before joining a snaking line of people at the refreshments counter.

'This is my final opportunity with Matt before he goes to

London,' Connie brought up her dilemma again on the balcony, searching for a place to sit. She picked a table near the front and the voice of the compère, Charlie Russell, travelled up from the floor below in waves. Two university chaplains passed by, here to supervise the dancers for immodest behaviour.

'God bless Lily,' one of them leaned over Connie to take me in and I nodded back awkwardly. It was just as well I was not in serious love like my beautiful friend, I thought. At least the priests would keep me away from Rory. But then, looking in Rory's direction, I saw him glance across and smile.

'The Mick Mulcahy Orchestra, 12-2pm, Admission 2/6d', declared a poster at the entrance as we stood in the queue and it must have drawn a crowd because, leaning over to peer down, a faint haze of cigarette smoke drifted across tightly packed figures, dissipating before a gleam of trumpets and saxophone and lines of black-coated musicians moving to the beat on a lit stage.

The jaunty tones of Lady Malone, the singer for the evening, bounced up. Swing music was making our feet tap and I squeezed Connie's arm.

'Matt will realise what he's going to miss if he goes away. Love always wins. It has with me,' I hinted, encircling her waist in case she'd leave me in the lurch like Rita, disappearing off with her boyfriend as if there was no tomorrow. As soon as Matt gets here with lemonade I'll tackle him about her, I thought. Across from us Rory was miming and holding up some bottles topped with glasses he'd bought, pointing to somebody he wanted to talk to. 'Stay as long as you like, my thoughts are on a war hero called Theo,' I mouthed back.

'*It don't mean a thing if it ain't got that swing. It don't mean a thing all you got to do is sing*,' Connie's feet began to tap despite my restraining arm. She was right. It was impossible to sit here another minute. Rita and I could dance a threesome and I stood to locate her on the floor below. '*Is you is or is you ain't my baby? The way you're acting lately makes me doubt.*'

'Take your partners ladies and gentlemen for a scintillating quick-step. We're in the mood for dancing,' Charlie's silken tones cajoled. 'And once more, to bring you lightly onto the dance floor, it's the one and only lovely Lady Malone.'

'The lads must be making the lemonade.' Connie leaned against the balcony's edge impatiently. There was a flurry of clapping. It was probably a forbidden jitterbug, dancers bending and dipping in quicksilver movements. The priests would soon put an end to that. About to stretch out further Matt brought us back by nudging brimming glasses of lemonade onto our table.

'Would you do me the honour Connie Brady?' He smiled and I heard a quick intake of breath. She was besotted. Maybe she was going to go with him to London and live in sin.

'Not if it means to say goodbye,' Connie flushed, suddenly serious. It was important to talk about love to give her support but the words wouldn't come.

'I'm sorry about going away Connie. It's better to break things off now while I'm still able. I couldn't tie you down.' Matt's face turned white.

'Did somebody mention a wedding?' The right words were out at last. 'If that's what's on both your minds why don't you follow your own instincts. I'm doing it. I'm marrying my soldier. You'll both have to follow the example set.' The effect of the remark was nasty more than pleasant, like getting a punch, or falling off Nellie onto hard ground. There was no time to think it out because the balcony dimmed. Some lights had gone out downstairs and whistling pierced the air. I dabbed my face.

'Shall we dance?' The pair beside me held each other's gaze. This was real love and if I was going to marry Theo I'd better buck up and look forward to it, I sighed. What was really needed now was harmless fun with Rory and, as if in answer, he sauntered over.

Putting the bottles down, he tapped a cigarette out of a box. Tobacco smoke made a wavering line. Blinking to keep it out of his eyes, hands extended, he executed a complicated jive.

'Ginger Rodgers take it away. Will we give it a twirl, Lily?'

'It's the only cure for a big talker if you ask me,' I said because a surge of rhythm had made my body sway and in the space of a beat, he had steered us down the stairs and onto the dance floor.

Mind your heart, I had the sudden thought when his cool hand held mine. Standing on the edge of the dancing crowd, heat mixed with sour sweat and a sickly smell of drink. An island of calm had developed in the centre of the floor it seemed because bodies were almost impossible to get through. Men's eyes darted, looking for a partner and girls chatted as if they hadn't seen them. '*Summer time and the livin' is easy*,' the tones of an invisible Lady Malone lilted, warm as a summer's breeze. Lights that had flickered before suddenly went out. The electricity must have failed and a muttered curse reached us as one of the priests from the balcony slithered past. An emergency ray shot from the stage area across our heads at the same time.

'Turn that damn thing off!' somebody called and there was a burst of applause. As I looked about for either of the girls, the beam picked out Connie and Matt. A space had developed around them. It truly is love, I thought, because their faces had almost blended and bodies were as one. The other priest a slim man with oily hair, veered towards them. It was too late to warn Connie and I saw her shoulder jerk back and something glittered on the ground. My gold brooch had fallen off and I rushed to pick it up.

'We'll have none of that indecency young man. Keep a respectable distance,' the priest's voice carried above the music, breaking my stride.

'Connie, over here,' I called to her urgently. The next thing I knew the brooch was in my hand. Stupidly I'd picked it up just as the crowd fanned away from us and now the light centred on me, shining and blinding, worse than any theatre. Words in my head were loud and clear but my legs were weak.

'Don't be upsetting yourself, Connie. You're no different from the rest of us,' I called at last and the priest shook his head and stared. Beside me Rory retreated with a look of wonder at my daring.

'I won't forget this kindness, Lily,' Connie trembled when my arm circled her shoulder. Even if the crowd had abandoned us once, now they surged forward. Matt held her from the other side. However much the priest heaved after that, dancers swallowed us up.

It only took a few seconds for the proper lights to return. Lady Malone dropped to a low E and I drew in a shuddering breath.

Connie and Matt had melted away but it was obvious the priest had only gone to cover. Soon he would spring forward again. But, darting glances around, there was no sign of Rory. It seemed that in just a few minutes he had forgotten me altogether because he was leaning in towards my priest shouting in his ear. He caught my look and his gaze went blank.

'My sister isn't getting married, I am,' I yelled to make sure he heard. '*Let him go let him tarry, let him sink or let him swim, for he doesn't care for me nor I don't care for him*,' the words of a song struggled out.

If this was the kind of respectable boy Mamma talked about I didn't want anything to do with him. I glared in the direction of the coward but, as if he misunderstood, quiet eyes held mine with a look of approval.

Chapter Thirty-six

The dance was over for us after that and I marched home boldly. But for the next few weeks I kept my head down. I had no choice or the college chaplains were going to haul me up and all would have gone well if Connie hadn't approached me in the library about a fortnight later. She slid a pile of books onto the table and spoke quietly.

'I've something to tell you, Lily. I'm leaving the job and going to England to work in a munitions factory.' Her lips had a pinched look as if she'd deprived herself of sleep but she smiled widely.

'You can't. They'd never agree at home,' I said and felt an instant glow as if she meant us both.

Connie shouldn't be so rash. She's set my mind travelling in completely the wrong direction, I was thinking later all the way to the hostel and I even stood staring at a new poster advertising a Hilton Edward's production, but not really seeing it, to try and banish my thoughts of a foreign shore. Connie needed a friend to go to London and it could be me. Rory didn't want to have anything to do with someone who had such a free-thinking sister and Theo still hadn't written. The Betty Highsmith Singing Agency, the words rang in my head.

At least a way was presenting itself for blackmailing Moyra. I'd write to say she needn't talk to me ever again if she didn't come. In the end I just knew she'd be grateful to be out of Ballyhale not to mention being in London. She'd need to bring one of Mamma's evening dresses and I'd wear my long white one. If she insisted on having the Clerys gown as a bribe, she could have it. So I continued my daydreaming.

'*There are three lovely lassies in Bannion, Bannion, Bannion*,' I sang and danced on the bedroom floor that evening to keep the fantasy up. Instead of three lassies this time there were only two: Moyra and me.

As I buttoned up my coat in the hallway at lunchtime the next day I was still daydreaming about my plans for the two of us. A cold draught blew around my feet and a broadcast came from the reception: 'The 34th American Division to lead attack on Eastern Front', a crisp English voice announced. The wind was making the old building creak and inside I could see Sister Angelica in her den, smothered in a shawl. Still listening, I heard the sound of a knock on the front door and pulled it open absentmindedly. A smiling telegram boy handed over his green envelope and saluted, cycling away. It was addressed to Auntie Terry but a sense of foreboding that I was the subject of the telegram told me to steam it open. My fears were right. The words spoke for themselves because it was from my mother. *On my way to Dublin. Expect me at noon today,* the telegram read.

The words were read and I barely had time to shout goodbye to Sister Angelica and pull open the door when I saw my mother looking across from the other side of the road. Sealing up the telegram with beating heart and throwing it on the hallstand I began to edge out to run.

But it was too late because, sporting a red pillbox hat and an impractical *baneen* coat, my dapper mother was skipping towards me. Rita had spotted her too as she came racing out after me. She stopped on the footpath and shouted: 'Good-day Mrs O'Donoghue,' and was gone. Maybe Mamma's up here to tell me something about Moyra. I could use the excuse to tell her Moyra would be better off leaving Ballyhale for a while. I pretended not to see the woman and skipped down the steps with my head in the air. Auntie Terry called from behind. I could pretend not to hear her too but the strap of my bag caught in a railing and my mother called out cheerfully.

'This is lucky, Lily. I was hoping to get you before you left,' her voice began to harden. Reaching the bottom step she patted that snowy coat. I remembered it was the one she'd worn when I last went with her to the Galway races. She had swished an imaginary riding crop through the air and cried gaily: 'Watch out everyone, I'm on the warpath.'

'Lily, you're looking marvellous. Stop trying to pretend you don't see me. Remember your mother always sees your little secrets,' she announced and then blocked me at the bottom of the steps, bestowing a hug.

Chapter Thirty-seven

'We'll go to Clerys and see what bargains they have,' Mamma announced an hour later. We'd had tea and scones in the nuns' parlour and now she tucked a tendril of hair under her pillbox hat and stared about with a self-satisfied air. Hanging from her arm was an impromptu gift from my aunt of a statue of Blessed Martin De Porres wrapped in brown paper and string. We were standing on the hostel steps again and spring had really arrived, I thought to distract myself, glancing across at the Rotunda trees. Chestnut blossoms carpeted the ground and birdsong drifted above the calls of children arriving late at the school next door. Maybe I should say I had a tutorial at the university to get away from whatever Mamma wanted but she caught my hand in a grip and swung me away from the hostel like I was a willing child.

Before there was a chance to say shopping could wait, we were halfway to O'Connell Street. Soon it seemed the weather might turn us back, because looking ahead Nelson's Pillar was obscured in mist. We'd rushed getting out but now began to look for a doorway. Splashing into a puddle Mamma's feet turned out, duck fashion. People began to stare at her unseasonable outfit. A flash of lightning in the sky was like a streak of gunfire and she threw her hands in the air.

'Your hat's lovely, missus, can I have it for a flowerpot?' A child appeared from a window. Umbrellas were unfurled and people started to run. Out on the road tramcars squealed.

'We can go into the Gresham,' I called out reluctantly and slid my arm into hers. Unexpectedly Eileen and her sister raced past. They could be introduced to Mamma to take her mind off whatever pronouncement she had to make, but their poor feet were streaked with grime and she'd only give them a few pence and move on. Tram lines shone wetly and, feeling in my pocket for sweets, I thought of little toes on cold and rough cobblestones. Fidelma stepped onto the road and a tram lurched close until Eileen pulled her back. I would battle on like them, I vowed, even if it means using Theo to get my sister to Dublin. Moyra and I will sing together and nothing will stop us, I buried the thought deep inside.

Warm air lapped about in the lobby of the Gresham as we shook off our coats. A group waiting to go out stood looking at the rain and we had to step around a set of monogrammed suitcases. Singsong American voices peppered the air. Catching sight of my mother's splattered coat a waiter hurried over to point to the ladies powder room, a gang of soldiers on leave from Belfast took up position in the seats facing me, near where we'd decided to sit. Their Northern accents travelled over. As soon as Mamma heard them she'd mention Theo's enlisting and hint about Moyra being upset for sure. Acknowledging the suggestion of help but staying put, looking as if she'd been relaxing in the sun, she nodded at the soldiers, sat and crossed her legs demurely and then looked round.

Sherry was ordered and served in tiny glasses. Running from the rain had brought a colour to my mother's cheeks and, pushing my bedraggled coat behind me onto a seat, I pinched cold cheeks to stay alert. One of the soldiers coughed to attract attention. Another bounced his leg in rhythm as if he wasn't in the room at all.

'Sherry is respectable. It's the kind of treat your father would approve of,' Mamma raised her glass and fluttered her eyes. 'This seat is not very good for privacy,' she said scowling. Instead of standing to move she took a handkerchief out and began to pat her eyes. Crying was a habit of my mother's to get what she wanted and I stiffened. *'My Belfast Rose,'* one of the soldier's voices lilted across.

'I've heard terrible things about you, Lily,' Mamma sighed. Bright patches appeared on her cheeks and she waved the hotel napkin. 'It's not good enough, my girl. Terry tells me you come into the hostel at all hours. She thinks you're keeping undesirable company.' The sniffling turned to a sob. 'You can appreciate your father is making many sacrifices to get you to university. We're going to ask you to come home. You can go with Moyra to Limerick to do the commercial course. It will be good company for her.'

'That's like one of Dado's ideas. I'm enjoying myself here,' my heart began to thump.

'You've hit on the problem precisely, Lily. You turn everything into good times and forget what you're supposed to be really doing.' Mamma was standing up now and taking a bow as if she was on stage. 'Moyra is pining about the house and if your father had his way she'd be gone tomorrow. We should never have let you go to Dublin in the first place. I don't know where all this is going to end,' she clasped her hands and blinked. 'You didn't want your sister to be involved with Theo. You wanted him to pay homage to you, but only from a distance. What that fellow needed was a few short sharp words from you and he'd have gone back to America, but you weren't prepared to do it. Your father is livid at you.' Mamma sank into the seat, deeper this time and thumped her chest. 'I've gone too far and hurt your feelings. Give me a hug, dear,' she said suddenly then and reached out.

A shoe touched my foot and I saw a lazy gaze. One of the soldiers had stood up to pass. Mamma squeezed me tight. 'Blessed Martin, thank you for this opportunity,' she murmured in my ear and held me apart.

'Of course there is one way out of this. Your Auntie Terry and I both agree. If you told your father you were marrying Theo it could be a long engagement. God knows we're all used to your stubborn streak,' she sighed. 'It might even make Dado so disgusted he wouldn't want you home.' Holding in anger at her words was like a pain at the back of my head. As I stared at the soldier, his laughing mouth pouted and a finger tipped in my direction as if to tell me off.

'You can't boss me that easily,' I told her. Bending forward, shaking out my nearly dry hair, my admiring soldier tried a low whistle. *There are three lovely lassies in Bannion and I am the best of them all,*' I hummed back. My mother wanted to take me over completely.

'You'll do it for your sister, Lily. Theo isn't interested in her. He only wants to bring his mother back to Ballyhale in glory. It's a pity he's so handsome. If this was twenty years ago Michael O'Donoghue wouldn't stand a chance. Sometimes that man forgets he only has a

Ballyhale because of me. Not to mention Auntie Terry and the cross she had to bear,' my mother said mournfully.

'Talent scout for HMV records looking for ballad singers'. I saw the notice outside the Irish Club as I hurried home. At the hotel I had finally burst in Mamma's presence and spurted out something about an essay to do. Running fast and then circling round by the club to regain composure, the sign had brought me to an abrupt halt. Mamma was probably storming up towards the hostel now but I had to go inside.

Auntie Terry was not at home but a note from Mamma had been left for me when this time I got back home from the Irish Club.

Meet me at the Clarence for tea at six. We have a lot to discuss about your future.

There was only one way out of Mamma's plans. I'd have to win the audition. That way I wouldn't need the family at all.

Chapter Thirty-eight

Dear Theo,

I hope all is well. You have been on my mind since you left. Mamma has decided we should get married. Make sure you get in touch the next time you have leave and I'll explain.

Yours faithfully,

Lily

Hopefully Theo would get this and I could warn him to be ready to refuse to take part in Mamma's plan. It was either that or marry him and so be able to stay at university. As soon as I mention the idea to Moyra she'll be up like lightning to Dublin. I smiled grimly at the thought. Picking up the carefully written lines, my fingers tapped nervously. The minute Moyra stepped in the door I'd make her beg to ask if we could go to that audition for duet singers.

I was in the basement of the hostel having a cup of tea. Mamma had gone home days ago. I still hadn't heard from her though and to take away the thought of what she might be up to, I let the soothing drip of a tap take over. Shaking the letter out the ink dried.

Hopefully Sister Angelica wouldn't come in or she'd be hearing another pack of lies. A big 'x' for a kiss would convince the censors not to keep it. I jabbed it on. Now Theo would think I meant every word of how I missed him.

Once Mamma had told me about our own cousins, the Fitzsimmons, who lived in a bungalow outside Castlebar. My Uncle Ned had gone from there to fight in the Crimean War. The letters he'd received from home had been sent back to my grandmother in a bundle when he'd been killed in action. Sooner or later this letter would reach Theo and it would be preserved in his pocket like a jewel to take out and look at when the day's fighting was over.

'I love you Theo,' I said out loud and shoved the note into a stamped envelope, lingering for effect on the word love. Anyone else would say he was a dreamer and a heart scald too, loving one sister and sneaking love from another and not caring who he hurt. A sound made me turn around. Annie was swaying in the doorway, waving a silk scarf in the air like a woman doing a harem fling.

'I found this in the shop today. Somebody had hidden it in a drawer and forgotten about it. It cost a packet but I bought it,' she grinned.

'Lend it to me for my next Irish Club appearance for the 'Three Lovely Lassies' song,' I said promptly. 'You'd never know, my sister might be able to come along with me,' I smiled and catching the scarf in mid-swing, danced it out of her hands.

Shortly after that, to make sure that I didn't put off posting my letter to Theo, I set out for the university. A crow flew off the Rotunda wall and pecked at a sliver of wool near my feet to help line a nest and waddled off. Spring was speeding up in the city, I thought, crossing the street to pass by the General Post Office. If I didn't make sure I posted it like this I knew I'd tear the note up and watch little pieces of paper float down the Liffey. But my footsteps slowed.

Reaching the Gate Theatre, one of the pillars provided a useful post to lean against to print the address and I took the letter out. *Theo Hynes, The American Naval Base, Belfast.* The capitals created an air of importance, like something that carried weight, bearing the romantic yearnings of a young girl in love. Still I stared at it dubiously. It should be thrown on the ground and get rolled over and forgotten about, but letting the foolish thing drop it wouldn't blow away. There was no time to waste. *There are three lovely lassies in Bannion, Bannion, Bannion,* the song was a balm for the heart, enough to remind me of how I'd planned so hopefully to go to London. This new enthusiasm should get me as far as the GPO and I sped up.

As I sauntered down O'Connell Street I saw a small crowd had gathered outside the main door of the post office and the surprising sound of bagpipes pierced the air. It was probably a ceremony to celebrate the new, much admired, statue of Cuchullain that had been installed inside, Cuchullain, the noble hero of *The Táin* story, who had been killed defending his country in battle. It might have been a long time ago and it shouldn't make me feel sorry for another soldier, but I headed for a posting slot all the same.

Proudly the note of the trumpet is sounding, loudly the war-cry rings out o'er the vale, the bagpipes droned. Reaching the edge of the crowd, it became necessary to push through. Before I knew it somebody had bumped in to me causing the letter to slip. At the same time I stared in astonishment seeing Eileen grin upwards. She and her sister must be living on the streets, I thought, we were meeting each other so much and before I could use this final chance not to dispatch the letter she bent and picked it up.

'I'll post this for you,' her child's high voice drew away and to the flourish of fresh piping from the band, she tipped the letter into a brass slit on the wall. 'Sing us a song like ya did before, Lily, and tell me how I'm going to be famous. You're better entertainment than that windy-bags piper.' This rescuer of a fallen soldier put her hands to her ears. She cocked her head to take me in.

'*Oh me father has forty white shillings, shillings, shillings, me father has forty white shillings and the price of a goat and a cow,*' I sang. 'It is a tune about a girl who is trying to convince a boy she has a great dowry. Not like me. I like to be free as a bird,' I shrugged. It was spoken to the air, though because alert to a policeman approaching, the girls had melted away, darting past strollers like quicksilver.

There wasn't much point in talking to Connie about London now but the escaping girls had set my heart singing.

'Say a prayer I'm doing the right thing. I'm giving my notice in to the Head Librarian this morning,' Connie whispered in my ear an hour later, as if she wanted me to change her mind about going. She was perched on a seat beside me in the library and began to line up books neatly. Despite the early hour the place was already full. Glinting bookshelves lined the walls and rows of tables stretched back and I heaved some books from my satchel onto the table. Behind their dividing counter, another librarian beckoned and Connie pretended not to see. In Ballyhale Mamma was probably already setting things in motion to talk to Dado. After a while she'd have the banns for Theo and I read in St Patrick's church, I had a sudden thought. I'd have to make a wedding cake in the hostel and all the girls would be green with envy. Annie would get a wedding dress and even if it wasn't a perfect fit Theo wouldn't notice, because I'd be his forever.

'Don't go to London yet, I want to talk to you about something. I might come along.' Turning to my friend to block out the scene I squeezed her hand and grinned.

'It won't be happening for another while,' she said, only frowning at my foolishness. Then she stood up, tidying steadily, when the Head Librarian began to wave.

'Hello, Lily,' a shoulder knocked against mine. Rory must have sneaked up on me. There was no time to talk further to Connie now because he was breathing down my neck. He thrust a newly transcribed music sheet into my hand as if I had nothing else to think about and began to hum the tonic solfa.

'I've been looking for you everywhere to show you this.' It was the first time he'd spoken to me since the dance and he rocked back on his heels.

'I must have been hiding myself so you wouldn't see me,' I shrugged.

'This song is called 'The Spinning Wheel'. It's published in a new book by Parkside Press called *Ballads with Music. Mellow the Moonlight, to shine is beginning*,' he began to nod to the words and a pair of students nearby who were in the middle of a *téte-a-téte* turned around.

'You have the morning free of lectures. Why don't we look at it somewhere else?' his freckled finger tugged at his hair. 'I'll see you outside in a half an hour,' he declared, walking off as if it was already decided.

Warm shafts of sun fell in through the doors of the college a short while later. I'd strolled over to look out but Rory was waiting. He seemed to think I'd gone there on purpose to leave, because he hovered in front of me. Standing on the steps it was hard not to go somewhere because a wind was whipping at our legs like an invitation to escape.

'Maybe we could find a sunny sheltered spot on Stephen's Green,' I said and he nodded eagerly.

Not long afterwards we found a comfortable bench that was conveniently empty in a sun-soaked corner of the park. Allowing me plenty of room to sit, Rory put his bag between us and leaned back. Children shrieking in play chased from behind a thick hedge and Tommy lolled over by the fountain. If the wedding was held in University Church I could walk out here afterwards on Theo's arm as a blushing bride, I thought to myself. In league with my despondent mood a wind shook blossoms down from a tree overhead. If she was still in Dublin, Connie would arrange a photographer. I pushed the image away.

Clumps of daffodils dipped in flower beds and the scent of wallflowers assailed us but love wouldn't stop appearing because a boy and girl parked themselves on a seat beside us, holding hands. Leaning towards me, Rory lifted the bag to take the sheet music out, taking my hand as he did so.

'You're a trick-actor. You wouldn't do something so daring if Anya was here,' I said promptly. You'd think the wind plucked my hair on purpose then to make it fly up untidily because he began to stare as if it was a pleasant sight. I should get rid of him straightaway to think about Theo but a music sheet fell to the ground and had to be picked up.

'Grafton Street is better than this,' I said abruptly. The excuse wasn't making him budge and I stood up. 'Race you to the gates!' I called out and dashed away.

This was freedom to be myself at last but away from our sheltered spot a bitter wind whipped across the park creating a tunnel of cold air. Beyond the trees smoke swirled from tall houses.

'You left the music on the bench,' Rory's voice travelled from behind and I pretended not to hear. The wind was in my hair and my feet hardly felt the ground. I was in Ballyhale, ready to warn Moyra about everything, I decided and the trees of the avenue were speeding past.

'I'm not singing anymore. I have to go home to Mayo,' the gale caught my words and flung them back to Rory. A tunnel of wind blew through Grafton Street but it was impossible to stop this delightful chase. Behind, a light pattering of feet kept up with mine. 'Race you to the hostel!' I shouted, not daring to wait.

Rounding by the Central Bank, Rory called out to me to slow down. Instead my feet picked up speed and when we reached O'Connell Street I was in my stride. The cool of Caffola's Ice-cream Parlour wafted out. This could be the holy well at the back gate at home. Further up Noonan's Café was Dinnie's kitchen with a slice of

Molly's hot griddle cake waiting for me. 'You'll never catch me now!' I called back gaily and a stitch in my side began to dig in. At the Aer Lingus offices I had to stop altogether. Rory laughed and spluttered, bending down and giving his cheeks a fighter's glow.

'You took off like a hare and I only wanted to go over a song with you. What's it all about?' he panted.

'I thought so long as we're here, I might as well enjoy myself and give you a race,' I blinked rapidly. Surely he'd see there was something wrong now, but he only grabbed my hand.

'I was going to let you know Anya and I are inviting you to a Walden's party. John McCormack will be the guest of honour. He loves to help young singers. You'll get a chance to meet him,' he breathed more slowly.

'I'm not going to play second fiddle to Anya. There'll be plenty of other chances to meet John McCormack without being made to feel under an obligation,' I asserted, but when a hot hand took mine I couldn't help squeezing it.

'Please yourself so,' he said airily. 'If that's the mood you're in you'd be better off staying away.' With that he dropped my fingers. The fleet-of-foot champion didn't even give me time to explain what had really happened but turned on his heel and left.

I could only stare at the retreating figure of Rory after that because an icy wind was pushing him away. There were hailstones in it and they began to bounce off the footpath. My cheeks had started to sting too and, despite being warm from the run, my toes were numb. That receding figure wasn't going to look back and I turned sadly. Goodbye to foolish games, I thought, and with a gloomy shrug

I faced the howling wind. Figures rushed past to get out of the sleeting rain and there were sharp yells of pain.

Serves Rory right he's got caught out in it. I gritted my teeth, trying not to slump. There was still time to catch up with him if I turned back. At least he'd been beaten in the run and I breathed noisily. A punching gust nearly knocked me off my feet but I was at the door of the hostel.

'Moyra it can't be you. How did you get here?' I stared. Somebody was here to help. My sister was standing in the hallway clutching a suitcase.

Chapter Thirty-Nine

Moyra will never agree to sing with me, she's too annoyed. She won't be coming with me to England either. The clear thought arose as I shut the hostel door to keep out the storm and took my sister in. She must have only arrived because hailstones clung to her coat and beret. Her eyes were bright, too much so, I decided as if she was hiding something, but I had troubles enough of my own and I hugged her, too cold to talk. She probably already knew about Mamma's plans for Theo and was blaming me for them because I saw the peaked face harden into resolve. Moyra was ready for attack. Hailstones melted in a small pool on the floor.

'Don't look at me like that. Mamma has her own ideas on everything. She's the one who made the suggestion about Theo,' I said. It was better to get the first word in. But instead of listening she looked around at a sound from upstairs.

Flexing my fingers to take away the cold, a warm glow began to spread after the onslaught of wintry weather outside. Moyra was my big sister, somebody who was supposed to look after me but her hot face was impassive. It flamed up more when she stamped her foot and a shoe squelched.

'The only thing you care about is a romance that's long over,' she said, yanking back my arm. Hailstones hit the hall fanlight noisily and girls who had been prepared to leave milled around. Moyra's coat clung to her tightly.

'You think you know everything,' I said. My sister had probably sailed out of Ballyhale without even bothering to say goodbye because the skeleton look of her gave the impression she'd hardly troubled to fling a few clothes on. Ignoring her plight, I rubbed my sore arm. Some of the girls arrived in the hall and began fixing headscarves before going out into the biting shower and, glad of something to do; I pulled open the door for them, shivering again in the icy wind.

'Look out, or she'll eat you alive,' Annie whispered in my ear, giving my sister an arched look.

'She'd better cut it out or she'll be sent back where she belongs,' I grinned. A few hailstones slipped in and bounced on the floor but I was suddenly at ease. *Mellow the moonlight to shine is beginning*; the first line of the song Rory had transcribed was back unexpectedly. Anything would be better than this row, I thought but just as quickly as the storm of anger had started it the appearance of my sister made it fizzle away.

Moyra slumped on the first step of the stairs. She stretched and yawned. Shortly afterwards she beckoned me to sit beside her.

Silence seeped back in after the scene of angry words and the clock in the reception ticked. One girl who had slept late trudged down the stairs and tipped against the case making it rock.

'Dado will be needing this for his next Lough Derg pilgrimage to pray for our tempers,' I nudged the case away and Moyra laughed.

'There's nothing sinful about this daughter's actions, whatever about the other cold-hearted one,' she said, pinching me in the side but the ice was broken. The sound of a voice from down the passageway calling out a command made us both turn. Sister Angelica was ready to poke her nose in and before we could run up the stairs she glided towards us, wrapped in a shapeless coat and carrying a small hold-all. She pulled an umbrella from the coat stand and stuck it in the air.

'Tell our surprise visitor to make herself at home, Lily O'Donoghue. Your aunt will be in from mass to take over shortly. I'm taking a short retreat with the Dominicans in Dun Laoghaire.' She flung the door open and a late glance pinned me to the spot.

Warmth was in the house after Sister Angelica left because a beam of sun hit the fanlight. It made a shimmering moon-shape on the floor. It struck me then that Moyra could have run away from home without a proper explanation, or maybe she'd heard something else about Theo. He could be on leave and she was planning to meet him. As soon as he came down I'd have to ask. I'd have to find some way of denying the letter meant anything, if he did appear.

There was a library of books in the Irish Club. They were bound to contain the new publication Rory had talked about. Singing always calmed Moyra down. If I could get her there she'd explain everything. One minute she was shouting as if she was in charge of the place and then all she wanted to do was disappear. *Mellow the moonlight to shine is beginning*, the refrain repeated itself.

We were out on the street, a few minutes later. Moyra was carrying her case saying something about finding a hotel to stay in for a day or two because Auntie Terry didn't know she was coming and I nodded wisely, steering her gently in the direction I wanted. Drifts of white still lay against sheltered walls. Her old suitcase bulged out and banged against her legs. Offering to carry it might soften her up. Sometimes they had tea and coffee for sale in the Centre, I remembered. It was another way to entice her in but she held onto her case and we trudged along, it seemed without end.

Soon we stood below the brightly painted door of the Irish Club and stared up. *Conrad na Gaeilge* a polished brass plate announced. It was the perfect cue to try out another air on her and I lilted 'Three Lovely Lassies'. Instead of being distracted, Moyra looked around warily.

'Look, there's a competition on.' I pointed because the old notice was still visible. 'We could win the prize money and stay in Dublin longer.' Instead of showing an interest, Moyra's eyes darkened. Her face grew still and she froze, like an animal caught in a beam of light.

'What's the matter? I'm only trying to cheer you up.' Glancing to where she looked, a priest had stopped on the other side of the road. It was Father Lonergan and I was forced to salute. This was out of my hands now. Auntie Terry would find out everything.

'There's no time to be frivolous, Lily. I have other things on my mind,' Moyra patted her forehead. I thought she mustn't be feeling well because she dropped her case heavily.

'You should have stayed at home if you're sick,' I had to say because this time she bent as if she was about to throw up her breakfast. A magpie bobbed his tail up and down and she whooshed it away.

'*One for sorrow, two for joy, three for a girl and four for a boy,*' I rattled off the old superstition as if we were just girls having a laugh and she put her hands to her ears and groaned.

'You'll be all right. We're sisters again on a big adventure.' I tried to get her to sit on the steps but she crouched, suggesting another spasm of pain. It was a doctor she wanted not a hotel, but if I said anything she'd fling it back in my face, such was her foul mood. She was like a girl expecting a baby. The thought made me stagger and I pushed it away.

'That *piseog* about magpies might be truer than you think, Lily,' she straightened finally, staring at me longingly as if it was the last time she'd see me on earth and then picked up the suitcase to walk on. It dragged at her hands. There was a chance for one last desperate effort. I pulled her load from her.

'If you're not feeling well you can get a cup of tea here. *'Mellow the moonlight to shine is beginning. Close by the window young Eileen is singing*,' I improvised carelessly but now Moyra was ducking behind me. Her head burrowed into my back. Father Lonergan was crossing the road to talk to us. 'In the family way'; the thought repeated itself, seeping in like a caustic drip.

'I'll have to let you into a secret, Lily. Theo is meeting me in the Clarence later. Then we're going to Belfast to get married,' Moyra tried to hobble off. Rescue was at hand, though, because a familiar voice sounded from the Irish Club.

'I believe the American warships protecting convoys are being hard hit in the Atlantic,' the voice said. It was Matt and I swung around to see him and Connie.

'There'll be no American sailors down here on leave for a while so,'

Connie said but before I could talk to her about going to England, Moyra was halfway down the street.

I had to follow her to the Clarence Hotel. Sitting in the lobby for the next two hours, even a wishful thinker like my sister had to admit Theo wasn't coming.

'Come back in the morning, please Lily. I'm going to Amiens Street Station to get the train to Belfast.' She forced a smile.

Chapter Forty

As soon as Mamma finds out about all this I'll be blamed and dragged home. I'll have to go to Anya's party and get John McCormack to say he wants to meet my sister, to get her back, I thought desperately, staring at the determined girl beside me. '*Mellow the moonlight to shine is beginning, close by the window young Eileen is singing*,' I hummed to try and draw attention to Rory's song but she was shooting along. It was a bright morning, and I had arrived at the Clarence Hotel at seven o'clock and now, lugging a heavy case, Amiens Street Station seemed a long way away. Dublin was just waking up. Unexpected overnight frost had crimped untidy patches of grass creating a tracery of lace on house windows and now the weather began to change. A drizzle was setting in but even that couldn't get Moyra to slow down. Children stood motionless outside a school with their heads down like cows in a field. We hurried beside a sluggish Liffey.

A streak of pink, bright as a girl's ribbon, appeared in the sky. When the cobblestones near Poolbeg Street caused us to stumble we had a much-needed pause. It was a chance to slow down and then the ghostly sounds of penned cattle waiting to be driven to a slaughterhouse made me push Moyra in front of me.

'We'll have to hide. One of Dado's friends might have driven those beasts here,' I looked around as if to suggest he might step out of an alleyway and grab at my hair, like a rope. A whimper escaped from my sister.

'You're going to get both of us in trouble drawing attention to yourself. Caffola's will be open now. You should go there when I leave. This running is making you hot,' she said quickly. An agonised moan from one of the cattle made her turn, but then a herdsman intercepted the unlucky animals and this allowed her to walk on sedately.

It was only when we reached a bollard beside a Guinness boat moored on the Liffey that Moyra let herself slow down. The large blue and cream porter barge bobbed gently and water sucked against its side.

'Are you sure you want to go to Belfast? Think of all the trouble you'll cause.' A brown face appeared from a porthole and I reached for her hand like sisters out for a stroll.

'There are worse things for a girl than running away and getting married,' Moyra said quietly. Ignoring the sailor, she leaned over and kissed my cheek. 'I'll write to you as soon as I settle and I know more.'

'Stay with me and we'll work things out,' I cajoled but my sister's grip grew stronger. Not even a curious sailor was going to stop her and then a horse and dray drew alongside to begin loading up barrels and men jumped down to get to work. A rope snaked past Moyra's feet threatening to whip the case into the river and she snatched it back.

'Cheer up *a grá*. Whatever it is can't be that bad. Tomorrow is a new day,' our sailor friend nodded and the boat beside us hooted a tune.

'My sister is running away from home but nobody is supposed to know,' I spoke too loudly and he tipped his cap.

'I wouldn't put it past you to do it, with those flashing eyes, but not that quiet one. A good life is ahead for both of you, though, with the help of God,' the sailor nodded wisely.

'You'll have to move on girls, or sail to Araby with the jolly tars,' another dark-faced man called down.

'We'll go on a pilgrimage to pray for help instead. If it doesn't kill us we'll come back fit for a convent!' I shouted above the noise.

Reaching the entrance to Amiens Street Station the shrill whistle of an engine sent all thoughts flying. An announcement called out the Belfast train and people milled about on the platform.

'Wait there, I have to get something,' Moyra urged me next and disappeared with her luggage. There had been a shunting sound and a puff of vapour smoke and I turned around blindly. Groping my way out I saw Moyra turning from the ticket office and wave one in the air. 'I'll invite you to the wedding. Tell them at home I've gone to Lough Derg like you said. Nobody will catch me until the week of silence they make you do is over,' she grinned and jumped through the dense vapour. Her case clattered onto a step. There was a bigger puff of smoke and she vanished.

Seagulls swooped in under the spacious station roof and the train belched and shot forward but she still hadn't reappeared. Soon it became small but no hand stuck out a window to say goodbye. Smut lodged in my eyes making me weep. But Moyra had solved another problem. Mamma couldn't say I was marrying Theo anymore. *What brings you into my house, to my house, to my house, what brings you into my house? Says the mistress unto Dan, I came here to court your daughter Mam, I thought it no great harm Mam. Oh Dan me dear you're welcome here. Thank you Mam says Dan,*' the song bubbled up.

Back in the hostel a few hours later I could see that Auntie Terry knew more than I thought. Her figure towered over me and I slouched trying to look innocent. We were in the hostel basement. Moyra might have already found Theo but nothing had changed here. Auntie Terry looked fresh as a daisy as if she'd just hopped out of bed and a smell of cooked food lingered in the room. A welcome heat radiated from the permanently lit double range at the top of the room and a sense of gaiety came from colourfully embroidered cushions on the long benches on either side of the big deal table. Snatching up a slice of bread as if I were the hungriest girl ever, I waited for the first question.

You'd know my aunt knew about Moyra from the determined look on her face. As soon I opened my mouth she'd have me on the first train back to Ballyhale and I shifted sideways concentrating my gaze on the window. Outside a bird swung on an old clothes line, singing madly.

Auntie Terry shook her head dolefully. 'I'm sure you've heard Moyra is missing Lily,' her gaze became keen. 'You must have some idea where she is. Try and think,' her cheeks tightened for a further attack. Escape, I thought, but as if she could read my mind my aunt began to pace over and back to the door.

'I'm not responsible for what my sister does. She's older than me. She's the one with all the sense. Now I'm going,' I said coolly, but my fingers broke the bread in front of me, unable to rise. My palms were sweating making me rub them on the seat cushion. This was getting to be like a nightmare and I flung my feet out.

'Things will only be solved if you tell the truth. Maybe we can help each other,' Auntie Terry said gently. Her eyes narrowed to slits. She clapped her hands sharply as if she'd caught a fly between them. It was all up. Maybe this was just a game she was playing, to take me off my guard.

'I don't know what you're talking about. I didn't sleep very well last night.' My mouth widened in a yawn. It was a last effort to distract her but she placed her hands against a thin nose.

'Your sister came here to see me. Am I right?' The nose narrowed into an accusing point. 'Let me give you some advice before you say another word. Father Lonergan knows Moyra. He's seen photographs of her many times. If you feel like lying to protect the girl I can understand that but if there's some way she needs help it would be of benefit if you let me know.' A hand landed on my shoulder before I could stand up and then my nail scraped at a name embedded in the table. I traced the words 'Mary Magdalene'. Auntie Terry shook her head understandingly.

'Moyra might want to talk to a priest. Perhaps there is something bothering her that she can't discuss openly. Girls can fall from grace when they least expect it. This wouldn't be the first time it happened to anyone.'

'If Moyra is in trouble there's nothing you or anyone else can do about it,' I shrugged.

'There are some predicaments girls get themselves into that have a different ending,' Auntie Terry said mysteriously and my ears went pink. At least Mamma wouldn't be dragging me home, if what I'd guessed about Moyra was true. Despite myself my feet began a silent tap dance. With this furore going on nobody would care what I did.

'I'd like to go. I have study to do,' I said, but Auntie Terry had started to sing a hymn like somebody in a trance. A kettle left on the cooker was hissing out steam, similar to a puff from Moyra's train and I drew in a sharp breath remembering her desertion.

'Dear Lily, you have a big responsibility now. For Moyra's sake, don't tell your mother anything until I can think what to do. Only a person who's been close to something like this before knows what it feels like,' Auntie Terry said at last. 'My darling daughter,' I was sure I heard her add, but it was impossible to know exactly because her shoulders slumped. If I wasn't careful we'd be kneeling and saying the rosary to get me to promise and I swung my hands rhythmically.

'Does that mean you'll speak up for me and I can stay here as long as I like?' *Come single belle and beau, unto me pay attention, don't ever fall in love, 'tis the divil's own invention*, the rhythm turned into a tune.

Auntie Terry hadn't time to answer because a figure blocked the doorway. Kindly eyes beamed but a black cassock created a sinister air.

'God bless all here.' Father Tierney was rubbing his hands and smiling fondly.

Chapter Forty-one

The smile on Father Tierney's face was more like something pasted on, I decided as he bobbed up and down in the doorway. Mamma was sending up a messenger to say I was being watched, as if her visit wasn't enough, and he was standing with his head to one side as if he sensed my thoughts. Stepping into the basement he swirled and turned with his back to Auntie Terry and me, stretching his hands over the cooker to get warm. Turning round abruptly he sliced the air in a blessing.

'For the lost at sea,' he said gently and reached out as if to take my hands. Auntie Terry didn't know what was going on because she shook her head at me and patted a seat to get him to sit down.

'This is an unexpected treat. I didn't expect to get both of Michael's family together without a search. I'm up in Dublin for a few days and decided to call in,' Father Tierney announced. He adopted a tragic air as if he'd really prefer to be somewhere else and looked longingly at the teapot on the cooker and then over at me and resumed his false grin.

'Nobody was ever so welcome,' Auntie Terry beamed. You must be thirsty after your long journey. Lily will make you a cup of tea.'

'Hello, Father, nice to see you but I can't stay I'm afraid. I'm due at the Legion of Mary,' I lied. Even if I wasn't right about him snooping, the air was choking me suddenly as if the room was crowded with people instead of just the three of us and I began to nod towards the passageway.

'God in his mercy is good, Lily. Like I said it's fortunate you're here because we have to talk.' The priest headed me away from the door. He raised a hand imperiously as if God really had sent him to us and lifted a long ladle on the kitchen table waving it vigorously.

'*For once I fell in love with a maiden so bewitchin', Miss Henrietta Bell from the Captain Kelly's kitchen*,' I hummed my song from the Rathmines concert, and grinned. At least there I'd been appreciated for myself. Sauntering over to the dresser to take some cups out, I cursed the man, eyeing the window as an escape route.

As if he really was only here to offer some prayers for our intentions, Father Tierney began to stride up and down, making a hole in the floor and making me dizzy looking at him. Auntie Terry poked a thin stick into the range to stoke it up and get the kettle boiling. Then she lit a taper and used it to ignite a gas jet on the wall. Thin as whitened bone, the delicate glass mantle glowed. Sooner or later one of them would forget about me and I'd have the opportunity to bolt.

'How is everyone in Ballyhale?' I asked brightly and Auntie Terry shot a grateful smile.

'The reason I've come, Lily, perhaps you know, is to find out where Moyra is. You might be aware she's run away.' Father Tierney clicked his fingers, casting an accusing glance as if I should know everything. 'I'm here on behalf of your parents. Moyra could be plunging herself into sin and disgrace and we need to save her. I can't stress the seriousness of this enough. Your poor mother is distraught.' Ceasing to pace, he leaned in, smelling like bad potatoes. Close-up, wrinkles had formed beside his flat nose and behind my back I joined fingers in the shape of a cross.

'You seem to think I hear everything,' I shrugged. Moyra couldn't accuse me of giving her away with such an innocuous remark but the priest leaped up and patted me on the shoulder as if I'd said the right thing. He beat his chest with a hand before returning it under the cassock.

'God rescue your sister from temptation.' His eyes glittered like pin tips and I stole a look at my watch. Jesus, help me out of here, I thought. At least there was the party ahead and I closed my eyes briefly. I twisted my hair into a curl to help me concentrate on the dream night ahead. Auntie Terry nudged me to bring me back. I just shrugged carelessly.

'*Happy Birthday to you, Happy birthday dear Moyra.*' The jingle surfaced of its own accord and I knew my aunt heard. Tomorrow was Moyra's birthday. She'd be twenty and we wouldn't even be together. I forced an indifferent smile.

'Don't drift away from us, Lily,' Aunty Terry's voice cut in. Her gaze had now become steely and her nervous fingers fussed with her bunch of keys. She shook her head, annoyed.

'Pay attention, young lady. This is a serious matter,' Father Tierney snapped. He really was on the attack because he crouched against the table. 'You know your father depends on us Lily. If you can offer some hope, he'll make sure you stay in Dublin. Sister Terry has something she wants to say to you. Isn't that so?'

The priest turned to my aunt and looked at her hopefully. She'll take my hand and tell me to leave because they want to talk, I prayed. But beyond her, for the first time, I saw a key turned in the basement door. This was a plot to break me down and I put my hands to my ears to cut out her voice. Over on the cooker the kettle continued to steam like that smoothly puffing engine. Moyra would know what to say, I wailed inside.

'Bless this house oh Lord we pray. Keep it safe by night and day'; a fault caused the jet gas to flare and an embroidered inscription framed on the wall leaped out and I stood up to plead my case.

'Prepare yourself for a shock dear,' Auntie Terry was over me. She took my hands from my ears firmly. 'I have some bad news. Moyra is going to have a baby. If she's gone somewhere to get married well and good, but it might not happen. This is stirring up memories for me too, ones I had hoped could be buried and forgotten about,' her voice began to crack.

'Magdalene', the word from before was under my fingers and was traced again despite myself. This was another trap to talk about Moyra and then throw suspicion on myself. Auntie Terry pressed my hand under her arm.

'You poor dear, it's just as well you're young and the world is full of promise.'

'Even if you don't tell us where your sister is she'll be found and brought back. We must follow God's will.' Father Tierney began to settle. He swished a string of rosary beads through the air.

'*There'll be blue birds over the white cliffs of Dover,*' Vera Lynn lilted from the parlour radio. It was my own world, tantalisingly close. Even music wasn't giving me strength though, because something made me say, 'She'll survive in Belfast.' Thankfully, Auntie Terry tipped her forehead with the sign of the cross and I stared at her face.

'A decade of the rosary wouldn't come amiss to guide a soul from the valley of darkness,' Father Tierney let out a grunt. He kissed the rosary crucifix. 'It's a pity you didn't let your family know before now how far this unfortunate liaison of your sister's had gone.' Button eyes dug into me, 'Your aunt mentioned marriage but I know, without a shadow of a doubt, it can't and won't happen.' I barely heard the last words because somebody rattled the door from outside. Whichever of the girls it was, this was rescue.

'Rita, I'm coming,' I leaped up. Everyone would have a laugh when I told them. I'd make up a crazy story about being pursued by a lovelorn priest. Behind me, Father Tierney hopped like a ceilí dancer.

'Prepare yourself for a different shock, Lily,' he warned. 'Dear girl, there is some information about your friend Theo I didn't want to have to break to you in this brutal manner. God help us, he has been reported missing in action. Now you can see why we need to find out where your sister is.' This was a trick, it had to be. I gasped stupidly and reeled backwards. If Auntie Terry hadn't caught me then I'd never have got out. She pushed me towards the door. Evil was propelling me from that room too, I sensed dimly, as if leaving a bloody battlefield, or hell and Lucifer.

'Come back, Lily, or you'll be tarred with the same brush as your sister. Archbishop McQuaid will insist on it!' Father Tierney roared.

'Forget what I said. She's not in Belfast and I'm going to tell her all about your lies,' I whimpered.

Chapter Forty-two

If Father Tierney is right about Moyra then there's no hope for her. She'll be put in a Magdalene Home and that will be the end of us, I realised. My feet had propelled me from the hostel and now they were like lead. Footpaths rose up to bar my way. That priest is a cod, he knows nothing, the words banged about in my brain. Forcing my feet along I reached O'Connell Bridge. A turgid Liffey rolled towards the sea and some out-of-work men begged by the stone parapets. As I shoved myself through the rolling mist a gaunt figure stepped up and pinned me to the spot. I stared around wildly. It was Father Tierney as a simpering angel but then two yellow teeth appeared. A frayed Aran sweater barely covered a bony frame and brown scapulars protruded.

'*An bhuil pingin agat a chailin deas?* Long life to you and yours, God be good to ye all.' The scarecrow turned into skin and bone and my shoulders lifted. This man spoke like Dinnie. He was from Mayo like me, a symbol of ease and good times and I fished out a penny and pressed it into his hand.

Eyes made small by too much drinking suggested a soul gone astray but the exchange had bucked me up and I held his hand to feel the warmth. Don't give up hope. Theo might not be dead. That was who the man's blessing referred to. It was what I would tell my sister too, as soon as she got in touch.

'Theo is missing but he'll be back,' I repeated the words until the memory of a priest's crucifix waving in front of my face began to disappear and I marched forward.

Hours later, and it seemed as if by some kind of miracle, my footsteps were leading to Anya's party because I was floating up the steps of a house close to the St Bernadette's Hall in Rathmines and saw her pretty head just before curtains closed on a party scene. Overhead a moon swung into view to light up the road and an imposing entrance gleamed cheerfully. Like another stroke of good luck the door swung open and, as I ran up the steps nobody came out to bar my way.

Rory appeared immediately. I'd had to lean against the doorway to get my breath and now he'd pushed out of the middle of a crowd. Behind him a brightly lit reception room blazed before voices retreated. He must have seen me from the window and felt sorry for me because he patted his cheeks and huffed and shifted. Conversation tinkled when the door opened again and Anya stepped out.

A wave of heat came with her from the party room. It would be impossible to talk to Rory with her beside him but a dimple came and went when he smiled, and I nodded back madly.

'Lily. It's lucky you got here. I've had a long talk with John McCormack about you and he'd like to hear one of your ballads,' Rory took one of my hands.

Trying to say thank you my grimacing face cracked into a smile. There'd be some comment about my wet shoes and dishevelled appearance next to ease matters more and I smoothed my hair down.

'I need to get to Belfast.' The words rushed out despite myself. 'My sister isn't well,' the madness flowed on. Coming in from the cold was making my head swim, because he was looking at me doubtfully. There was a cough from behind as if Anya wanted to join in. I had a muddled thought of a boat to Holyhead mixed in with homes for fallen girls.

'I might have to go to England for good as well,' I declared and shook my head as if there was wool inside.

It was obvious that Rory wanted to look away because the fool went out of focus and through the music Anya called out. My hand was dropped.

'Money will be a problem if I have to go.' I nodded vigorously but a chill struck despite the heat of the house, as if I was back in the night and I had to pull my cardigan around me. The action caused a prick of pain. It was the brooch my father had given me as his going away present. I'd stuck it on in a hurry getting dressed and now it glinted like a new coin. The brooch could be pawned and used to help Moyra. I gripped the sharp thing tightly. I'd get in touch with her using the number for Andrew that Theo had given me and arrange to get her to London before she found out I'd told on her. My mind ran on, grateful to have found a solution.

Matt would be in London any day now. He might be working class but he was kind, I decided. After that I'd go to the Betty Highsmith Singing Agency. It would be like a dream come true. In a far off way my legs were beginning to buckle.

'Come back in Rory. The guests are looking for you,' Anya took his arm. Looking me up and down, she looked unimpressed. A burst of song came from the party room.

'There'll be blue birds over the white cliffs of Dover, Tomorrow, just you wait and see.'

'You got here in the end slow-coach. Some people don't know what they're missing,' her voice was cold.

'The fun isn't over yet. I'll be back. Ask Rory who he likes to talk to.' Just then my body tipped forward. It wasn't intended. I realised I hadn't had anything to eat and Rory's arms felt delightful. Now he'd know I really was the tattered street girl he secretly liked and because the part of Cinderella called for it, I left him longing to leave his party scene.

Chapter Forty-three

A week had passed since Father Tierney had left and I still hadn't heard from Moyra. But that wasn't the only trouble because a nightmare of mine was starting to recur now to compound matters. I shifted on the pillow of my narrow hostel bed. Theo, pale as a cold-hearted moon, was drowning. Swimming against steely waves to reach him, they surged back. This was like hovering on the edge of a whirlpool about to be sucked in. All around me girls slept normally, not like me, half dead in a dream. Blinking to get rid of water, the bed came into focus. Stale air crossed the room in waves from so many girls stuck together in one room and I coughed and shot upright.

'I'm coming to get you *a stór,*' I said weakly still half-asleep but I was the one needing rescue and I stared wildly, pulling the blankets over my head.

I remembered that Granny Lloyd had kept the telegram about her son, my Uncle Ned, telling her he'd died at war, in her bible. It was pressed between the pages like some people preserve butterflies. If a notice as devastating as that had arrived at Ned's house about Theo, they would have wanted to rush over to Ballyhale straightaway to tell the news, I thought. I should have been there too and I leaned back weakly.

If I had a lock of Theo's hair I'd put it in my prayer book and look at it every day. Watching the dark strands fade might keep these dreams away. Otherwise it was all lies and he needed a good kick, holed up somewhere on the deserted Irish coastline keeping his whereabouts quiet until the war blew over and draping his arms around another nice girl like Moyra, to help pass the time.

'Rita, are you awake?' my voice rasped and the sleeping girl beside me turned in her bed. Yawning, she opened a crusted eye and glared.

'Sorry to disturb you,' I said loudly to keep her awake. 'I had a nightmare about Theo,' my hair must have looked like a bird's nest because she was staring at it oddly.

'Think of Rory instead,' she said and closed her eyes. She was being smart. It was because she was remembering the last time we'd seen him. The two of us were talking in the corridor in university when he strolled up with a cut of cake wrapped in a white napkin and proffered it in my direction like somebody giving a peace offering, as if he realised he should have followed when I left the party.

'I kept this for you when you didn't get back to Walden's the other night,' his mouth turned down in an apologetic grin.

'Lucky for some people to have a lover chasing them bearing gifts,' Rita had piped up beside me and I hit her with my bag and he stood back as if he was being attacked.

One of the girls in the dormitory laughed in her sleep and I turned abruptly. I could hear the musical bells of the Black Church coming into the room too as first light crept through half-open shutters. Stretching out, my hand hit against a picture of Moyra on the locker, Moyra on her first pony, smiling as if she was the most beloved girl in the world, but really wanting to unseat anyone trying to take her place.

As soon as Theo was found he'd come to Dublin and accuse me of letting Moyra go to Belfast.

'He should know she couldn't have been stopped anyway,' I said aloud. There was a sharp jerk of the shoulder from Rita and to calm myself I riveted my gaze on the white ceiling boards overhead. Instead the pale face of Cathall Plunkett appeared.

My cousin Cathall was my age and I'd attended his wake last year. He'd been driving the family motor car when the brake cable snapped. It crashed into a bridge on the River Owenduff and ended up nose deep in the water. He had a broken face when I saw him laid out, God rest his soul, but it was his look of determination to stay alive that had held me, fighting to hold onto life until the bitter end.

Switching a desperate gaze to the top of the wardrobe, that ashen face wouldn't go away. Theo had the same kind of willpower and even if his ship had gone down there must have been survivors, I thought. But it was cold comfort in a room where it would take a bomb to waken one of the girls and I rocked on the bed to make the springs rattle.

At least it was morning now and time to rise. Pale light almost obscured Dado's brooch lying on the locker and I stared at it moodily. Today I would go to the pawnshop in Marlborough Street and then get Matt's address from Connie. As soon as I arrived in London it would be straight to the War Office to begin a search for Theo. The idea of that would get Moyra over in a flash. Between the two of us there were bound to be results.

'It's too early to get up. Go back to sleep.' Rita looked up suddenly.

'Can you let Auntie Terry know I've gone to university to do some early study?' I asked. If a missing soldier's life depended on me the least I could do was work hard to prove myself. After that I'd sneak back to the Irish Club to plan some songs to bring to England.

As soon as the hostel was left behind, skipping into a wide-awake day, I was hungry. A milkman was ladling out his treat of creamy milk fresh from the country at doorsteps and I began to think of the upstairs Carlton Cinema restaurant breakfast. Reaching O'Connell Street my mouth was already watering. It was impossible to resist glancing across the wide road towards it and I fancied I saw a waiter open a window at the other side and imagined rows of snow-white tables. To increase the attraction, large raindrops splattered the footpath. A stiff breeze blew up from the direction of the Liffey, bringing showers, and I spied my poor tramp Tommy sleeping in the porch of the Savoy Cinema.

Is there any fear of me, when you see his plight? I'll get something simple to eat at the university I thought but hunger wouldn't go away. I could get Tommy some fried bread from the restaurant; my footsteps had brought me as far as Nelson's Pillar and I paused.

'*I am a little beggar man, a begging I will be. Three score and ten and a lass upon my knee.*' As if to help the bright idea along an air surfaced in my memory that I'd once heard Matt play.

It would cause a chuckle at the Betty Highsmith Singing Agency and I hummed louder.

Chapter Forty-four

Running back up the middle of the wide street to the restaurant after making my secret promise to Tommy to get him breakfast, a tram splashed through the rain, wetting the new stockings I'd borrowed from Annie. At Nelson's Pillar a repair man with puffed out cheeks and carrying a large tool box went through the railings of the monument and pulled open the entrance door. As soon as he did a snowy dove flapped out.

'Sail away beauty,' intoned the worker but the bird couldn't rise. That was my heart weighed down with sorrow because of Theo, I thought and sighed. A church would be a better place to go to pray for forgiveness for sending a man away to war, instead of stuffing myself with food. But another song was in my ear and an arm was stealing over my shoulder. An umbrella swung up to cut out the punishing rain and a smiling face dipped towards me.

'*There are three lovely lassies in Bannion*,' Matt lilted.

'*Bannion, Bannion and I am the best of them all*,' I chirped along. Here was a friend just when I was at my lowest. He must know a person was hungry just by looking at them because he steered me towards the Carlton breakfast treat, like a fellow conspirator.

'I heard you'd gone to London,' I poked my head out from the umbrella, pointing it away as if to stop him.

'Not yet, but His Majesty can expect the pleasure of my company any day. It might even call for a celebration,' Matt joked. He took a passport out of his pocket and waved it in the air. 'The real problem is leaving Sadie behind on her own in this country of hypocrites, always butting into everyone's business,' he scowled.

Seated in a window alcove in the spacious upstairs restaurant a few minutes later, I eased off wet shoes, wriggled my toes and settled back. Out on the floor a waiter flitted between pristine tables. My nightmare morning was far behind but as soon as I got the chance to tell Matt he'd hear everything about Theo. An enticing smell of rashers lingered in the air. Slices of soda bread instead of the usual black variety the war threw up, sat neatly arranged on the white table cloth. Cold raindrops slid along the window outside but I was too busy thickly buttering a slice of bread to care.

'I don't know if Connie told you but Theo has joined the American Navy,' I said lightly. Matt reached for a helping of bread and his eyes narrowed.

'Are you alright Lily? You don't look well,' he said at last. The observant man must have noticed one of my eyelids quivering and I raised a hand to stop it. A waiter looked over and nodded.

'It's nothing. I slept badly last night,' I shrugged. This wasn't the way it should be, I was supposed to be complaining about Theo and how he was wearing me away with anxiety since he'd gone. This breakfast would have to be finished quickly if I was going to make the first lecture I decided. Words were beginning to rise inside too and I squeezed my eyes shut.

'Theo is dead and it's all my fault!' I gasped and felt my hands lift like an exclamation. 'Or he's missing, he might be dead.' Moyra had something to do with it too, I should have said, trying to find a means to run off with him. I laughed shakily.

'That's terrible. How do you know, Lily?' Everything was alright because the man before me was pouring tea as if the news was the most normal thing in the world. A waiter placed a silver teapot on our table and his white-coated figure melted away.

'Our parish priest Father Tierney told me yesterday. It's all a trick probably.' Up at the reception the waiter was swinging a piled tray from a dumb-waiter and I focused hard. He dived about, placing plates here and there.

'If you're worried about Theo you could get in touch with the American Embassy, or somebody who might have more information. You owe it to yourself.' Matt nodded his head. Pouring the tea he concentrated on the amber liquid. 'There's a phone at the desk. Tell them it's an emergency. They won't mind if you explain why,' he leaned back as if he was used to asking people to read from a dead list every day of the week and I stood up abruptly.

'Ballyhaunis, The Gateway to the West', a poster for the Great Western Railway hung beside a recess for the public phone which the waiter indicated and I remembered Mamma. She'd be hard on the heels of Father Tierney, supporting him all the way if I couldn't make up another lie about Moyra. The thought held me for a moment. Looking back at Matt to see if he was watching or I could return, he nodded approvingly. Sitting at the table I'd kicked off wet shoes and now my stockinged feet sank into a soft carpet.

It was easy to fish Andrew's number out. A hole in one of my socks was causing the waiter to glance too closely and it was impossible to speak into the receiver without a tweed coat in the recess getting in the way. That jacket was similar to one of Dado's. If he was here he'd tell me not to be making a nuisance of myself.

'Hello, Andy Deasy here. Can I help you?' unfamiliar American tones barked in my ear. A hand on the clock over the phone jumped and the voice on the other end of the phone breathed lightly. This was worse than having a sleeping Rita snoring or being at a funeral because, as if in commiseration, a cup of tea arrived from the waiter on a nearby shelf.

'My name is Lily O'Donoghue. You haven't met me but I got your name from Theo Hynes. I was wondering how he is.' The words were surprisingly easy and there was a sudden need to giggle. '*Three Lovely Lassies*,' I hummed to keep the laughter down. The tweed coat had an overwhelming smell and I sneezed. 'Theo said I was to ring you if there was anything I needed,' I stammered. 'Tally-ho, follow that fox', a hunting call of Dado's was confusing my thoughts. Dado's coat was his favourite for following the hounds.

'I'm sorry to have to be so plain-speaking about this. Theo is missing at sea. We don't know any more yet. One of our ships on convoy protection was blown up. There have been some survivors but his name hasn't come through.'

It was like Father Tierney said and now the tweed odour was the same as from hyacinths beside the laid-out Cathall to disguise the smell of death.

'Can you hold on for a moment Lily, I got a letter this morning that might be useful. It's from your sister Moyra. Theo told me about her. It's news to me, but she says they were secretly married before he left for sea and that you would explain.' A sharp tap came from the other side.

There was a rustle of paper and the American spoke to himself, as if he'd love to reach out and strangle me to get at the truth. 'There can't be a mistake I suppose because she signs herself Mrs Moyra Hynes.'

This time, along with Dado's hunting horn I saw a pretty fox, a tawny blur running for cover, like my sister being chased and about to get away. Moyra was safely married and she didn't care who she got into trouble covering up for her. I banged the receiver down.

Dear Mamma,

I'm sure you'll be delighted to hear Theo and Moyra are married. My studies are going well and Miss Hourigan says I should get into second year easily.

I started a letter to my mother that evening. It was my last chance to continue singing and I experienced guilty elation giving my sister away.

Chapter Forty-five

Dear Lily,

Come up to Belfast. I've found somebody who'd love your Irish tunes and will put you on the bill in City Hall. Mercifully there haven't been any air raids since arriving but the city is on a constant state of alert and it would be lovely to have you around. There's no word of Theo yet but there has to be hope. Until then at least we have each other,

Your loving sister

Moyra.

Moyra wasn't married after all. The letter had been addressed from The American Naval Base in Belfast, and I'd read it quickly in a hostel toilet cubicle before leaving for university.

'You're looking pale. Is there some trouble?' Rita had said before I left.

'This is the parting of the ways. You won't see me here tonight,' I joked and she laughed and shook her head. It would be better than having to explain about Moyra getting in the family way. I should have said that my sister is on the slippery slope to perdition and is going to drag me down with her. Rita's laughter had continued with

Annie on the hostel steps as if I shouldn't have a care in the world and now, as I lay in the Iveagh Gardens taking the sun, I longed for some company. I wanted to tell Rita everything.

The first person in sight is going to hear my confession, even if it's a stranger I thought, squinting in the sun. An empty space met my gaze. Mamma hadn't made any response to my letter either and that made matters even more critical. Any day now she'd have me with her, sunbathing under the sycamore in the kitchen garden.

'I want to be a singer but instead I'll be the sister of that bad girl who got herself pregnant and then went around pretending she was married, getting fatter and fatter for all the world to see,' I practised the words I would say out loud to whoever came and there was a call that sounded like my name. It came with a sense of carbolic soap, but nobody was near.

It was a calm afternoon, the air had been cold earlier on but now the sun was shining enough to create a holiday feeling. The clickedy clack of a lawnmower and a sweet smell of cut grass created a timeless air. I closed my eyes and imagined myself walking into the Betty Highsmith Agency in Holborn. It would make up for my treachery over Moyra by getting her to London. First thing we'd find the War Office and ask if they knew anything about a missing sailor. She could explain how she needed Theo, that he was her dearest love and he had to be found straightaway and then she'd burst into tears.

'If you don't find him Moyra and I will end up in the Magdalene laundry,' I'd say to waken them up more.

Goodbye Tom, and goodbye Jack, and goodbye Kate and Mary, the anchor's weighed and the gangway's up and we're leaving Tipperary, the emigration song would be a great choice for us both to sing for an audition, even if it had nothing to do with a missing soldier.

It was hard to be serious in this glorious weather. Whoever had been nearby crunched on gravel path but then I made the mistake of calling out and had to duck, scratching my face on a prickly bush. Miss Hourigan was on the warpath, searching for students who should be in class.

A student with a limp like Theo's passed by and I gazed mesmerised, nearly giving myself away. Any minute now I'd hear an American lilt in my head, 'I love you, Lily.' It seemed more real than imagined and I put my hands to my ears. It was becoming impossible to stay in this place. Instead the face of Rory came into view. Rising jauntily, I picked at needles of bush in my hair.

'John McCormack would love this peace. I believe he's still in Dublin,' Rory announced as if we'd been talking for ages. His had been the carbolic smell. His face had an innocent look as if he'd never sneaked around and he started to throw a coin in the air playfully.

'I'm sure you and Anya will both get around to talking about it. I'll see him in London,' I said boldly. When I went into the Betty Highsmith Agency I'd have to mention meeting the singer, but before I could crow more, Miss Hourigan was back. Rory waved to bring her over and I froze.

'Why don't we get out of here?' I shoved books into my bag letting half of them fall but, reaching to retrieve a stubborn sliver of bush from my hair, Rory pressed me to him.

'Heads I tell Miss Hourigan about London or tails we go to a café,' he whispered and doffed his cap towards her, like Dado being suave at a race meeting.

'Wait there Lily O'Donoghue, I have news from your family to discuss,' Miss Hourigan called loudly. She had to be avoided, even if it meant telling Rory about Moyra and before she could call louder I scurried from the gardens like a scalded cat.

Stepping into the flowery oasis of Stephen's Green to take a shortcut to Robert Robert's, a café in Grafton Street we'd agreed on that often had music, the park was looking its very best. Cottony trees swayed in the breeze and blossoms dropped lazily. Hyde Park in London would be just as good. Mamma often spoke about its appeal from her summers spent there and I concentrated on that memory to stay focused. Rory jingled coins in his pocket.

Close to the park bridge a model plane landed and its owner, a soldier in Irish uniform, began to fix it fussily. The noise was enough to make anyone cower and think of warplanes overhead, but only small clouds drifted by. I was taking deep breaths of sun-filled air, concentrating on vibrant flower beds, when a boy ran towards us. It was a reminder to be true to Moyra because, just like Theo, a lock of the boy's hair fell engagingly over one eye. The child grasped my hand trustingly.

'Keep your eyes on the ball!' Rory called. The boy had thrown a tennis ball and now Rory lifted it and flicked it forward.

'Catch me if you can, slowcoach!' a girl called sharply. Before Rory could stop her she'd snatched the ball and with her hair bobbing in the wind she leaped across an expanse of grass with her prize. That would have been Moyra when we were young, grabbing whatever I was playing with. Forget about your sister and stay here, I thought, and bumped against the man at my side, shyly.

The whole of Dublin seemed to be out taking the air, making the most of the day. Robert Robert's café in Grafton Street was awash with noise a short while later and a waitress dipped between tables. Rory ordered tea. The spoon he was using to stir it made a soothing pattern on the surface. I'm not going to say goodbye to him and say 'I'm off to England.' The thought brought instant relief. For all I knew he might have set up a meeting with John McCormack here. It would be just like Rory's thoughtfulness but I refused to meet his eye. Turning to look at him then I could see a smile tugging at his lips. While I watched his face changed. He frowned and reached for my fingers.

'How is your sister? You seemed to be very concerned about her at the party,' he said bluntly. 'Anya would like to help. Her father wants to meet me this afternoon to talk about joining the firm. He'd prefer to see us more than good friends,' he glanced away stormily.

'Moyra is fine but I'm afraid I have to leave now. I have to go into Clarendon Street Church to say a prayer for a poor sinner.' I dragged myself up. Rory had already had a chance to judge me and now the final rejection was about to come and I lifted another cake, unable to resist the temptation of taking it with me as I left.

'Carnations for a white wedding,' a flower seller called outside the church a few minutes later, but I noticed a pawnbroker further down the lane and fingered Dado's brooch on my coat. Going to England was too extraordinary a step and I entered the church gratefully.

Chapter Forty-six

Sin, the word began to reverberate in my head. It had been waiting to pounce and now the walls seemed to echo it. I'd gone into church to get away from Rory but my heart quailed. Moyra and I were both sinners. I knew I shouldn't be the one to take all the blame for telling Father Tierney on her, but guilt was beginning to pierce like a dagger and I looked around, hoping for solace. A few beggars had come into the back of the church and '*Tantum Ergo*' sounded from the choir.

Whatever about my receiving forgiveness, Moyra would suffer the stigma of disgrace forever. To add to her problems she was at the mercy of people who cared only about the sin she had committed and not about her own turmoil. This was how I reasoned it all but my guilt wouldn't leave. Digging my nails into the pew in front, turning to see if Rory had followed to explain all to him, only the soothing music filled the air. Two girls arrived giggling in the pew behind and it seemed as if I could hear Rita's amused tones beside me.

'Find a priest and confess your sins. As soon as you kneel down he will ask what sort of stuff you and Theo got up to,' she'd say. Somebody tapped me on the back but looking around it was only one of the girls and she just shook her head and grinned as if she'd enjoyed giving me a fright.

'I love you Moyra,' I muttered instinctively to take away a shivery feeling. This was prompted by a glance at a statue nearby which seemed to represent my sister's face, as pious and real-looking as if she was staring down at me. Another memory followed quickly, of a photograph in Auntie Terry's latest *Capuchin Annual* of a Belfast street, a patchwork of terraced houses dwarfed by a giant shipyard with people dotted about looking more like dolls. This was a way of telling me that Moyra would only feel like an outsider in such a foreign place. At least in England we'd be together. She'd forgive me there, I thought.

A priest swished into a confessional beside me and one of the girls from the pew moved across to take first place. Rory was the one to take my mind off all this. He was probably still in the café and so, plucking up courage and avoiding rows of saints with their accusing faces, I drifted out.

I went straight back to Bewley's and saw our places had been taken. Before the impulse could die down and, despite my better judgement, I sauntered into the pawnshop and sold my brooch. Now that I'd taken this step perhaps I should buy a ticket for the boat in case I really decided to go. Remembering that the shipping offices and shop were in Westmoreland Street I braced myself and set out, all the time using the excuse that Rory might have gone in that direction for Walden's shop.

I arrived sooner than I wanted to and immediately saw a line of customers snaked outside the shipping offices in Westmoreland

Street. Slowly, I drifted into the queue. Finding out how difficult everything would be was a sure way of preventing me from going to England. An old man shuffled in front. Nervously, I held a hand to my coat over the place my brooch should have been and I tapped him on the shoulder.

'Is this where you queue to get a ticket to London?'

'Yes darling, but go before the blitzing starts again or you'll be fried alive,' he slapped his knee as if I should laugh at his joke.

'Next please,' a sales girl announced from behind a partition and I was pushed forward. Separated from a diminishing pile beside her, a ticket appeared on the counter.

'I only want to make an enquiry.' I shoved the ticket back.

'Don't mind her. She has a sweetheart in London. It's only ten pounds. Don't let her away with that excuse.' the man whom I had spoken to before lit a cigarette. He'd parked himself in a chair reserved for the elderly and coughed between his words.

'University students shouldn't be wasting our time, there are people here who need to get back to work,' somebody else contradicted him. Then I saw that my diary, which had the name of University College Dublin written on the front had fallen out of my bag. The only thing to do was pay and opening a secret pocket in my purse I took the money out.

I wasn't really going away of course, but even so, after I crept into the hostel later I packed a bag and then went out again, wandering aimlessly in out-of-the-way streets to keep from being recognised. This would be practice for when I would leave but the happy faces of children playing, even the smell from the Liffey making me hold my nose, told me it couldn't happen.

'*Goodbye Tom, and goodbye Jack, and goodbye Kate and Mary,*' I hummed a song for parting. I could busk in London in the future, I decided, or try getting work in a theatre. Crossing a street, a puff of exhaust from a faulty bus made me wish to be anywhere but Dublin until the driver waved and stuck out a cheerful hand.

Reaching Dun Laoghaire the skies were already darkening. Having got as far as here I might as well check out what to do for the next time and I began to follow the signs. A ship's horn blared and I panted onto a dockside. Orders were being shouted, a thick rope was snaking off a bollard and as I stood back a hand gripped my arm.

'Leave it, Lily. Nobody is going to London. This is a dangerous time.' Rory was standing beside me. He must have followed me from the café, keeping behind me all the time and now he was here to save the day. A sailor reached for my hand as the gangway rose.

'Goodbye Rory, I'll write to you from London,' I said. Helplessly I allowed myself be pulled forward.

'Rita told me about your sister and that she's in Belfast. I'd love to meet her, we could go together,' Rory called out hopefully. He'll try and meet my mother and father next, I thought, and to prevent such a calamity, at the last minute I tried to jump on. Missing a sailor's hand I fell back. I looked around in case the failure was spotted, but Rory had disappeared.

Nobody had noticed I was missing when I got back to the hostel and it was just as well because a letter arrived from Dado the following morning.

Dear Lily,

God and his blessed mother help us. Your sister has let everyone down. What did we do to deserve this disgrace? Your mother and I have talked it over and come up with a decent solution. You know Jack Murphy, Alf's tearaway son, is settling down and getting married. You remember he went to school with your cousin Larry; well now the couple are going to join him in New York.

I'm selling the butcher's stall to Alf for a song if he agrees to get his son and new wife to take Moyra's bastard to America.

Don't say a word about this to your Auntie Terry. The fewer people know the better.

Yours sincerely,

Dado.

Mamma hadn't told him yet about her plan to marry me off. It was just as well I hadn't left for London. The Betty Highsmith Singing Agency rang in my head like a summoning bell.

Chapter Forty-seven

The boat ticket stayed in my pocket for months after that. Sometimes I looked at it and laughed at my foolishness but often I took it out and held it fiercely, determined to live my dream on London's dangerous streets. Rory never mentioned going to Belfast again and there was no word from Moyra. I thought about Theo constantly. It didn't matter that the croppy boy was fighting with England — something my father gave out about so much — only that he'd put his life in danger and now, because of me, he was missing.

'*Twas down by the glenside I met an old woman, a plucking young nettles 'nor saw I was comin', She listened a while to the song I was singing, Glorio, glorio to the bauld Fenian men*,' I sang in the dormitory once because it reminded me of him and then repeated it for a week nearly driving Rita mad. The Glenside song was about an Irish rebel who was captured and shot and it was easy to transfer the scene to a bleak battlefield or torpedo-infested sea. If Theo was in a prisoner-of-war camp at least I'd know I hadn't driven him to his death. He'd be safe and I could knit him socks or write letters but there was no news at all and that was worse.

He came back to haunt me badly one sunny Dublin evening. It

was shortly after our last exam of the year and the dormitory was alive with excitement. I was replacing a button for Rita on a skirt she'd chosen to wear to a ceilí being held in the Aula Maxima for an end-of-year celebration and now she was hovering, ready to grab it out of my hand.

'It's hard to believe it's June already.' She put the skirt up to her with a whoop of delight and began to flit about. All around at least half of the girls in the room were getting ready to celebrate.

'No more study. We'll knock sparks out of the floor tonight,' Rita called gaily. Outside the city would still be warm after a day of unexpected heat, but Rita was right. I'm going to enjoy myself whatever happens, I thought and pushed aside the image of a pleading Theo.

A short time later I turned around to have a good view of my own dress and as I watched the sweeping hem, knocked the boat ticket off the locker. Rita changed her tune when she picked it up and saw what it was.

'You'll be using this to visit Connie next, I suppose,' she looked at me curiously. 'Your old pals won't be good enough for you when you're swanking around with your Ireland-mocking friends.' Before there was a chance to smooth things out, she left.

There was no time to talk to her before the dance but arriving at the Aula Maxima that evening the world brightened up. Rory had joined us at the corner of Leeson Street. He'd help me talk things over. But instead of waiting for Rita to catch up he grabbed a messenger-bike from a railing and despite my squeals of protest he heaved me into the commodious basket and we wobbled off.

'This is the way things should be Lily, without any complications. I've started to work in Walden's shop in South Frederick Street. Now that we're neighbours we can make an arrangement to go to the Irish Club together to talk about a singing date for you,' he called out, dipping dangerously. At the same time Rita joined a gang on the Hall steps and my plan to make it up with her was foiled.

A poster announced: 'The Delahunty Ceilí Band'. Sweet fiddling poured out the door and the bedlam inside the Aula Maxima made talk impossible after that. A heaving push of bodies carried me onto the dance floor, we formed dance lines and I looked around for Rory.

'The Siege of Ennis,' Peadar called out from the stage and a spotlight made his slicked down hair glisten. Music poured over us and floorboards started to resound, bringing us all into the swing.

'Dance with me!' Rory called from a retreating line until we got separated. Packed in tightly the orderly rows began to sift through the hall, weaving from top to bottom. A mood of happy release flew about, bodies swung in tight circles and we leaped and stepped between each other. Rory's line of dancers descending towards mine was bound to face me soon and in this easy mood he was going to be hard to be ordinary with. Sit out the first dance, I thought instinctively, because at that moment the college chaplain appeared. Any sort of kind look would make me confess to my betrayal of Moyra, but letting myself be danced towards the exit, Rita manoeuvred me back.

'Got to you at last,' a warm arm was slipped into mine. Rory had made his way through the packed lines. In a controlled spin beside him Rita's cheap skirt filled out. Rory's shoulder bumped mine and his lips brushed close but before a deep flush gave me away, Rita bumped him out of the way.

'When your dancing line gets up as far as the stage Peadar has told them you want to sing a song.' She took my arm. A kiss landed on my cheek and she swept on. It meant she'd made an effort to stay friends but before I could point out the priest she'd disappeared.

Led forward relentlessly after that, the stage approached. At least Rita was up there to get rid of nerves and I willed myself to swing. The best way to get on was from the side and, trying to resist their efforts, a wave of dancers unexpectedly lifted me up. Looking over the heads of the crowd, there was no priest. Soon I saw the commotion had drawn his attention because he'd been hidden beside the podium. A *bodhrán* beat a steady rhythm and fiddles struck up.

'How are you Lily? We haven't spoken for a while,' a lull in the music allowed the priest to come closer. 'We need to have a talk about your sister. She can't be found,' he bellowed. Everyone seemed to know about Moyra and I began to sweat. Dabbing his own forehead, the priest stepped onto the stage. 'Never mind the singing. I believe that scandalous girl, whose name doesn't deserve to be spoken, is leading you on with a different tune. We all know Moyra is a bad girl. Your parish priest has told me about it. She needs to go into a home and maybe you'll be going with her if you don't keep out of mischief,' his voice lowered. Hot breath on my face was like a blast from hell.

'I don't know what you mean Father,' I said. An arm was tugging me from the side. Rory had moved towards us, forcing the priest to break his grip. He would hear everything the priest had to say and ducking between bodies I slid towards a wall. The sun-swirl of a dancer's dress made me feel dizzy. Then I had reason to feel worse. Unable to tear my eyes away I saw that a picture of somebody who looked just like Moyra was pasted to the wall, as if to hammer home the message of the priest.

'Missing: Moyra O'Donoghue. Report any sighting to the chaplain's office', it read and her face smiled out defiantly.

Now I was staggering out of the Aula Maxima and a cold wind blew in the door. I stared into the darkness. There was no escaping from what Moyra had done. The mess she'd got herself into was becoming clear for all the world to see. She was dragging me in so deep there was no way out and I gulped air gratefully. Breathing more slowly a woman on the footpath had stopped to adjust her headscarf. Tall and elegant she swished the cotton square neatly. Something familiar about her made me peer out. It was Nurse Kennedy. The gaslight caused her eyes to glitter. Somebody called from the porch of the University Church next door. It was my sister's voice, you couldn't escape it and she was about to get caught.

'Go away, Moyra,' I called shakily.

'Did you tell Rory to come out for a bit of a court?' Rita was beside me and linked my arm, determined this time to stick close to her friend. She lifted her skirt to let air pass between her legs and I tried to signal about the priest behind. He was staring past her, though, to where my sister had spoken.

'*Goodbye Mike and goodbye Pat and goodbye Kate and Mary, the anchor's weighed and the gangway's up and I'm leavin' Tipperary. There's the steamer blazing up I can no longer stay, I'm bound for New York city boys, ten thousand miles away,*' I sang to put him off, a hue and cry until I felt his nose up against my neck, sniffing like one of Dado's foxhounds.

'I've made arrangements for Rita and yourself to delay your holidays for a few weeks to help clean the hostel,' Auntie Terry said the following morning. It was still early but we'd managed to struggle out of bed and Rita stifled a yawn.

'Don't. I want to leave for Ballyhale at once,' I said immediately, imagining my sister's demanding face. Moyra's sudden appearance had caused another dream about Theo that night. He'd been pulled from the waves by her but was lying prone on a lonesome shore calling out my name.

Struggling awake I fell out of the bed with a thump, pulling the boat ticket off the locker with me, like a reminder of his ship returning.

Chapter Forty-eight

The next morning it was hard to drive away thoughts of the dance.

'You belong with Anya,' I had started to say to Rory at the dance, after the priest disappeared. Shortly afterwards Anya did arrive and I had glowered and leaped about as if I hadn't meant a word of it.

There was no time for gadding about with Rory now, until I plucked up the courage to keep the chaplain off my back. But still the lesson wasn't sinking in because as I got up and splashed cold water on my tired face I remembered his missed kiss when our dancing lines came together and I saw my own grinning face looking back at me from the mirror. Then — as I was thinking of a few hints I could give to Rita so we could talk about it —Auntie Terry called up the stairs sweetly.

'It's good to hear you up, Lily. Yourself and Rita can get early mass and start the spring-cleaning this afternoon.' She called until somebody spoke to her and cut off her voice.

'Peader, come and see this sleepy head,' I was pulling at Rita at the same time. Auntie Terry might be looking after our morals but I could have told her that love was in the air too. Then I leaped on the sleepy-head, rolling her out of the bed.

Moyra didn't make her presence known again until later that week. She should know she was being watched and have some sense but instead she nearly gave me away. I'd been walking down O'Connell Street when she stepped out from Clerys doorway. Before there was a chance to ask her about the missing person poster she slipped a key into my hand.

'Number 31 Clonliffe Road,' she murmured and walked away. She needn't think she can boss me around. I called after her sharply. Shortly afterwards a couple coming from McDowell's Happy Ring House blocked my view of her entirely.

There was another reason to be careful. Archbishop McQuaid's palace was just around the corner from Clonliffe Road and there was a priests' seminary beside it. The minute I got back from my visit, Father Lonergan would arrive at the hostel, or worse the college chaplain, and read my face and guess everything. Moyra was lucky. Any sister under the pressure I was would let the other one stew in sin. Swishing a duster over already gleaming bed-ends I pushed the key out of sight and then my sister looked back at me from her picture on the locker and I had to grin back shaking my head at her - quite easily done.

It was possible to put off the visit for the next couple of days but then the memory of Moyra's face wouldn't go away and I decided to go to her on the hostel bike. It would allow for the chance to get the meeting over quickly and, singing to keep my spirits up, I dashed along city streets. As soon as I arrived she'd complain about how it had taken me so long and then she'd give me a list of things she wanted done. I had all these thoughts but I kept pedalling.

Clonliffe Road was long and narrow, almost disappearing out of sight. Concentrating on looking for her number, I had to jump off and walk. Once it was necessary to turn at what sounded like my name but I was distracted again by insistent waving from a girl on a garden path with a makeshift pram and a doll tucked round with rags. Partially obscured by a trailing clematis, Moyra's number was on the house beside her. It was one of a terrace of single-storey homes and, watched by the silent girl, I opened the garden gate.

At least my sister had picked somewhere pretty because already purple flowers were smothering the red-brick front. There was a sharp tap on a window and I saw her quickly withdrawn face. Moyra was determined to stay hidden. Well it was time to face the world and I lifted the key high for all to see. Remembering her picture on the locker and how much I missed her, I drew it down.

'The girl you're looking for is married to a soldier but he's never at home,' the child on the footpath piped up. She'd picked up her doll and stared at me curiously.

'Lily up to her old tricks again, letting the neighbours know everything,' I could hear Moyra saying and I nodded trying to look wise.

'I'll just knock and see if anyone is home. I'm from the Vincent De Paul making charitable visits in the area,' I lied and when the nosy child wasn't looking I put the key in a rusted lock and turned it sharply.

At first, only darkness lay behind the swinging door.

'Moyra, stop hiding, I saw you already,' I called softly, there was a warm hug ahead too, I was sure of it. My voice echoed in silence and then the gloom dissipated and luminous green eyes shone. Here was the beaming smile I loved so much but a harsh cough followed.

'You look wonderful, Lily. This is such a treat.' Moyra's rounded eyes drew back into the gloom again and I tried not to notice a stale smell.

'It's great to be here. You're looking well, Moyra,' I shook my head extending a hand to feel the way, touching a slimy wall. She'd introduced light at the end of a passageway and, as I moved forward, a stained carpet squelched under my feet. Wax polish lingered over a musty smell and I nearly fell, stepping down into a coal-hole for a kitchen.

This is in a worse state than the hallway, I decided, looking around as grey light filtering through a narrow window showed up the cheerless room. The only furniture was a rickety chair pushed sideways and a scrubbed table. Dado would get a sledgehammer to the place if he saw it and I tried not to stare at the threadbare curtains and concrete floor. Showing some brightness at last, a yellow laburnum flapped against the window outside.

We sat awkwardly. A watery concoction that was supposed to be tea was pressed into my hands and then Moyra began humming, her old self returning. Casting me sunny smiles she was talking non-stop as if I was about to disappear. She sped about, wiping some crumbs from the table and rattling a dead cooker with a poker to produce a spurt of enticing heat.

'This house is all I could get. Please don't tell anyone in Ballyhale where I am, Lily.' A direct gaze met mine at last. 'We have to talk about Theo. Missing in action doesn't mean he's dead. What do you think?' she smiled weakly. Tears came into her eyes. 'Andrew believes I'm married and as soon as Theo comes back I will be,' she grinned brightly. I sipped the tea loudly.

The poker had clattered from her hands as if she'd driven it too hard and black streaked her dress. She's burrowed into this hole like a rabbit to make it her own, I thought, and it will be impossible to get her out. Sooner or later she'll be dragged away helplessly. To drive the message home, outside poison laburnum flowers from the yellow tree tapped on the window.

'Father Tierney thinks Theo is dead,' I said. It was wrong to be so blunt because my hands began to shake and Moyra grabbed the cup before it spilled.

'We only have each other now and you can depend on me, Lily,' she said and my face grew still.

'Theo did the right thing by going to war and God will look after him. He can respect himself for his decision,' I said. 'You know he loves me instead of you,' I tried to add but those words wouldn't come out.

'Don't be upset. We should go for a walk to work things out,' Moyra extended a hand.

'Fairview Park is nearby. Anything is better than this mouldy house in the middle of a street of spies,' I exclaimed. She'd be congratulating me on being an aunt and telling me my duties next if we didn't go and I stood up.

'A heart-to-heart sounds lovely Lily. The main thing is we have to help each other to keep the baby. It's what Theo would like,' she smiled in a queenly way as if I couldn't possibly have an opinion and put on her coat with an effort. If she could push to get her way so could this sister. Theo had never wanted to marry her and I studied a button on my own coat and waited.

Chapter Forty-nine

Fairview Park had seemed vast to me from a tram one day on a visit with Rita to her relations in Howth, but reaching it now the green was just the right size for an intimate chat and I pushed my bike slowly to let Moyra go ahead.

Guarded by a line of trees from the road, dandelions grew in the verges. A freshening wind tossed the seeding heads and, because the rain had stopped and grey clouds had retreated we could walk at our ease. Stretches of green bloomed towards a distant sea and, like somebody in a dream and still remembering my sister's threat, my thoughts escaped to Rory. With a bit of luck he might have been the person who followed me and called my name on Clonliffe Road. A laugh and a song from him would take all this away.

Arriving at a kissing-gate Moyra slowed to a crawl, she swung through awkwardly, as if there was nothing the matter with her size and I parked the bike to give her time. Chestnut blossoms showered from overhead and nesting birds plucked at worms but she kept her head down. My lunch was in the bicycle basket. A picnic would take her mind off her plans and suddenly ravenous from the cycle I was ready to unwrap the sandwiches. I watched her slide onto a park bench and seize the arm rest as if in pain. By the time I reached her she was breathing normally.

'I have nobody to speak to, Lily, and everything is going round and round in my head. I'm sorry about bringing up Theo, really I am. At least I've managed to convince people I'm married,' she squinted up at a bird on a sprouting branch overhead with a contented sigh.

Look after Moyra for me, Theo had requested. What he didn't realise was that Moyra would use any excuse to tell me exactly how she thought it should be done. Sitting beside her with one of my books as a tray and ignoring her soulful eyes, I noticed her bump move imperceptibly. It was the future telling me not to betray it and I stared mesmerised. She should have thought of the consequences when she behaved like she did instead of dragging me into this. The only thing to do for the moment was smile and I concentrated on the oversized blossoms falling on the ground, sticky and plain.

'Nobody believes you're married,' I said and tried to hold her eyes.

'It wasn't meant to be this way you know, Lily.' Moyra dipped a hand into my bag daintily. She was ignoring my remark and removing a jam sandwich. She sniffed at it and started to eat. 'I suppose I've always lived in a bit of a cocoon. You know what it's like in Ballyhale. The main conversation is the price of tillage and cattle and who died and who was born. The war would need to be happening in the next parish for people to think about what it means. It's as if getting our independence from England was enough fighting. You've heard Dinnie say it often,' she grimaced.

'If you're going to keep the baby what will the world think?' I burst out. Somebody had to say it. I had romance to consider.

Recently I'd begun to imagine a honeymoon on board a ship. A mysterious stranger and I were bound for America. The air on deck at night was like ice.

'This baby is the best thing to happen to Theo ever. He's alive. I know it. Saying we're married is only a delaying tactic until he gets back and then everything will be put right,' she said stoutly. She picked up another sandwich but her hand had begun to shake. Soon her whole body was trembling. A gang of children ran into the park. They set up goalposts with their coats and kicked a ragged ball around.

Boy or girl? The words popped into my head like picture face cards.

'I'm sorry to bring all this trouble on you, Lily. None of it is your fault,' Moyra shrugged.

'Don't apologise. I know about life,' I said. I was sailing away on that ship of the unknown, perched like a hotel on navy waters. If it was too exposed on deck the stranger and I would go to the ballroom and dance the tango.

'It's getting cold here, we should go back.' Moyra stood up. Another attack of pain had made her cling onto the back of the bench and I walked to the kissing-gate. Drops of water from a rain drenched tree splashed onto my face and while I was wiping them off, Moyra passed me and crossed the road.

Glancing over, a forceful wind pinned back her clothes and the bump showed like a cushion. I'd left my satchel behind and as I turned to fetch it one of the boys in the park carried it in my direction. There was another urge to leave, to turn towards the sea like that fairy tale ship, but, retrieving my bike, a darker vision presented itself. Nurse Kennedy was rounding a street corner on the other side. Unable to shout a warning, the woman Connie said was a murderer had reached my sister. Pedalling madly towards them at last, she had Auntie Terry's baby photograph in her hand.

'Don't listen to her, she kills unborn babies,' I called out. My voice had a strangled sound but Moyra hadn't noticed. She was looking at the photograph and listening intently. Overhead a noisy plane nose-dived from the clouds, only righting itself at the last minute and emerging through the gate, the children extended their arms stiffly, miming wings and laughing and darting through traffic as if nothing was the matter. Unable to tear my gaze away, the nurse's hand rested on my sister's shoulder, taunting me until I pedalled away.

Avoiding Clonliffe Road and all that was said there, I headed home. When I reached the North Strand, the area where a bomb had dropped a year earlier, I gazed into the skies for signs of trouble. Now was the time to tackle Fidelma's mother, to find out more about the babies she cared for. The thought took over but as I turned towards Rutland Street the passing funeral of a child made me stop. A group of wailing women in black shawls carrying a small coffin emerged onto broken-down steps. Moyra's baby might die and there wouldn't be anything to work out. I shrank back and strained to keep the funeral in sight in case Nurse Kennedy appeared, before cycling reluctantly towards the hostel.

You let yourself be followed to where I live and now you'll have to take responsibility for Theo's baby. Say nothing to Auntie Terry until after your next visit, an abrupt note arrived in the door from Moyra shortly after.

Chapter Fifty

A few days later I was stretching to feel less cramped in the narrow lavatory beside the attic dormitory where I'd gone for some privacy. Another letter was hidden up my sleeve. My elbow disturbed a bundle of newspaper cuttings hanging on a string and I squirmed around on the hard seat to pick them up, it caused me to drop the letter. '*I've been a moonshiner for many's the year, I've spent all me money on whiskey and beer,*' an American drinking song had been on my mind and I hummed it, bending down. '*I'll go to some hollow and set up my still, and I'll give you a gallon for a two dollar bill.*' The song had a perfect chorus for two. If this was from the Irish Club accepting my application for an audition then I would have to contact Moyra straight away.

Opening the letter before anyone knocked on the door I saw that it was from Rory.

Lily, this is your lucky day because a HMV representative has been in the shop enquiring about family acts to make recordings and I mentioned you and your sister. Let me know as soon as you can when she turns up and I'll set up a date, the typed words had a matter-of-fact look.

The last sentence was underlined and I began to twirl the paper about. Rory was still thinking of my career. This was a much better chance than the Irish Club and I hugged the sheet. It would mean bringing my sister to him but he'd be so impressed by her singing he wouldn't even notice her small bump.

'Come out, Lily, I can see you. How about doing some cleaning instead of reading that letter?' Rita's cross voice carried into the cubicle.

'I don't know what you're talking about. As a matter of fact I was checking this place for acoustics,' I said airily. She was somebody else looking for information. Yesterday she'd said something about Moyra's poster on the wall of the Aula Maxima. Rory's note was a godsend and as if there couldn't be a better place in the world to sing than a girls' toilet I emerged, dipping the letter in the air.

'Read this. There's nothing the O'Donoghue sisters can't do once they put their minds to it.' I couldn't stop the grin on my face, as she snatched it away.

I'll go to some hollow in this country ten gallons of wash and I'll go on a spree. My song was back again. Our morning's work was over and Rita and I were in the basement for lunch and the words of 'The Moonshine' rose and fell pleasantly. As soon as she mentions the poster I'll mysteriously hint that my sister had put it up as a joke to find out if she'd pass as a singing star and see if she believes me, I thought. A sizzling sound of onions in butter came from the cooker and I had a sensation of Moyra in her poky room cooking a meal for one. A bird singing sweetly on an abandoned clothes line in the yard created a welcome distraction. Then the appetising smells drifting through the air pushed thoughts of Moyra away even further.

Jigging to my song over at the basement range, Rita cracked some eggs to fry. Instead of flipping them over though, her back stiffened and I saw her beckon madly.

'Come and look at this, Lily. It's twins,' her flushed face beamed as I sighed and sauntered across. A double yolk had fallen from a shell on the black pan and she tipped it up to try and separate it.

'Did you ever hear of a girl who had a baby and wasn't married?' I said shyly. It had come out despite myself but those odd-looking eggs would remind anyone of birth and Moyra hadn't gone away. It wouldn't be right to talk about her of course and I renewed my song shakily. Rita poked at the twin yellows with a knife. The raised tones of my aunt talking on the phone in the reception broke our silence and my heart beat uncomfortably. On the pan the double-egg sizzled merrily.

'Only a girl called Lizzie Dunne, a neighbour of mine who had a baby in a coal shed at the side of the house. Why do you ask?' Rita barely glanced up.

'I found our dog Bran with a litter of pups in the turf shed one day and nobody had guessed she was going to have them,' I gabbled. Something about a sister getting into similar trouble had been about to come out and my gaze slid away. She flicked out a hankie and dabbed her eyes.

'I know something is wrong with Moyra, but don't worry if you don't want to talk,' Rita said suddenly. She'd pushed the egg around on the pan making the yolks wobble against each other and I grabbed the cooker rail. This was going a step too far. Only a blabber-mouth would keep on at it.

'You're too close to the onions and it's making you cry,' I said brightly. 'My sister is expecting a baby. She's trying to keep it for herself and I'm supposed to help her. Sister Angelica and Father Tierney would prefer to have her in a County Home.' The words rushed out like a torrent.

'I thought so,' Rita said coolly, 'but even if she is in trouble, life can still go on. You showed me the letter from Rory. If you like I can go for the audition and pretend to be a forgotten stepsister. You've got me to do things like that before and it would give Moyra a laugh.'

'That's a terrible suggestion. Auntie Terry would be bound to find out and butt in. She's determined to make Moyra and me stick together one way or the other,' I said hotly.

Chapter Fifty-one

'Moonshine, dear moonshine oh how I love thee, you killed my poor father but dare you try me,' I projected my voice down to the wash hand basins on the back wall a few days later, putting a sense of yearning into the words that would draw an audience. It was Friday afternoon, about time for Rory to come around asking if I'd spoken to my sister and I began to flick at some holy pictures with my duster. As I made an instant decision and was on the point of leaving to go and tell Moyra I didn't want to have anything to do with her baby, I heard somebody sneaking up the stairs. It could only be Sister Angelica coming to poke her nose in about the spring-cleaning and I picked up a goose wing and began to swish it around.

A cobweb stood out over the window and I gave it an extra wallop. There was a shout from the street below. Peeping out the window I spied Billy, a friend of Sadie's who told me he'd joined the Voluntary Defence Force to protect the country from a German invasion. He was looking up and waving to get somebody's attention to be let inside.

'Close up that window, you'd find any excuse not to work,' Sister Angelica had glided in blocking the doorway and now she stood with legs apart at the end of my bed.

'It's only Billy, Sadie's friend looking for a bite to eat. He's back from patrol in Ringsend, thinking he'll keep the Germans away single-handedly. Hitler could come up and shake his hand and he wouldn't know him,' I grinned. That was what Sadie said when he visited before and she took me aside afterwards with a pleading look. 'Never tell anybody about what you saw when you came to our room or I'll lose my job,' her fingers pinched my arm painfully.

'Hold on Billy, I'll be down to let you in,' I called out the window.

'That's no way for a young lady to behave,' Sister Angelica raised her voice.

Down below a drunk had rounded the corner and draped himself around a lamp post. Adding to this sorry pantomime Billy was trying to prop him up but then he slipped. A man with a worn-out appearance crossed the road to help. He looked like a scarecrow and was probably coming to the hostel for food as well as Billy. I pushed my feet into my shoes.

'The dormitory is as dirty-looking as ever. It looks as if Father Tierney was right about your slovenly Protestant character.' Sister Angelica jutted out her elbows in an effort to block my way and I sidestepped nimbly.

'Come down quickly until you see this,' Rita called next from the room downstairs. She must have guessed something was up and before the nun could object I flew past her, whacking the door shut on her voice.

Beds in the first floor room were pushed to one side so that the floor could be scrubbed but Rita had lost interest in that. She was ignoring me and gazing out the window. A fly buzzed across in the cleared space between us and a finely decorated ceiling of doves and violins created a busy air. Outside the man who was drunk had stumbled and fallen on his way across the road. That wasn't what held Rita's attention though, because Auntie Terry had arrived on the spot and was now standing over him. For some reason she'd stepped from a taxi as if she'd been on a long trip but that wasn't the alarming thing. A rather becoming velvet hat covered her grey hair and when her coat swung open she was wearing my long white dress underneath. Rita gripped my arm and pointed.

'She looks ridiculous. It must be fancy dress,' I shrugged in disbelief. The only thing to do was make fun of the situation until I found out what was going on. Auntie Terry closed her coat quickly. Before there was a chance of another glimpse she looked up and we both had to draw back. She must have guessed someone was watching because she disappeared from view and soon there were voices downstairs. Sister Angelica had nabbed her and unless they were in cahoots, everything would all come out. Rushing out, I crouched at the top of the stairs to listen.

'Lily, I'd like you to come down for a cup of tea,' Auntie Terry called up as if she knew we were spying.

'*There's moonshine for Lisa and moonshine for May, moonshine for Lou and she'll sing all the day,*' I sang aloud to distract her. Suddenly it was all becoming clear. Auntie Terry had found out where Moyra lived and had gone there pretending to be me so that she'd let her in. Walking down the stairs as sedately as possible I strolled into the nuns' parlour, ready for a fight.

Inside the elegant room some books which Auntie Terry must have been reading, had been lifted from a chair onto the floor as though I'd been expected and the two holy sisters flitted about as if nothing was the matter. No tea was visible. After a while Auntie Terry stood at the mantelpiece and Sister Angelica took the window seat. The sound of Billy talking drifted in from the hallway. A candle flickered over my aunt's head and bunched lilac in a vase sent out a cheerful scent. Auntie Terry looked flushed as if she had just run a race but Sister Angelica was smiling primly. Covered by the coat, my dress which she wore was no longer visible. Auntie Terry tucked tendrils of hair into her neatly coiled bun. I noticed a wad of pound notes lay on the table. It was a considerable sum, impossible not to stare at and placed within easy reach like a temptation. I dragged my gaze away.

'Your sister needs to see you. She's agreed to go into a convent and have her baby,' Sister Angelica said suddenly. Her back was to the light, obscuring her face, and she hissed out air as if suddenly punctured. 'Your auntie and I have come to an agreement. The money you see is yours. Do what you like with it so long as you make sure she plays her part.' The nun bestowed a blessing on the notes furtively and pushed them in my direction. Here was another trap to weaken my sister's position further and I gripped the empty chair. As though the bargain was made Sister Angelica took some mints from her pocket and proffered them around. She sucked on one loudly.

'Moyra trusts me. I can't act unless she agrees with it,' I said shakily.

'Girls in trouble have no rights,' Auntie Terry said, 'you must advise her to do what Sister Angelica says.' She couldn't have meant it however because she shook her head at me, catching my eye and glaring.

There was no time to make any decision because another well known voice came in from the hall. Mamma had arrived to add to the confusion. It was an unexpected visit but she arrived in the nick of time to save me and I called out her name.

'I've come to take you home, Lily,' my mother rang out. She sailed into the parlour. Her arms were held out towards me as if it was where I really belonged. Nobody noticed that by then I'd already tipped the money into my curled-up apron and I smiled falsely.

Chapter Fifty-two

Autumn was in the air and I'd arrived back in Dublin scared out of my wits after my summer holidays. I'd fled from home. Mamma had her way and got me to Ballyhale all right and sometimes the weeks there were wonderful. Grass turned feathery in boreens, brambles flowered and deepened into purple. I tried to forget about Moyra and her predicament, singing and daydreaming in my look-out spots of old. In the meantime Mamma was working herself up to a different goal. She wanted me to stay at home. Things got really bad when she stepped on a rotten apple in the orchard one day and twisted an ankle. A week later, to save myself nursing her every daylight hour, I had to pretend Ned needed my help to save hay. Afterwards I was sorry for being so abrupt when I saw her staring at a photograph of Moyra and putting her head on her arms to cry. The following morning I went with Our Lady's Sodality from Ballyhaunis to climb Croagh Patrick as a way of making amends.

Disembarking from our coach at a wide path, the way upward sloped gently. A salty Atlantic smell swept over us and Clew Bay stretched beyond. Nearing the top, Clare Island and the sea beckoned like a fairy tale land outside loss and war. As we knelt on the rocky summit the rosary was chanted and all I felt was an ache in my legs and my cut knees. My mother had won; she could keep me in Ballyhale for as long as she wanted and I lay on the stones, gasping like Bran - wanting only a welcoming hug home and a hot meal.

There was still no word of Theo and I forced myself to remember him, as if it would keep him alive. But most of my time was spent on Nellie, visiting neighbours or galloping through fields. The money had stayed tucked away in the bottom of my trunk, in case it was needed to run away and a few weeks before I was due back to college it seemed the time was at hand when I found a note about my sister from Auntie Terry. Mamma had left it openly on a shelf behind the butter churn.

Moyra has moved into the Ellesmere Nursing Home in a place called Cadogan Street near The North Strand overlooking the Royal Canal, the note said and I pushed it further out of sight, mooching around to find Dinnie so I could learn a new song. The money might be another singing opportunity to help me escape my sister's predicament and I remembered Theo's fabled nightclubs in New York and heard a train in my head thundering across American plains.

As if she guessed what I was thinking, a letter arrived from Rita.

You might as well enjoy the rest of your holidays. Nobody is around. Rory is off to England very soon to look into the recording business for Anya's father. He told me to tell you he didn't know how long he'd be away. He held a party last night to celebrate. John McCormack was an unexpected guest. The first person asked to sing was Anya and she launched into one of your own songs copying your style.

Barely able to finish reading I threw the letter down. This was my last chance to avail myself of the audition Rory had talked about. One thing my friend couldn't guess though was that because of her information I would sneak away from Ballyhale. That evening, feeling very guilty, I bundled some clothes into a case.

The following morning I was still half in a dream when I got out of bed. The case bumped on the stairs, but nobody wakened. If I hurried I'd get a lift with the post-van and I could take the first train from Ballyhaunis. I stood at the back door and shivered. At the same time a gush of wind threatened to close it and I knew I couldn't stay.

Chapter Fifty-three

The peace and quiet of my summer rushed back to soothe me. It was just a few days after my return to the hostel. Mamma had written demanding I go home but Auntie Terry, keen to get me to help had quietened her down and I now continued to worry about Moyra. The sight of the hostel bike, leaning invitingly against the hostel railings one day eventually made me give in to the urge to go and see her. Better to get my sister on my side first before checking to see if Rory was still in Dublin, I decided, and telling Auntie Terry I was going to be at the university all day, I set out. I got to Summerhill in no time and as I was about to cycle on, a hymn arrived on the wind. It was one I had once been put out of St Patrick's choir for singing badly, 'Sweet Heart of Jesus, fount of love and mercy'. It was probably a procession and I shouldn't delay but the singing was infectious and I stopped to look.

There was barely time to pull over to the side of the road when a cherry red Sacred Heart appeared aloft flanked by men in lines with scapulas swinging on their chests. Behind the bearers a priest dipped a stick in holy water and sprinkled it on a growing crowd.

'Oh take my heart, so cold and so ungrateful,' I hummed and tried to press forward.

It occurred to me that Moyra would have a right laugh at me, dancing a bike to a hymn rhythm and I tried to imagine her, happy as Larry in her new home. I had another thought. This was the moment to go to Rory while he was in the shop and ask him about the audition. Imagine having to visit his flat otherwise and being greeted by smirking Anya. The idea made me turn the handlebars. Rita could be the second half as she suggested. Moyra would never agree to singing anyway, instead she would use it as an excuse to get what she wanted. With that I put my bike into reverse. At the same time a gap appeared like the parting of the Sea of Galilee. There was no choice but to move forward to my sister's side of the street.

Making my way quickly after that, the Ellesmere Nursing Home was one of a group of imposing redbrick buildings flanking the canal close to the Fairview end and, after I parked the bike out of sight, my body felt exposed and awkward peering through the front railings. I sidled up to the garden path and the front door swung open. Moyra was really in need of a visitor all right, because all at once her plump figure rushed out. I had a feeling of being crushed, overwhelmed in a hug and, before there was time to talk I was pulled in and dragged up stairs.

'Don't be so rough.' I had to strain away, gasping for breath. Down below in the hallway a head peered from a doorway and a woman with a sideways gait looked up. It didn't matter what she saw because suddenly I felt tired and I let myself flop onto a narrow bed in the room where my sister had brought me to and, putting my hands out, I grinned as if we'd never been apart, making her sit down.

It would be easy to forget I was supposed to get Moyra to leave for an audition because looking around, everything was much better than Clonliffe Road. The room had a neat appearance. Floorboards were bare and the bed hard but she'd cut out pictures of flowers and tacked them on the wall. A sense of peace was added too by sounds of ducks quacking outside. We swung hands and she put her finger on her lips and we bounced and pulled faces to make each other laugh.

'We're doing a singing trial. I've come to take you away from here,' I said solemnly.

'Leave your surprises for a minute until I get used to you being here. You look marvellous, Lily,' she said with admiration.

'If I was to put make-up on forever I'd never match the glow of your skin, show-off,' I said and she simpered. Glancing out her window for a look at her view, dark waters disappeared between reeds. I'd knocked against her vanity set upsetting their order on the dressing table and, as I was getting ready to tell her about the money and how we could use it to find Theo, she picked up her hairbrush.

'Some things don't change. That mop of yours is a right-looking mess,' she grinned and swished the brush through the air, brandishing it wildly. A blotched mirror was so spotted you could hardly see yourself but she pinned my black curls up in an expert twist.

'Let's get out of here, Moyra, and we'll be together again. You can get somebody to take the baby after it's born and everything will be back to normal.' My voice had a hysterical note and I gripped the brush handle for better effect. We were both in the same mind because her face darkened.

'Over the hills and far away, is that it, Lily? We could go to the Betty Highsmith Singing Agency you've always talked about,' she smiled and let my hair tumble down. 'It's strange in a way. You were the one Theo always liked and now look at me.' This time she pressed her hands over the front of her dress and lowered her gaze. Beads of sweat appeared on her forehead. 'Help me to bring up his child, Lily. I know I shouldn't think like this, but I can't help it.' Her lips puckered as if all she had to do was pout to get her way.

'That's what I'm trying to say now.' I grimaced, appalled at my own words. Rory would still be in his shop if I left but it was hard to tear my gaze from that trembling mouth. About to retract, voices sounded outside and a heated argument flew about. It was only a flash of movement to duck under the bed because the door had opened. Too late, Nurse Kennedy stepped inside. Moyra had kept me here too long and the sneak from downstairs had called her to investigate. A hand was reaching for my bag on the bedside locker and I swung up.

'We need to talk, Lily. Moyra will sing with you if you pass your money to me. I'm the one Sister Terry meant it for.' The nurse grasped the bag. Close-up her gaze looked soft and caring.

'To do the same to her as happened to Sadie, is that it?' I shouted and my fingers closed in a desperate grip. With a heave, it was done and I bolted.

Cycling madly to the hostel, I blurted out the terrible event to Auntie Terry some time later.

'How careless can you get about your sister's happiness? Now the child will disappear in America,' Auntie Terry exclaimed.

'If Nurse Kennedy caused Rosie Ryan's death she won't stop short at murdering Moyra's baby,' I said bleakly.

Chapter Fifty-four

'Behold the working man,' Rory announced and I turned around sharply. It was a few days after my visit to Moyra, I was about to go to her again to explain about Nurse Kennedy, even if it meant I was stuck with doing what she wanted. I stared at him blankly. Just when I'd stopped thinking about him, here I was bumping into him on his way to lunch hour and I stood undecided. A dog on the street came to sniff at my feet and shoppers swept past. Now there was no need to worry about going to his shop and I blinked. There was no point in pretending I'd forgotten about the note.

A line of nuns pushed us closer. Rory doffed his hat with a flourish and put on a comical air, waving a parcel with a string in his hand to and fro.

'If mademoiselle would care for a morning coffee I can drop this into my flat and then we could try the saddle-room in the Shelbourne?' He bowed slightly as if he was in the habit of asking me out every day of the week and put on a pretend snooty expression.

'Miss Hourigan expects us to study every spare minute of the day,' I said and peered past him. As if about to go, Nurse Kennedy had come into my mind too. These days it seemed to me that I saw her at every corner.

'*There was a young maiden and her story was sad. For once she was courted by a brave sailor lad. He courted her truly by night and by day, but now he has left her and gone far away,*' Rory's whistling filled the air and good manners required I should hum. He had picked on one of my tunes, probably the song Anya had sung at the party but I wouldn't say anything about that in case he'd wonder what I knew. Moyra can wait to hear about the danger she's in. She's only getting me into deeper trouble anyhow, I thought moodily, and I stepped up to Rory and took his arm.

Some time later an American-sounding voice called from the street just before Rory put the key in his door. It made me think of Andrew and that I should be at the university writing to him to hear if there was any news about Theo but, inside a calming silence made me perk up. I had been tired for days. It was caused by rising at dawn to prevent another conversation with Auntie Terry about the money until I could decide what to do and now I yawned and stretched. '*If I were a blackbird, I'd whistle and sing,*' I hummed. Worse than that, glancing over at it, the possibility of a nap on Rory's bed was calling tantalisingly.

I noticed immediately that since the last occasion I had been here the narrow bed had been pushed against the wall to fit in a newly-acquired ancient piano. There was a gleaming gramophone too and I edged over. Already a pile of records was stacked up. The Harlem Dixie Band the top label declared. About to lift it carefully to read, Rory nodded and grinned. I would have asked him to play it, anything to forget where I was supposed to be, but a painted face materialised at the window outside. It was only a passer-by, but I jumped. This woman could have been sent after me. The business of Nurse Kennedy was beginning to unnerve me and I turned from the sight abruptly.

'Hold the back of the chair please, Lily, I want to try this light before we leave.' Unaware of the snoop, Rory had taken the string off his parcel and positioned the only chair in the room under a dangling flex in the ceiling. Opening the parcel a gleaming bubble nestled in shredded newspaper. 'The wonder of the modern world,' he said brandishing a light bulb aloft. 'You look very pale, is everything all right, Lily?' he said looking concerned.

'We'll need to stay for a while to make sure it stays working,' I pretended to smother a yawn, drawing further away from the window. Now it looked as if I wouldn't be able to go to meet Moyra anyway because my face seemed different. It had a rubbery feeling, like something steeped in suds and I rubbed it hard. Standing on the chair to insert the bulb, Rory swooped down and pecked me on the lips. It was a wrong-way-around kiss and his chin got in the way.

'Thank you for your help, Lily,' he said.

'All we did was go for a walk,' I blushed. Despite myself, my legs were acting up as well as my face and I stood stiffly.

'You didn't have to come here after the foolish way I've sometimes behaved,' Rory said and added to the upside-down kiss with another one. The look of his closed lids was smooth as a baby's and leaping from the chair he was suddenly beside me. Two bright spots on his cheeks glowed and a puff of heat came from his chest. He raised shy eyes and this time those lips lingered. Really I should write to Andrew to ask him to save another sister from compromising herself instead of pestering him about Theo's whereabouts, because my arms with a will of their own were about to cling to the man in front of me and I jerked backwards falling on the bed.

'You're beautiful, do you know that, Lily?' Rory smiled shyly.

'I love you, Theo,' I whispered inside. It was a desperate measure to make me keep my head but tiredness was overwhelming. Above me, sea-green eyes shone and a nearby church bell boomed continuously.

'It must be a funeral mass in The University Church. I should be there,' my voice shrilled. A rackety noise like a car engine and then a brief explosion from upstairs provided a better distraction and I gripped the counterpane thankfully.

'Don't mind the noise. It's only medical students making *poitín*. We should go and have a sup,' Rory laughed. Rising from the bed though, I fell backwards.

My blouse had opened and there was a flash of the lace underwear I'd borrowed from Annie. A Knock medal glinted, put on in the hostel at the last minute.

'Marry me,' Rory said.

'It's too late. I'm promised to someone else,' I said. I had to because the painted woman was back, peering at herself in the window's reflection to dab on lipstick but really peeping in this time.

'Whatever you say won't stop me loving you, Lily,' Rory said. He might be the one to spring me from the Magdalene convent. When the funeral mass was over, the University Chaplain passed the flat's exposed window.

Chapter Fifty-five

I told Rory I really had to study and stepping out of his flat before he could stop me, I stared across at the entrance to St Stephen's Green, determined to get as far away as possible. My skin began to prickle and my knees shook. That painted woman was really sent by Nurse Kennedy, I thought, the nuns' money is proving to be my undoing, and then I stopped. She could still be watching. When I least expected it she'd tap me on the shoulder.

I paused at the railings of St Vincent's Hospital thinking vaguely about getting something to help me sleep for a week. Briefly my eyes closed and I saw heaving waves. Theo should have fought on land, at least then I wouldn't be going around the place seeing the sea every time I blinked.

Nobody had told me the effect a missing person would have. Andrew could be down here organising a search party for him, instead of helping me. He was probably with Auntie Terry right now. I'd have to wear an armband to let his people know I was on the lookout and when Theo was found we'd all stick our hands in the air as a victory sign. Laughing at my own foolishness urged me to move. The need to keep Theo in the forefront of my mind was going too far when I found myself pushing away thoughts of Rory's kisses. Even if I couldn't allow myself to dwell on the way he liked me I should be pleased at the thought of the conquest, I sighed.

Swinging my arms as if on parade got me as far as O'Connell Street and the next time it was necessary to clutch onto something was outside the Happy Ring House when, not watching the way ahead, a sandwich board on the footpath nearly tripped me up. In the window a photograph of newlyweds provided a setting for a display of rings. The girl was dipping backwards and her face had a heavenly look. Doldrums must have hit the street as though an invisible wave of water was rising and circling overhead. I clutched my arms. Rita would have a right laugh at all this. She'd stick her tongue out at the bride and start a silly swoon. If Connie was here she'd put on a serious expression and take my arm and bring me for a cup of tea and say, 'look after yourself!'

Journeying on, my lips felt swollen, too big for my face. As I held my breath there was a lingering feeling of warmth from when Rory had bent close. Up ahead a child was begging and I dropped a penny in her cupped hands. This was the kind of starving mite Moyra's baby would become, or maybe worse if Nurse Kennedy had a darker purpose. My mother needed a good talking to as well as Dado, but they were such snobs they wouldn't listen to anyone and Father Tierney only cared about immoral behaviour.

I should have been sighing because of all that was against me but instead a light-hearted feeling came over me as I thought of Rory and, of course, a song wouldn't stay down. '*Mellow the moonlight to shine is beginning, close by the window young Eileen is singing*,' I hummed.

'The Spinning Wheel' was new, picked up from a tinker ballad-sheet seller on Henry Street. I'd also joined the National Library in search of catchy airs and found an Italian version of the same tune, as a Neapolitan folk song.

The pain in my chest began to ease as I rested for a moment in a doorway opposite the Rotunda Maternity Hospital. A crowd of boys wearing Belvedere College blazers galloped past. Traffic halted and an ambulance bell clanged. I watched as it ground to a halt in front of the hospital gates and a woman was lifted from the back of the van. The baby in her arms wailed and a gaping crowd rushed forward. This would be Moyra if she was taken bad in the nursing home. I'd have to step into the breach and tell them I'd look after the baby until she got better. '*Close by the window young Eileen is singing, Bent o'er the fire her blind grandmother spinning*'; starting to sing again, the words dried up.

It looked as if the weather was on Moyra's side, pushing me towards her because squalling rain began to fall. Bracing myself against it was no use. Using a tram sign to straighten up, I started to quiver like a leaf. 'All aboard for Howth,' a conductor called, jumping off and swinging me onto the platform. There was no time now to disembark. I was on my way to Cadogan Street.

There were beads of rain on the gate of the nursing home and a bay window downstairs was fogged as I plunged my hand into the bag to make sure the money was still there. One good thing, since getting on the tram my head had cleared, in fact everything around was so vivid I might have had magnified vision. I'd be able to talk to her honestly about getting away. Moyra would love 'The Spinning Wheel' too, I decided.

'Tell them you're married,' I murmured under my breath. It might be enough to get us out of the place and I imagined her packing her case and the two of us strolling by the canal as if we hadn't a care in the world. When we got to London and the child was born it could be left outside the London War Office with a tag that said *c/o Theo Hynes*, the saving thought made me grin. This was her last chance to have a life of her own and I strolled up the garden path of the Ellesmere Nursing Home.

The front door was on the latch as before and I stepped into the hall. A stale smell of cooked cabbage lingered, mixed with newly-quenched candles. Somebody had just come in because an umbrella shone with rain on a stand. Voices came from a partly opened door and about to slip upstairs I froze. Familiar tones reached out.

'She can't keep the baby. It's out of the question,' my father's voice was followed by a sob.

'The girl will be excommunicated. She's flaunted the law of the church and now she wants to show off the results to the world. Sister Angelica tells me Lily's virtue is under threat too. She thinks the girl is a danger to herself and should be locked up. Speak to her before it's too late,' Father Tierney murmured.

'Nurse Kennedy will look after the child for a fee,' Mamma began but my father interrupted.

'Andrew and I have our own arrangement. America is not far away enough for the little bastard.'

Moyra needed to be told all this. I began to back away.

'Hail Mary full of Grace, the Lord is with thee. Blessed are

thou amongst women. And blessed is the fruit of thy womb, Jesus,'
Father Tierney's prayer reached faintly as I bolted into Moyra's room.
He'd produce a consent form for a nun's novitiate for me, as soon as
the rosary was over.

'Hurry up, we have to get out of here,' I called, loud enough to
waken a bishop and rushed to the window to jump down.

Chapter Fifty-six

Only a miracle will bring Theo back now, I thought miserably, as I jumped from the nursing home window and peered back. There had been voices in the corridor behind me, but now squinting upwards only closed shutters met my gaze.

'I'll be back. Get ready,' I mouthed as if to my sister looking down for help.

I could only hobble away, beginning to nurse a sore ankle. I crossed over to Amiens Street at the Five Lamps where a policeman was holding up the traffic. A loose horse had escaped and was skittering about in the centre of the road, darting this way and that, trying to find a way out. The policeman approached and the horse jerked its head back and kicked out behind making onlookers exclaim and scatter. A brown-faced man finally managed to sneak up and slide a halter over its neck and draw it away.

The thought this gave me of escaping by riding off on Nellie made me smile. Tomorrow I'd sneak into the nursing home and my sister and I would run away together. She'd get out by lying and saying she was going to get married and we'd flee to London. As soon as the baby was born we'd play with it for a while and I'd listen to her accounts of the painful birth and let her go on about how like Theo the baby is. Then I'd tell her she'd have to give it up for a short time. At that stage the miracle would have happened, Theo would be back and they'd get married in a secret ceremony. In a short while we'd be able to sing together. I clutched my bag tighter and let uncertain pleasure bubble up.

Reaching O'Connell Street my feet turned towards the university. It was a way of avoiding Auntie Terry and Connie might have a break from work. We could have a chat about how the war was affecting Matt in London and her planned visit and I'd announce my sister and I were going over.

'*There are three lovely lassies in Bannion, Bannion, Bannion, there are three lovely lassies in Bannion and I am the best of them all,*' the light-hearted air tripped out. It was necessary to push away the returning numbness that had gripped me and I breathed deeply. Maybe this time it was different, caused by that jump from Moyra's window and, as if to prove it, a woman walking ahead let a key drop on the street and I was instantly distracted. She hurried through the gates of Trinity College with a bag swinging open and not hearing my call, I started to run. The dead feeling in my chest was replaced by trembling legs from the spurt of action but then she passed through an archway and disappeared.

I followed, dark surged about in the deep recess and green glimmered beyond an exit opposite. All along the walls there were glass cases displaying information for students. 'The Harlem Dixies. Lunch time concert in aid of war widows', my heart skipped a beat at the notice. They were the darkie singers on the record in Rory's flat.

'Volunteers needed to help at door', a smaller line of writing declared.

Here was another chance to help Moyra leave. The miracle had happened and I began to rock with growing excitement. Any American who read the notice would come along to see the singers and I'd manage to get on the stage and make the announcement about a missing sailor. If that didn't find him there and then it soon would because the word would be out. Students came from all over the world to Trinity. The plea was bound to get to him, even if he was lying low, thinking of coming back to me when the war was over.

My hands clapped by themselves. A pain in my side distracted my thoughts and students crowding the passageway forced me against the wall. Catholics weren't even allowed inside the gates of Trinity College and here I was, larger than life, planning to go on stage. Suddenly a prickly fear surged up in me. When I looked at it differently, once word went out about my singing at a Protestant university it would be the end of any chance of a light-hearted student life.

I moved into some shadows in case I was being followed and a playful sun warmed cobblestones ahead and, behind, an indifferent city clattered and cranked. A priest peered in the archway. Soon he was reading the notice and taking details down on the back of an envelope, pretending his only interest could be a pagan Dixie Band and I retreated further, looking for refuge in this heathen stronghold.

Chapter Fifty-seven

It was a few days later and the morning of the concert had arrived. Sudden thoughts rushed into my head as I leapt out of bed.

'I can't do it. I'll never see a face I know again. I'll be enrolled in the county home in Ballyhaunis tomorrow.' A clock chimed nine faintly and I sat back on the dormitory bed. Stale air wafted about in the room and I readied to talk myself out of it with Rita. Her laugh came from the first floor landing and there was a hum of voices. Grabbing a dressing gown I chased down after her.

'Here comes the dark horse. Nobody knows what you're up to these days, Lily. Any chance of a chat or would that be a miracle?' Rita said too loudly. She was lolling against the window in the middle room when I arrived and then put a finger to her lips like a warning sign and shook her head. A curtain sectioned off one of the beds in a corner of the big room and she jiggled her body and pointed over.

'Sister Terry slept here last night to stop girls sneaking out to dances,' she whispered and called out again, 'wait for me, Annie,' and waltzed away. The curtain twitched. If Auntie Terry was praying all night for girls with impure thoughts Moyra would be looked after by her instead of needing my help. As I started to follow Rita, a hand emerged.

Unable to tear my eyes away now a foot had followed. It was Auntie Terry all right and she murmured and stretched.

'There you are, Lily,' she paused and frowned as if we were being overheard. 'I'm so glad you made proper use of that money,' she said loudly and without waiting for a reply, dashed back to her enclosed space. Next to appear was that bundle of loosely gathered stolen letters from the past, crumpled as if they'd been slept on all night, with my photograph as a baby on top. Coming close she pecked my cheek, brought the photograph close to her chest and whispered; 'Say a prayer, dear. I had a message during the night. Moyra has started. Thanks to you giving the money to Nurse Kennedy, everything will be all right.' Two spots of red appeared on her cheeks like she was someone in sudden pain and she patted her front and grimaced.

'It hasn't anything to do with me,' I said coolly but my heart gave a thump. She hadn't listened to me when I told her about the nurse. I could follow her example and abandon Moyra to her fate too. God couldn't stop his miracle now though, especially when all the O'Donoghue sisters wanted to do was sing; '*There are three lovely lassies in Bannion and I am the best of them all,*' I hummed shakily.

'Nothing will have changed with Moyra after this. She cares about her sister first off,' I said calmly.

'Stay close at hand, Lily. You might be needed,' Auntie Terry added sweetly, as if she hadn't heard, and then she plodded off.

'The Three Lovely Lassies' stayed in my head, lasting all the way to Nelson's Pillar. That missing person announcement would have to be made, I thought. I was now panting and moving so fast I had to grab onto a gaslight standard. Pain lodged deep in my tummy and I paused again at the Happy Ring House. The picture of the happy bride had been replaced by a couple with a baby. Breaking into a trot it felt as if a high tide out in Dublin Bay had spilled into the street because my feet were cold as if moving through water.

'This is all about you. Marry Theo, even he has to come back from the dead,' I groaned to get myself to stop but ahead the green verges of Trinity College rocked gently.

Chapter Fifty-eight

In the archway of Trinity College there was no sign of the priest who'd taken down the information about the Dixie Concert. He was probably waiting in a doorway to pounce but I walked through boldly. Arrows indicated an imposing entrance to the concert location but inside the space was pokey. Black drapes made the lobby look more like an entrance to the underworld and disembodied voices could be heard. Somebody had tacked up sprays of pine over a doorway to create a more pleasant effect, but it only served to deepen the gloom. A gent with a dickey bow barely glanced up from a ticket desk.

'If you're here to volunteer it's too late,' he grimaced and returned to study a list of names. It was just the excuse I needed to give up. Moyra could get Theo back by herself and I gripped the edge of his desk.

'That's your worry. Here's the one who came,' my voice said coolly. Standing awkwardly, my back began to ache. You'd think I was the one having the baby and I snapped upright. 'Just as well for you I know a war widow who needs help,' I announced and my knees wobbled.

'Let her through. She's the best singer in the world and I'm putting her with me on the programme,' another voice interrupted. I should have known Rory would want to see his band and now he'd pulled the entrance curtain aside. The county home here I come, I thought, and followed his disappearing figure like a prisoner in chains.

It was unusual to see a spotlight creating a circle on a tiny stage and I should have realised Anya would be here, decked out in one of her figure-revealing dresses. You'd think she was the Queen of Sheba floating around and pretending not to see me and then she kissed me on the cheek.

'Delighted to see you, Lily, you're a brave girl to sing in the chambers of hell,' she said gaily. It was the last straw but, as I attempted to ease past her and leave, she blocked the exit as if really she was glad I was there.

A poster of De Valera on an ass and sitting backwards - supposed to represent neutrality - drifted before my eyes on a backstage wall when Anya had disappeared to put on make-up, a short while later. Another picture showed the same Dev dressed like a Roman emperor lording it over his subjects. 'We want free speech and a free press', a wit had scrawled underneath. They might believe in freedom of speech here but real life was different and if the priest who'd stepped in to look at the poster in the Trinity gates arrived, I was done for. He could be out there at this moment, skulking behind an empty seat. A drawn curtain lured me forward.

As I was looking about to see if it would be possible to leave at the back of the hall, a storage door leading under the stage materialised.

It would be a good bolt-hole but, as I fumbled at the lock, Rory called out. 'The programme will be starting soon. We've been picked to go first, Lily,' he grinned and linked my arm. Maybe somebody in the audience will put the priest out if he starts his shenanigans, I thought, and I blinked back cheekily.

'Douse the spotlight, we don't want her to be seen yet,' a solitary voice sounded. It was all too late and I'd been pushed onto the stage. Despite the glare some American soldiers lounging in the front row stood out. Worse than that, my instincts were right, because a priest had plonked himself beside them. The hall began to fill as the buck from the ticket desk pranced onstage.

'Welcome Ladies and Gentlemen to this special Trinity College fundraising event for the war effort.' His big teeth created a false grin and he tittered and leaped about as silence descended. 'There has been a lot of talk recently about the Gaelic Revival and "the bog Irish" in us, as it were, and what Mr Yeats calls our Celtic Inheritance,' in a second the show-off went on. He caught hold of my arm and raised it up.

'Pigs in the parlour,' a thin voice at the back squeaked and there was a spurt of laughter to egg him on. My eyes began to dart about seeking a last minute reprieve. Any minute now the priest would make his move.

'From the bogs of Mayo, slumbering under the thraldom of the *Tuatha Dé Danann*, where comely maidens get up to all kinds of high-jinks at the crossroads, I'd like to present Lily O'Donoghue. With a good Catholic name like that we all know whose side she's on, so give her a rousing welcome!'

Thoughts of the storage area under the stage thundered inside as a distinct possibility but as I looked behind I saw Anya was going through the motions of clapping.

'*Dia is Mhuire dhuit. Tá athás orm beith anseo,*' I stammered and tried to step off the platform onto a front seat.

'You show them girl,' an American voice drawled. It was the smell from a pine cutting wafting onto the stage that proved to be my undoing, I realised afterwards. I was back in Ballyhale and Dinnie might as well be here. I could see him tipping a cap in greeting in the back row. Rory's piano was placed directly under a side light, his hair shone like coppery leaves to lure me on and a few notes dangled in the air. Now a slow handclap travelled up.

'*There are three lovely lassies in Bannion, and I am the best of them all,*' Rory started to croon. He was the biggest *oinseach* of all. Anya would be having a go next to show off and reluctantly my shoulders went back.

'*Oh me father has forty white shillings, shillings, shillings, me father has forty white shillings, and the price of a goat and a cow,*' the words of a marriage promise of a dowry for a farmer's daughter were pouring out despite myself and the priest in front stood to clap.

That deceiver in black would be up on the stage before the last word was out but still I belted on. Barely visible from my standpoint, a commotion had started in a dim recess. Another promise of escape I thought and began to perspire faintly. I could get off the stage, drag an American with me and then run to Moyra bursting to tell her about the money and the possiblility of success in London. It was all part of the miracle. My voice soared. Instead of deliverance, disaster struck. I'd been nabbed. From the middle of the audience, my father was leaping towards his so-called fallen daughter.

Dado raised a stick in the air as if he was bringing in cows. Mamma followed in his wake and then Father Tierney appeared. A fierce pain, not the phantom one when I thought of Theo's moon-painted face, pierced my side.

'I'm sick, Rory.' My legs buckled next and Rory extended his arms. The audience clapped. Somebody whistled. As if it wasn't bad enough being on a Protestant stage I found myself in a lover's clinch.

'Get out of here unless you want eternal damnation.' I struggled but he cut the words short, pressing his mouth to mine as the cheering grew.

Chapter Fifty-nine

It's too late to change things. Moyra's baby can go to America or we'll both be sentenced to lives of chastity, I thought dimly. I struggled from Rory's arms but the cheering got louder and he took me back in them. My parents must be close to the stage and for a minute I snuggled close, not wanting to see.

'Rescue us before we all perish Theo,' I groaned. The unfortunate musketeer beside me coughed harshly but stayed. As soon as the 'bauld' Theo made himself known of course he'd tell me how much he appreciated what I'd done for Moyra. Saying he was only a lost soul dipping up and down on sea waves would show more honesty, I thought, and the room began to jump.

Below us there was a clattering noise as my parents got entangled in some chairs. If Anya came on stage and attacked Rory for holding me so nice and close I could take the chance to slip away. I looked around hopefully.

'You're a disgrace to the family; somebody who had the best of everything!' my father was shouting above the din and the crowd booed. Now that they were on my side, with a bit of luck, he'd start to storm about and make matters worse for himself. Mamma had such a love of the stage she'd be too busy taking everything in to be of any assistance but Father Tierney would make up for her by calling my name and bringing attention to himself, as if he was on the pulpit in Ballyhale making an example of a sinner. The noise of cheering grew and Rory nibbled my ear.

'Your singing was wonderful, Lily,' he murmured.

'It's all thanks to a miracle,' I said confused because my toes were lifting, with weakness or the heady embrace, I didn't know which, and I lowered my head. With a bound the Dixie group came on. I could blacken my face and be one of them. I'd mime the numbers I didn't know and when they left I'd go as well. The thought cheered as I watched them spread out, but Rory's chin was stuck to mine and wouldn't let me.

'Kiss, kiss,' a slow chant started in the audience. There was a flash and a crackling sound and descending darkness stilled both of us. Rory nearly knocked me down in some sort of struggle and then his arms let go. Beyond this bedlam, outside heedless sunshine was pouring down and people were chatting I knew, but, lifted up I was pushed to a side wall.

'You can't hide forever, Lily O'Donoghue,' a new voice hissed. The paradise world slipped away. There was a choking sensation and Father Tierney's tobacco smell clogged the air. Only a desperate effort could save the situation and I dived towards the concert entrance.

'Rory where are you?' I looked back breathlessly. Welcome fresh air spilled over me but nobody had followed. Leaves rustled on a tree tinged with autumn and the calm sound of a voice on a telephone came from a nearby office. Propelling myself into a sun trap beside the door of the hall it seemed every minute Rory would appear. Even if the lights had blown they must have decided to go on with the concert and, as if to confirm it, a loud burst of singing wafted out into my passageway.

'That silly girl tripped on some wires and pulled them loose. Serves me right for letting her appear.' The smart-alec Master of Ceremonies was outside. Taking a peep I saw he'd been talking to himself, and was leaning against a wall with a cigarette stuck in his gob. Through an office window in my secluded space an elderly lady caught my eye. Her brow furrowed and she flicked her head as if to draw me in.

'She's a disaster, I scrimp and scrape to give her a university education and she sings songs on stage like a corner boy,' the voice of the college buck was replaced by Dado's. My father had come for me and Father Tierney must be with him because another low voice growled and my palms grew clammy.

'Hello Father. I can't believe you're here. It's amazing the different people you can meet in Dublin,' I gabbled a speech inside and practised a smile. The real solution would be if an American came and we could make a run for it and it looked as if it was about to happen. A stocky sailor with cropped hair appeared at my hiding place. He peered in.

'You have to get in touch with Theo Hynes and tell him it's time to come back. Take a taxi to the Ellesmere Nursing Home on Cadogan Street off the North Strand at twelve o'clock tonight and don't tell anyone. Bring a box big enough to fit a baby in,' the words came out like a dream. The next person to turn to was the lady in the office, who was now opening her door and crooking a finger at me.

'Is everything ok, can I get a doctor?' the soldier enquired but I'd fallen inside.

She'll keep me talking and then my parents will walk in, I thought, but the office lady was bestowing a lingering look on me as if I was an emergency case. Dropping onto one of the seats, too tired to care if I'd been seen, she made me lie on a sofa. If they didn't barge in here the next place everyone from Ballyhale would go to was the hostel and I started twisting to get up. It seemed essential to get to the library. I had remembered Connie talking about rows of library books in dusty back rooms where you could get lost for a month. It might also be a good move to hide in the Pro-Cathedral. Devotions might be on, to keep the saints on my side.

'You're praying so much you'll get squinty-eyed from staring up to the sky.' I could hear Rita's laugh. It was the kind of fun a girl needed.

Chapter Sixty

I'd got out of the office by saying I'd visit a doctor and for the rest of that day a sense of being in a dream took over. Instead of hiding I went around in a daze. By the time darkness fell I hadn't eaten for hours. Even if it meant abandoning my plans to see Moyra, it was necessary to go back to the hostel. But first I found myself standing at the Pro-Cathedral. Trying to think clearly I wandered in. As well as my hunger, tiredness was hitting home. The residual heat from a large congregation I'd seen leaving after a men's confraternity caused me to yawn. Moonlight penetrated stained-glass windows and, now aching from stiffness I stretched out willing myself to sleep, as if I was in Ballyhale, or a babe in her sister's arms.

When I woke up an image of Mary in a dimly lit oil painting fleeing to Jerusalem to have her baby caught my eye. There had been a loud noise and, only half awake, I shook my head. A crashing sound resounded from the back of the church.

'The spirit of Theo revisiting his love,' I imagined Rita saying with a laugh and she might be right because the dim interior became forbidding as real footsteps were approaching up the centre aisle.

'This way Edwina,' my father's voice boomed in the stillness.

Taking a quick glance back I saw Father Tierney prowling beside him. He must have stuck his head in and decided to pray and, keeping in line, Mamma brought up the rear. She slipped into a pew near mine and bent her head. Any escapade with Moyra was as good as over if they saw me. I froze and my teeth began to chatter.

Turning around an oil lamp created an aura bright enough to light up Mamma. It would bring me into its glow too. Please God let my tummy shut up, I pleaded. It had begun to grumble like a volcano and I rubbed it roughly. Maybe I should speak up about it being a mistake to sing in Trinity but my lips stayed shut.

In front touches of gold on a statue of the Virgin Mary lured me forward irresistibly. It was having the same effect on Mamma because she groaned helplessly.

'We'll do the Stations of the Cross for a safe delivery,' she said aloud. The stations started on the wall to my left and I slid down on the seat. She was now lighting a candle at a minor altar and I took the chance to slip sideways, edging my shoulders back.

She'll keep me by her side forever. That had been my thought leaving Ballyhale and the feeling of being captive wouldn't leave. I had noticed her frail look when she bowed her head. If Theo could really be a ghost instead of pretending to be alive all this could come to an end and I wouldn't have to be sneaking out of a church while the rest of the family prayed. *Oh Mary we crown thee with blossoms today, queen of the angels and queen of the May,* the words of a hymn welled inside. It was Mamma's favourite. She would lilt the words in Ballyhaunis church and as soon as she heard my croaking accompaniment she'd call out lovingly. Just as I was about to open my mouth to speak Dado gave a shout. Standing out on the aisle he spread his arms wide.

'God preserve us all, we're letting Moyra down!' he wailed.

'Don't upset yourself. Keeping the baby would let the American Lloyds step into the farm. We can't let that happen, for Lily's sake. They probably know she's not who she seems already,' Mamma circled his waist. I stood up and yelped. The sound hung in the air. It wasn't true. Mamma was being crafty again. She should be told off for being too smart. A priest arrived in front of the altar as I rushed forward. I paused.

As well as my cry, a pooka wind had blown Mamma's headscarf up and caused her to exclaim. She raised her hands to tidy her hair into place. The priest looked suspiciously like the Trinity spy. It would have been possible to argue with Father Tierney but not with two men of God and I backed out carefully.

As I ducked and weaved through homeward-bound workers, later a warplane which had gone off its route droned overhead. Hunger overwhelmed me and I concentrated on it to keep Mamma's dismissive words at bay. I was helped by the sight of an actor swinging out from the Gate Theatre wolfing down a sandwich. At the hostel, Mary Mullens, was waiting outside. She was a beggar woman we all knew and had her new baby wrapped in her shawl. She often came for alms and this time she provided me with an opportunity to slip inside. A comforting smell of wax polish filled the air and I sidled towards the basement.

Rita was my saviour then because I'd started to fall in a fit of weakness and she scooped to pick me up. She must have been getting ready to go to bed and come down because her hair was pinned on her head as artificial looking as any statue and she frowned.

'Everybody has been looking for you. Your aunt was on her knees all day. Annie heard her say something about your sister having her baby. Is it true, Lily?' Her face went pale.

'Pretend it's all in your imagination and that Moyra is the same girl as you met last year. Don't be afraid if I disappear after this. Unless there's a miracle and I'm not who you think I am,' I blabbered.

'We'll have to go to see her. She is your sister, even if she'll have to give the baby away,' Rita looked at me strangely.

This is all Mamma's doing. Now she has Rita believing I'm a fake, I thought.

Chapter Sixty-one

'Your sister will want you to visit,' Rita's words came into my head. It was the morning after my vigil in the church. Even though I'd fallen into bed it seemed only a minute since I had blacked out and I groaned and half opened my eyes. Rita was leaning over me, pulling me up.

'You know where Moyra lives. We'll have to go before Sister Terry sees us,' she advised. There was barely time to dress before she'd dragged me to the top of the stairs. Sister Angelica's voice could be heard from the basement and Rita put a finger to her lips. We tripped over each other trying to pull back. Falling together a fit of the giggles made us roll about and I hugged her close. If Moyra wasn't having this baby, Rita could come to London with us. We could explore the dance halls together, I fantasised. I could say I was a Protestant and we'd get into any party we wanted. *Dear Auntie Terry*, I'd write, *I want an explanation about Mamma's remark that everybody knows who Lily is.* Something made me shiver inside, like peering into a murky hole, and I shoved the thought away.

A beggar sang raggedly at the entrance to the National Ballroom when we slipped outside, *I like the way you walk, I like the way you*

talk, you're so good to me honey. You know that I can't leave you alone.'
I was stuffing a slice of apple cake into my mouth, given to me by Rita
from her locker, and was savouring the tart flavour when still tired,
my eyelids began to droop. The beggar became Father Tierney in the
church, his face lit by a candle. He was sliding towards us and the
glow gave him the look of a charming Beelzebub.

'Let's go Rita. This street is haunted,' I said and, not caring who
was watching from the hostel, we stumbled across the road.

Stones got in my shoe and I tripped over an iron bar and grazed a
knee, before we finally reached the nursing home. Apart from Moyra's
window being open, the house had a quiet air. I dodged behind Rita
and waved up at my sister's window in case she looked out. All around
us cheerfulness prevailed. A bright sun dimpled the waters of the
canal and ducks quacked. The weather was behaving in a peculiar way
because a few raindrops fell from a cloudless sky and a colourful drake
dive-bombed towards us. Rita shook me vigorously to move on.

'My sister and I would like to audition for the Betty Highsmith
Agency. We've travelled all the way from the West of Ireland,' I
murmured inside like lines from a play. The thought of being in
London already was necessary for what lay ahead. If the soldier had
come though and taken the baby the miracle would have happened.
Otherwise I could grab the child and pretend to be a nurse, turning
my coat inside out to make it into a nurse's cloak and running to the
station to give it to him, before they all got on the Belfast train. I was
grasping the gate now, still unable to move, and Rita went first. *On the
wings of the wind o'er the dark rolling deep, angels are coming to watch
o'er thy sleep, angels are coming to watch over thee, so list' to the wind*

coming over the sea. The Connemara Cradle Song Mamma used to sing was going around in my head, as though my sister was perfectly safe.

'We'll be thrown into a black hole for floozies if Sister Angelica finds out we've been here,' Rita looked back and grinned. 'Whatever bad thing your sister did, she needs you now,' she said and pushed in that door that was forever open.

As I crept after Rita indicating upwards we moved further into the house. Moyra mustn't have had the baby at all because outside her room, silence reigned. After turning a smooth door knob we could see her lying on her hard bed, arms resting easily. She wasn't even awake. Her face had a pinched look but tossed hair spread across the pillow like a chestnut sea. Beside the bed, a bundle in a shawl stirred in a drawer across two chairs. It was the baby that had caused all the problems and I put my finger to my lips.

'We're in deep trouble if we don't get out of here,' I whispered, but Rita was stealing over. Straightening her back she poked a finger at the child's shawl. A little fist curled up prettily and eyeing the window, praying I'd be able to run and jump in time, I edged forward.

'Theo, it's a boy,' Moyra murmured at that moment. She was sick or dreaming and it wouldn't help any of us but before I could shake her to be quiet she shot up. 'Lily, you've come to get the baby before it's taken from me. Thank God,' she said. Red flew to her cheeks when she noticed Rita and she glared as if she was the enemy. Her nightdress was torn in places and caked with blood and she began to thresh about. 'Take him and hide him before they come,' she struggled out of the bed.

'You look like you've been dragged through a mangle. Give us a hug and we'll all go,' I said to slow her down and like a ball deflating, she sank back. 'Have this and put it on,' I began to take my coat off, shivering to show her the depth of my sacrifice, but she fell back further.

'I knew you'd do this for Theo's sake, Lily. It's what sisters are for,' she sat up with a sigh. Pouting her mouth, slipping out of the bed and trying to cover up her blood stains she picked up the neat parcel in the drawer.

'Lily, I'd like to present your new nephew,' she said shyly. 'Look how perfect he is. Say hello to Auntie Lily,' she caught the little hand and waved it. 'You and she are really going to know each other.' A hot gaze swept over the child to me, barely taking me in and the bundle was thrust forward, 'Hold him *a stór*, you'll love the little *maneen*.'

A squirming bundle landed in my arms and she leaned further and hugged us both and grinned dopily. '*On the wings of the wind o'er the dark rolling deep, angels are coming to watch o'er thy sleep, angels are coming to watch over thee, so list' to the wind coming over the sea,*' she crooned my lullaby. 'He's so beautiful. You'll be asking me next if you can keep him, Lily,' her voice broke.

'Don't worry. An arrangement has been made with an American soldier to take the baby,' I said but the loud quacking of a duck, like mocking laughter, cut me short. She's right, this baby should be Theo's and mine. The thought had come just as she spoke but the sense of a shadow in the doorway made me turn. Nurse Kennedy stepped inside. Father Tierney tipping his forehead and prancing like a goat followed after her.

'Run Rita and catch the baby from the window,' I gasped but my bundle was too heavy somehow and my feet stuck.

'This is all your fault, Lily! You knew they were here and took the baby so you could give it over. You were always jealous!' Moyra screamed. Backing to the window, she tensed, like a cat ready to pounce.

'Your sister is right, Lily. If you'd given me Sister Terry's money when I asked, the nursing home would have looked after the child. Now he's going to America,' Nurse Kennedy said calmly.

'Theo is drowning,' it was my first reaction because Moyra's mouth gaped open. A force had wrenched the baby out of my arms and they swung forward light as thistle-down. Father Tierney imprisoned them and my sister howled. Her burst past us to close the door was too late and Nurse Kennedy vanished with the baby as noiselessly as she had come. Father Tierney turned the key. Launching backwards, Moyra kicked and roared and threw herself against him. Blood formed in pools from thin rivulets veining her legs and a mewing sound entered the room like keening at a Mayo wake.

She could be expiring unaided because since that first scream of hers I'd been suffocating. This was Theo's ship, bodies writhed in pain and we were tilting to go under. It was what Mamma meant by being unwanted, not being me at all. Moyra slumped like a barely alive person and I held her head and crushed it tight.

'Nobody dies if I can help it,' my voice roared.

'Marry Rory and adopt the baby, Lily. However bad it looks, he'll understand,' Rita fell down with us, sobbing.

Chapter Sixty-two

'I'm bringing you to see Rory, he's the only one who can help you get over this shock,' Rita said over and over again. The landlady and Father Tierney had evicted us, and we floated, numbed, from that house of pain. Without a will of my own, her words kept me going. Traffic rumbled and people crowded the streets but I remained a senseless rock. As we passed through St Stephen's Green the weather was turning fine. It could be snowing for all I cared but Rita said to turn my face up to feel the sun and she made a satisfied noise, inhaling the decaying scents of autumn.

'Stop blaming yourself. Everything will be all right when you have a chat with Rory. He's a modern man. No matter what happened, he'll understand,' she nodded happily. Then she was silent for the rest of the trip, probably thinking what a coward I'd been.

When we knocked on the door, Rory walked smartly out of his flat as if he'd been waiting.

'Nice to have the pleasure of your company, girls,' he declared breezily. Ignoring me, drawing Rita aside, he took her by the arms. 'It's funny. I've just had a visit from a forlorn-looking Romeo. If you hurry, Rita, you'll catch Peadar going into the university,' he announced.

Before he could be stopped he was twisting my ally around and shoving her along the street.

'Don't go, Rita, we haven't said goodbye,' I tried to pull her back.

'Remember what I said to tell Rory about the baby,' the traitor began to draw away. *'There was a young maiden and her story was sad, for once she was courted by a brave sailor lad,'* singing 'The Blackbird', her voice came back faintly.

Rory's flat had a damp smell that hadn't been noticeable before and he added to a sense of being under water by drawing a curtain across to keep out the sun's glare. A curl was peeping over one of his stuck-out ears, itching to be tucked into place. This was farewell to him too, as far as I was concerned, and I gazed at the curl indifferently. Looking for a drink would give me time to think and I sat on the rickety chair and held my head.

'Now that I'm here I'm feeling thirsty,' I lied to distract him.

'We always seem to meet in strange circumstances, Lily,' Rory ignored me. He must have guessed I was playing for time because he filled a cup at the sink too slowly. Warmth began to invade his voice. 'Don't stir. You don't look well as a matter of fact.' His next glance was soft.

'I wouldn't be here if it wasn't for my sister. She's taking me away to London and Rita brought me to say goodbye,' I clicked my fingers to look perky but instead of a drink Rory's cool hand was resting on my forehead. He stuck his face close and pretended to be a doctor feeling my pulse.

'Better not go yet. Your temperature is up. This could be serious,' he grinned. 'Lie down when I'm away and have a rest. There's not much time for me, I'm afraid. I only have an hour for lunch,' an upper lip curled disdainfully as if he was already regretting his decision to invite me in and he began to pick up his coat about to leave.

'You'll be asking next why I have to go with Moyra,' I said abruptly. If I didn't want to tell him the whole truth, talking might keep him in the place for a while and keep away thoughts of her abandoned in her prison house but he only tinkled the piano before closing the lid and tucked back that loose curl.

'*He courted me truly by night and by day, but now he has left me and gone far away*,' Rita's Blackbird was on his ear and he was trying it out.

'The world is full of songs about girls who are left behind, but the opposite can also be true too. You know what I mean, Lily?' he said coolly and before I could react he lifted a bunch of keys, shaking them like a tambourine.

'You said once some people never forget who they love,' I hit back. It was supposed to hint such feelings had to be put aside because I was a girl with a special mission, but my sickness must have spread to him because he pressed the cup to his cheeks as if he was too warm.

'*My parents they slight me and will not agree, that I and my sailor boy married should be*,' I sang loudly to press the point home.

'If you like I could stay, Lily. This could be the half-day I'm due to take,' a flush crept up his cheeks.

'Whatever you do, don't say we'll have a sing-song. It never lasts between the two of us,' I grinned weakly but my heart leaped. If I didn't go to my poor sister now though that would be a final rejection and I struggled from the chair. Tears came to my eyes.

'You're crying because nobody cares about lonely girls and their abandoned babies,' Rory said in a matter-of-fact way. Dry lips touched mine before I could fight them off and my head felt light.

'You'd be upset too if you'd caused your sister's baby to be snatched away,' my tears began but the cup had tipped in Rory's hands and cooling water splashed like a blessing.

'We're not responsible for the evil done in the name of God,' he said, 'that's the fault of the Catholic Church.' My head landed on his chest with the shock. Breath from his words singed my neck.

'*My parents they chide me and will not agree that me and my sailor love married should be, but let them deride me and do what they will, while there's breath in my body he's the one I love still.*' The remainder of a song for a sailor rose up. Mamma was wrong about one thing. I was her daughter, willing to sacrifice anyone to get my way and I glanced about coldly, ready to stay. That's when I had an image of Moyra, riddled with loss, stretched on bare floorboards like a dying swan and I had to sag in Rory's arms to keep myself from her, kissing and kissing to take that saving thought away.

Epilogue

Toby Murphy disliked his hair. It had a way of uncoiling itself, like a bunch of tight springs on his head when he dried it after a shower, or when he'd come in from the rain. He'd grown up in New York and had lived in the same secluded suburban street in Queens for twenty-four years and now was on a visit to Ireland. He worked for American General Electric and they'd sent him over, for a fee, to help bring improvements to the Irish Electricity Supply Board's expanding grid.

His hair mattered at this moment because he was about to meet his real mother. She didn't know what was in store for her. He didn't know himself. He'd told no-one. He couldn't inform his parents, Jack and Kitty Murphy because they'd died in a car crash when he was eighteen. They'd never told him he was adopted. Somebody wasn't telling the truth because Kitty Murphy's name was on his birth certificate as his natural mother. When he began to inquire seriously about it he heard stories of how doctors back in Ireland had been known to substitute the real mother's name with the adopted mother's at the request of the natural mother's family, to avoid scandal. It was conceivable that this could have happened in his case.

In many ways he wished all this wasn't taking place. Although it was only six years after his parents' death he was beginning to lead a full life. Shortly before his planned visit a letter with an Irish stamp had arrived. That was how he found out his life had been a sham. As well as discovering he was adopted the letter was accompanied by a picture of two little girls; one a toddler and the other, a cute baby leaning back in a pram. 'The O'Donoghue Sisters, Moyra and Lily', was inscribed on the back of the picture. There was a bundle of other letters as well, yellowed with age, that had belonged to a nun, his Great Aunt Terry, now deceased. She'd felt guilty and had wished him to receive them, he was informed. The sister Lily had married someone called Rory and had a family of four. Moyra, who was supposed to be his mother, had never married and now had plans to become a nun and go to the missions. 'If she really is who she says, it serves her right for abandoning me. Why should I let her off the hook now?' Toby decided. It was hard to dismiss the thought.

The sender of the information was a Franciscan priest called Father Lonergan, also quite old, Toby guessed, from the wobbly signature. He had known of his existence and whereabouts since he was born, the priest had stated bluntly and there was an urgency about him meeting his natural mother. In the circumstances, because his birth had been irregular and she might not want to be reminded of it, he did not have to reveal who he was, but it was important to make contact with her. It was the last wish of his dying grand-aunt. The priest printed 'Moyra O'Donoghue', his mother's name, in brackets after his own signature. The whole thing might be an embarrassment to a man of the cloth but he was determined to press home his point, Toby thought.

Toby Murphy felt a drop trickle down the back of his neck and put a hand up to trap it before it went under the collar of his coat. It had been raining all day in Dublin and now he was in the foyer of the Clarence Hotel. A dark Liffey rolled by outside and poorly dressed Dubliners were going about their business. He didn't like this city. It had a dismal feel to it he'd decided when he'd strolled from his quarters after his taxi had brought him from the airport. It didn't matter that no skyscrapers reared upwards to baffle the eye. He liked elegant Merrion Square where he'd been lodged and beyond it too, the simple delights of a showy Stephen's Green. What he didn't savour was the dispirited air the city exuded and a lassitude of manner amongst its people, as if the grey place could never house dreams and the only hope of a better future was to get away.

Arriving in the city Toby had contacted Father Lonergan straightaway and now he had to find a means to stay incognito, blend in with the audience at a farewell concert he'd been asked to attend. The event was to celebrate his mother, the priest had explained. Both she and her sister were singing, Toby saw from the poster above the reception of the hotel. He would be just in time to meet her, the priest had emphasised at their meeting, because his mother had already received a letter of acceptance from the convent she wished to enter.

Toby's coat lay damply on his knee when he sat down in a compact ballroom, converted for the occasion and he placed it on the back of his seat. The small performance area soon filled up. He had intended to stay at the back but another row of seats was added behind and he was hemmed in. To give his legs room to stretch he moved to the edge of the row. An olive complexion - which he was unaware was an inheritance from his father - gave him an exotic air. His dark expressive eyes were filled with mistrust.

'And now the moment we've all been waiting for. Expect fireworks ladies and gentlemen, or if you must, shed a quiet tear for a singer about to depart to faraway shores. I'm speaking of Moyra O'Donoghue, singing alongside her sister, the irresistible, the one and only Lily O'Donoghue.' Toby sat up with a jerk and his chair skidded sideways onto the aisle. The floorboards had been too highly polished and now his eyes shot open. Overcome by jet-lag he'd fallen asleep only to find a pretty auburn-haired lady on stage looking down curiously. A pianist beside her diverted attention, launching into a flowery introduction and Toby began to pull back. She had seen him clearly though. 'I don't want to be here', an idea he'd had from the beginning took more shape. 'My own mother loved me dearly, this counterfeit won't even ask how I managed growing up,' he thought. As soon as the lights went down he'd bolt. Father Lonergan arrived on stage next. The priest mentioned sacrifices and how it was God's will that Moyra O'Donoghue had chosen the path she was about to embark on. He threw his hands out as if to embrace the audience and Toby crouched, ready to sprint.

'Pray for her to change her mind. She's made a mistake,' a man beside Toby shouted and there were feeble claps.

'Perhaps you're right. If there's anyone here who thinks they have a reason why this marriage between a girl and her maker should not take place, let him say it now or forever hold his peace,' Father Lonergan quipped and Toby ducked down. The priest meant him. He covered his face with a leaflet from the chair. The auburn-haired woman who seemed to be Moyra, was providing a distraction. She'd begun to speak about poor babies in South Africa and what little chances they had. She'd never had a child of her own, she told the listeners and wanted to dedicate herself to them. Once she was going to get married and hopefully have a family but the Lord had given her a different pathway to walk. Toby sat mesmerised. She turned to beckon her sister onto the stage.

'All Lily wanted was that I should sing,' she said cheerfully and the audience clapped. Unable to move, Toby watched a vivacious raven-haired creature saunter from the wings.

'Hello everyone. It's great to be here. Welcome to "The O'Donoghue Sisters",' Lily said and everyone cheered.

'Give us "The Blackbird",' a man beside Toby shouted.

'Don't mind a word Moyra says. Even if, for arguments sake she had a long-lost son it wouldn't keep her from singing. I'll test it out,' Lily flung a hand in the air for emphasis. Diverting his face, Toby noted a rich brogue. 'Let's see what we can do. If there's anyone in the audience who'd like to be Moyra's son, just for convenience sake put your hand up and we'll see whether she'll leave the stage and claim him, or continue to sing,' she grinned at her sister and the audience laughed at her humour but Toby gripped his seat in panic. Surely he'd get away soon.

'Try the stranger who landed in the aisle a few minutes ago. He doesn't seem to know who he is,' Father Lonergan took up the theme. Sweat was beginning to copy the sensation of Dublin rain on Toby's neck. The audience turned to stare at him.

'It's a trap. She never wanted me before,' he said weakly to a